YOU HAVE TO UNDERSTAND HOW EMBARRASSING THIS ROOSTER business is for me. I am Ford Falcon. I have just pepper-bombed a solar bear. But this blankety-blank rooster gets the better of me. And no matter how hard I fling him or Toad "fetches" him, he always comes cackling back. Somewhere in me I admire him. But most of all I would like to admire him on a big plate surrounded by boiled potatoes and cooked carrots.

MICHAEL PERRY

HARPER

An Imprint of HarperCollinsPublishers

The Scavengers

Copyright © 2014 by Michael Perry

Library of Congress Cataloging-in-Publication Data

Perry, Michael, date

The scavengers / Michael Perry.

    pages cm

  Summary: With a neighbor's help, twelve-year-old Ford Falcon learns to survive in the harsh world outside the Bubble Cities by scavenging for items to use or trade—skills she needs when her parents unexpectedly go missing.

  ISBN 978-0-06-202617-0

  [1. Survival—Fiction. 2. Family life—Fiction. 3. Ragpickers—Fiction. 4. Missing persons—Fiction. 5. Science fiction.] I. Title.

PZ7.P43538Sc 2014   2014001878

[Fic]—dc23   CIP

                                                                        AC

Typography by Torborg Davern

16 17 18 19 OPM 10 9 8 7 6 5 4 3 2

First paperback edition, 2015

For my daughters

INTRODUCTION

THE OLD CAR WAS SUNK TO THE BUMPERS WHEN I DISCOVERED IT, but my first thought was how good it would be to sleep in there and hear the rain drumming on steel rather than splattering against our tattered old tarp.

I was Maggie back then. Maggie, the name my parents gave me. A nice name. But these weren't nice times. We were tired and hungry, and the GreyDevil bonfires were burning brighter and the solar bear howls were getting closer, and every morning as I strapped my SpitStick across my back and set out to scavenge, I found myself thinking I needed a better name. A stronger name.

I mean, the name Maggie was fine, it just seemed kinda underpowered.

So when I scrubbed the moss from the side of that old car

overlooking Goldmine Gully and saw the chrome letters—
Ford Falcon—I climbed up on the hood and stood there with
my steel-toed boots planted wide and I wedged my fists on
my hips and I announced that Maggie was yesterday, and
from this day forward I would answer only to Ford Falcon.
Ford, because we had a lot of rivers to cross. Falcon, because,
well, if you have a lot of rivers to cross, a pair of wings can't
hurt, and then once you get across the river it's likely you will
need sharp eyes and an even sharper beak.

Yes. I know. I named myself after an old dead car. Worse
yet, it's not even a cool car. It's a station wagon. Station wagons were how parents hauled kids around during the time
between covered wagons and minivans. These days you
won't see a minivan unless it's being pulled by a horse, and
even horses are hard to come by.

But if you see me you will know me because I wear a vest
made from the hide of a beast that tried to kill me and lost.
I skinned that beast myself, and also I skinned the lettering
from that old dead car and stitched it to the vest across my
shoulder blades using copper wire so that in polished chrome
the world can read my name and know it: Ford Falcon.

1

"COCK-A-DOODLE . . . *AAACK–KACK–KACK–KACK*!"

Way down in Hoot Holler, Hatchet the Rooster is rul-
ing the roost. It's tough to rule the roost when all of your
cock-a-doodles sputter out like you're gagging on a crossways
caterpillar, but Hatchet's ego is twice the size of his multi-
colored mop of a tail, and I guarantee you by the time that
last *kack*! echoes off Skullduggery Ridge he's already fluffing
his feathers and strutting around like that's exactly what he
meant to say.

"Cock-a-doodle . . . *aaack-kack-kack-kack*!"

Hatchet belongs to our neighbors Toad and Arlinda Hopper. They live a half-hour hike away, down the western side
of Skullduggery Ridge, but even though we can't see their
farm from here the crowing comes through loud and clear.

That rooster has brass lungs. And once he gets started, he doesn't stop. He'll crow at noon, he'll crow at the moon, he'll crow any which way the wind blows. Most of all, he'll crow whenever he feels the need to remind the world that he is a *rooster*, which is about every six minutes. That bird is as loopy as a ball of snarled yarn.

"Cock-a-doodle . . . *aaack-kack-kack-kack*!"

Guess I'm done sleeping. I crawl out of the station wagon and climb onto the hood. Dawn is still a ways off, but even as I pull my quilt tight around my shoulders birds are twittering in the darkness around me—that is, when they aren't drowned out by all the cock-a-doodle-*ack*ing.

On the horizon before me there are two faint gray smudges of light. One is the first hint of sunrise. The other is the glow from the lights of a Bubble City. I've never been to any of the Bubble Cities, but once when I was helping Toad tear apart a junk car I found a brochure under the backseat that said *Your Bubble City!* Inside, it had a lot of pictures of happy people laughing and playing volleyball and eating ice cream cones. The brochure unfolded like a map to show more happy people doing more happy things—swimming, dancing, walking through flowers, laughing on rides in an amusement park, jumping on trampolines (Toad had to explain to me what volleyball, amusement parks, and trampolines were)—and when it was all the way unfolded you could see a shiny bubble shimmering above all the people. I told Toad it looked pretty neat. He just shook his head and said something about not believing everything I read.

As the gray horizon oozes over to pink, the glow of the Bubble City fades and the landscape takes shape, sloping sharply away to the east from the Falcon's front bumper before rumpling itself into foothills that bump along for many miles into the invisible distance. I wonder sometimes what my life would be like if Dad and Ma had stayed UnderBubble, as everyone out here calls it. Instead, they chose OutBubble, and believe me, there is no volleyball or ice cream cones Out-Bubble. As the last of the glow disappears into sunlight, I wonder if there are girls my age waking beneath the Bubble, and what their day will be like compared to mine.

Now the parrot flocks are squawking. This makes me grin, because it means Hatchet is getting some competition. Dad and Ma tell me there never used to be parrots here unless they were in cages. Now they swoop around all over the place. My parents say the world has changed a lot since they were children. Back then, people argued about whether the earth was warming up or cooling down. Well, the weather did get warmer—we don't really have winter anymore—but mostly it just got weirder. The seasons are all skittery. Sun for a month, then sleet for a week. Snowdrifts on Tuesday, puddles on Wednesday. Our oak and pine forests got more jungly and leafy. The parrots moved in, and other newcomers followed. Wild hogs, alligators halfway up the Mississippi, sky-blocking flocks of turkey vultures, and, scariest of all, solar bears. Solar bears were created when government scientists tried to save polar bears from extinction by crossing them with grizzly bears and splicing in a dab of coyote DNA. The result wasn't really a polar bear or a grizzly bear, but a four-legged experiment with white fur and caramel-colored stripes, big teeth and bad breath, and a howl like its tail is caught in a crack. One thing the scientists maybe hadn't kept in mind is that bears can range hundreds of miles, so after the weather changed it wasn't long before they migrated down into this area. There is a reason I never go anywhere without my hunting knife, my SpitStick, my ToothClub, and a sack of pepper-pea pellets. I made all of those weapons myself, and they're on the car hood beside me this very minute. Well, except for the knife, which was given to me by Toad and I carry sheathed in my boot top.

The sun is nearly up now. In the lower valleys I can see smeary patches of smoke drifting from the last of the Grey-Devil bonfires. Nobody really knows where the GreyDevils come from, but we'd all be happier if they went back. Toad says they probably started out as humans like us, and that's why we should try not to kill them, but they're pale and dirty and instead of talking they moan and howl like sickly solar bears. Creepy. Every night they build big bonfires of whatever trash and wood they can find, and then gather around to get all hopped up on PartsWash.

PartsWash is homemade hooch. It's fermenty and disgusting and got its name because it smells like something a mechanic would use to strip grease from old engine parts.

Plus, based on the way the GreyDevils look, if you drink it long enough, it'll pretty much wash away *your* parts.

PartsWash is brewed by gangs we call Juice Cruisers. The GreyDevils steal anything they can lay their hands on and trade it to the Juice Cruisers for PartsWash. Then the Juice Cruisers turn around and trade and sell the stolen things wherever there is a market, which is pretty much everywhere, because these days, here in OutBubble world, there's a shortage of everything. I've never met a Juice Cruiser, and never hope to. Toad says they are outlaws who will leave you alone if you leave them alone.

I don't know exactly what the Juice Cruisers put in PartsWash, but it must be powerful because the GreyDevils will do pretty much anything to get more, which is why they're dangerous—at least until evening, when they start drinking. The bonfires burn all night long until the PartsWash is gone or the last GreyDevil has collapsed. From up here, the countryside looks all soft and gentle and newborn. But those smoke smears remind me that this is not paradise.

"Cock-a-doodle . . . *aaack-kack-kack-kack*!"

Also, there is that rooster. No sound like that would ever be allowed in paradise.

Uphill from where I am sitting, I hear a noise. I turn to look and see Ma step out of the shack with her pans, ready to cook breakfast.

It's time to begin the day.

2

WE ARE A FAMILY OF FOUR. THERE'S ME, OF COURSE. I'M AT THAT age where I'm not sure who I am, but then again, in the world we live in, there isn't a lot of time to wonder. Mostly we are busy scavenging, scrounging, and surviving. It's not like I have a lot of time to sit around thinking in cutesy, heart-dotted curlicue letters. I love my family, but I choose to live in an old car a hundred yards downhill from them. Maybe that tells you something.

My first chore every morning is to let the chickens out and gather eggs for breakfast. The path takes me right past our outdoor oven, which is made from mud and stones. Ma is stoking the fire.

"Mornin', Ma."

"Good morning, Maggie." Ma refuses to call me Ford

Falcon. She also refuses to say "mornin'." She is precise about these things. "When we drop our gerunds, we drop our standards," she likes to say. Ma studied English and writing in college. To me, *gerund* sounds like the name of a teensy African antelope, but it really means the *-ing* sound at the end of a word. "Just because our *life* is rough around the edges doesn't mean *we* have to be rough around the edges," says Ma.

I still like to say "mornin'."

The chicken coop is small, square, and solid. Before I open the "people" door, I drop a tiny drawbridge hatch and the chickens come clucking and blinking out into the daylight. I never get tired of watching them go flapping into freedom, fanning out to peck and scratch and turn their heads sideways to give a bug the beady eye before snapping it into their beaks. Our flock is all hens, no roosters. One Hatchet is rooster enough for miles around.

Inside the coop, I wait a moment for my eyes to adjust to the dimness, then reach into the nesting boxes one by one. The eggs are still warm, and I like the way each one feels in my palm. Solid and delicate at the same time. Some of the eggs are white, some of the eggs are brown, and some are pale green. They all look the same in the frying pan. I am placing the last egg in the basket when I hear a noise behind me. Just as I turn to check it out, a figure leaps from the darkest corner of the coop and into my face.

"FLABBA-SHAMMY!"

The eggs go everywhere. My heart is flopping like an electrocuted fish.

"DOOKIE!" I yell, but the little creature has already scooted out the door and is running off to Ma, flapping his arms like chicken wings.

Dookie. My little snot flicker of a brother. He drives me nuts. Always popping up here and there, scaring the bejeebers out of me. Grabbing one of the unbroken eggs, I sidearm it out the door and it smacks him—*pop-shmush!*—on the back of his head.

"ZABBA-ZOO!" he hollers, and leaps into Ma's arms.

"MAGGIE!" Now it's Ma hollering. She's holding Dookie and he's looking up at her with his sad pony eyes. Dookie has never been able to speak with his mouth, but he figured out how to talk with those eyes a long time ago.

"Ma, he . . ."

"Enough!" says Ma. Right about then she runs her hand through his hair and discovers the egg goop.

"For shame! Both of you!" She sets Dookie down and now he's looking at me and his eyes have changed from sad pony to sneaky weasel.

While I gather up the remaining eggs, Ma goes back to cooking the bacon, and Dookie goes spinning off in circles, humming to himself.

Dookie has never been right. I love him, but I love him the way you always love stinky little brothers: a little bit goes a long way. I know it bothers Ma that he can't talk the way he should, but there's nothing to be done, and he seems happy enough as long as he gets to drive his sister up a tree now and then. I hand Ma the surviving eggs. As she cracks them into the pan, I turn to get the dishes from the shack and meet the fourth member of our family—Dad—coming out the door. He blinks as he steps into the open, then rubs his eyes slowly. Dad was always an early riser, but lately he sleeps in more often. Sometimes when he comes out of the shack he looks like he didn't sleep at all. Ma gives him a worried look she thinks I don't see. Dad hugs her. Dookie leaps out of the bushes and hugs them both.

"Mornin', Dad," I say.

"Oh, mornin'," says Dad, like he just noticed me.

When the eggs are done, Ma serves Dookie first. He takes a mouthful, stands up, spins in a circle, then sits down and does the same thing again. This is not unusual. This is just your basic breakfast with Dookie. We're used to it.

Before Ma hands Dad his plate, she chops up a wild garlic plant and sprinkles it over the eggs. I wrinkle my nose. Dad eats garlic on everything. He says it helps him stay healthy. I say it just makes him smell funny. But by the time he's half-way through his eggs, he does seem better.

"You ready to hunt for gold?" he asks me, smiling in his lopsided way.

3

I ONCE LIVED IN A REGULAR HOUSE WITH REGULAR PEOPLE IN A REGULAR place. I remember cars and television screens and telephones and green grass and at least one birthday cake. Most of my memories from those days are gone or blurry. But one memory I carry as clearly as if it happened yesterday. I am standing in a field with my father. He is holding a red balloon. There is a white bandage on his cheek. He kneels down to hand me the balloon but he lets go too quickly and the string slips through my fingers. The balloon rises, sliding sideways across the sky, higher and higher until it is a colorless dot that I can't see anyway because I am crying. Dad takes me into the house and blows up another red balloon, but when he lets go of this one it doesn't float, it just drops to the floor with a soft bounce and sits there. I stomp on it and make it pop.

And then I remember we got into a car that smelled brand-new and drove into the country. Dad said we were going camping, and I was excited but Ma was crying. Dookie was just a little bundle in his car seat. We drove for almost a whole day. I remember the radio was on, and right when it was starting to get dark I heard a man on the radio talking about a red balloon, which made me grumpy again. And then right after that Dad stopped the car and said it was time to start the camping trip.

It wasn't a very good camping trip. Mostly I remember rain and walking. And walking. And walking. Day after day. I remember being cold and damp in the mornings and hot and hungry in the afternoons. I remember bug bites and scrapes and itching and blisters and the sound of howling solar bears. I remember Dad's white bandage turning brown from dust and sweat. I remember eating cold beans from cans. And then one day I remember Dad telling me we would be camping for a very long time. I remember yelling at Dad and running to Ma, and both of us crying while she held me. I remember Dad standing there with a pack on his back and Dookie strapped on his front, and I remember Dad had tears in his eyes too. Dookie just blew bubbles through his drool.

In the beginning, at least we had a tent. But one night in an awful storm a tree branch blew down, ripping through the tent and stabbing the ground right beside my head. The next day Dad found an old tarp snagged in the brush beside a flooded stream, and that became our shelter. By then we were out of canned food and scrounging for whatever we could find, like cattail roots and green apples, and Dad's precious wild garlic. Sometimes Dad was able to kill a rabbit or a squirrel and we fried the meat over a fire. And we were always searching for water. I remember begging Dad to take us back home. He just very quietly said, *We can't do that, Maggie*, and when I begged Ma, she said the same thing, even more quietly. When I asked why, they looked at each other and then Dad said someday I would understand. And so we stayed hidden in the woods, rolling up that tarp and moving every few days. The days became weeks. The weeks became months.

Ma did everything she could to give me little moments of a normal life. We played games like tic-tac-toe and connect the dots. She sang songs to Dookie. She read to me from a book called *Little House on the Prairie*. Ma said no matter how we were living she couldn't imagine her daughter being in a world without books, so she had slipped it in her pack at the last minute. We read that book over and over, until I had every chapter memorized. Every time I heard about the hardships little Laura Ingalls and her family went through it helped me a little bit with understanding ours. Ma said I should learn to read too, and she began teaching me the alphabet. We didn't have a blackboard or pencils and paper, so she'd clear away the leaves and I'd draw letters in the dirt with a stick, or use a piece of charcoal on the smooth side of some birch bark. Other times she'd have me study tree branches and find *V*s and *W*s, or press an acorn cap into mud to show me the shape of an *O*. Then she had me pick out words in *Little House on the Prairie*, and then whole sentences. Pretty soon I could read the book on my own, although I still liked it best when Ma read to me.

I remember plenty of scary times, too, like when lightning split a tree right beside our shelter and the thunder was so loud I felt it in my teeth. Sometimes the scariest things were the ones you couldn't see, like wild hogs snuffling through the camp in the middle of the night, or solar bear howls in the distance. One day I happened upon the skull of a hog that had been killed by solar bears. I pried out the tusks, wedged them in one end of a split stick, and wrapped the split tight with woven runner vines. I called it my ToothClub, and practiced swinging it at imaginary solar bears. Even though I knew it wouldn't do me any good if a real solar bear truly wanted to eat me, carrying that ToothClub made me feel a little better.

I don't know how long we wandered. Maybe Dad and Ma kept track, but for me it just seemed like it was the only life we'd ever known, and that those other fuzzy memories belonged to another girl. Ma was growing skinnier. There were dark circles under her eyes. Back then, she was the sickly one and Dad was strong and tough. Once he twisted his ankle on a rock and it swelled up and we didn't know if it was broken. By the next morning it was back to its normal shape and he could walk fine. Dad was weird that way. He was really healthy, and he healed really fast. Maybe the garlic really did work. He never got a cough or a cold, and if he got a scratch on his arm in the afternoon, by the next morning you could hardly see where it was. I asked Ma about it once, and she just said, "Your father has a remarkable constitution." I asked her what *constitution* meant, and by the time she got done explaining that one, I had forgotten what I asked in the first place.

We wandered for a couple of years. We moved a lot and scrounged our food from the woods. My hair grew long and tangled. I outgrew my clothes and Ma had to patch them together with pieces torn from one of Dad's old T-shirts. Sometimes we would stay in one place for a few months, then we'd pack everything up and move again. One day after we had been wandering again we were scouring the hills for wintergreen berries and windfall apples—and still more wild garlic—when we came to a sharp cut in the earth. Dad walked to the edge, peered over, and hollered, "It's a gold mine!"

I ran to his side to look. And there below me I saw piles and piles of . . . junk. Bedsprings. Rotting lumber. Cracked rubber tires. Rusty soup cans and empty oil cans. Broken bottles. Pipes and chunks of iron and gears from old machines. A cracked cast iron stove. This wasn't even fresh junk. It was old junk, half-buried, with trees and brush growing out of it.

Dad clambered over the edge and started tugging at the

piles like a man who'd just discovered a pile of loose money. "We don't have to *scrounge* anymore!" he said. Now we can *scavenge*!" I remember thinking, *Is there a difference?* Neither one sounded very thrilling.

Ma was kinda hanging back. But down there in the junk Dad was scampering around like a little kid. "Hey!" he said, bending down. When he stood up he was holding a window frame high above his head. It had all the little squares, but the glass panes were missing. "A window! For your mother!" Ma was always saying that of all the things she missed from her old life, most of all she missed drinking tea while reading a good book beside a window.

Dad scrambled back up to where Ma was standing and surveyed the scene one more time.

"Goldmine Gully!" he declared. Then he hugged Ma. "Marlene, we're stayin' put!"

For the first time since I don't know when, Ma smiled. Then a darker look came over her face. "But, John . . . can we? Dare we?"

"We don't really have a choice now," said Dad, his face turning serious too. Then he noticed how closely I was watching him, and he switched quickly back to a smile. "And what better place?" he said, nodding toward the ravine and switching quickly back to a smile. He raised the glassless window so the sun passed through it and fell in squares at Ma's feet. "I'll build you a cabin! With a window, for reading! And a bookshelf!" Of course he had no idea how he would do this,

17

especially since he had no tools. And Dad wasn't even very good at rigging up a simple shelter with our tarp. But I could tell he was more excited than I had ever seen him, and Ma's smile returned.

"It'll be just like *Little House on the Prairie*," said Dad.

"You mean *Little House Perched Over the Junkpile*," said Ma, but she was still smiling.

"We're staying put, kids!" said Dad, gathering us into his arms.

Over the next few weeks we dragged enough lumber and tin out of Goldmine Gully to build a sleeping shelter. It wasn't very sturdy. Everything was just propped up and tied together with vines and woven grass and old rusty wire, and the roof was the same old tarp we'd been sleeping under when we were moving camp every day. The window Dad found was still leaned against a tree with not a pane of glass in it. Ma had gone back to looking as tired as ever. We were always hungry. Dad would dig in the junk for a few days straight and tinker on the shelter, but then he would seem to lose interest and wander off into the woods for the rest of the day. Sometimes he didn't come back until late at night. The next morning, he was always grinning his goofy lopsided grin and was ready to scavenge again.

One day when Dad had walked off yet again and I could see the worry in Ma's eyes, I went for a walk of my own to think things over.

I was angry. Angry with my father for wandering off.

Angry with Ma for not standing up to him. Angry with both of them for making us live like wilderness hobos and not telling me why. Part of me wanted to run away, and part of me knew I had a responsibility to help my family. I guess I was learning you can love your Ma and Dad and still get angry with them sometimes. I didn't want to leave, but I wanted to be alone. I stomped off downhill from Goldmine Gully, not sure where I was headed. I didn't make it very far when I came upon that old Ford Falcon. It was half-hidden behind a clump of brush and sunk into the dirt, but when I tried a door it opened. The car smelled funky inside, but it was in pretty good shape and not all chewed up like I thought it would be. The middle seat was folded down, and there was plenty of room for me to stretch out. Looking back up the hill I could still see our shelter. At that moment I realized that this old car would let me hide out but still be where I belonged, and that's when I stood up on the hood and declared myself Ford Falcon forevermore.

And then I saw the old man standing in the trees.

4

HE WAS SUPER SKINNY. LIKE A PIECE OF BEEF JERKY WITH LEGS.
His narrow face was tan and wrinkly, and his eyes were bright
as a bucket of sparks.

"Eetings-gray!"

I just looked at him, confused.

"Ig-pay atin-lay!" he said, as if that explained everything.
His voice was half yell, half laughter.

"Dow y'hooin'?"

"D'wha?" I said.

He was grinning ear to ear. "Spit's an oonerism! A flop-
flip! A verbal mishmash in honor of the Reverend William
Archibald Spooner, door as a deadnail for bass-not-tenor a
penny-ury or embroider, but still a-lip in our lives!"

Now my mouth just hung open.

Suddenly the man stepped forward and extended his hand and, in a completely normal voice, said, "Greetings. Name's Toad. Toad Hopper. Real name, Thomas. But I was born legs first and Daddy said I was kickin' like a toad, and, well, the name stuck. For seventy-eight years now."

I reached down from the hood of the car and shook his hand. It was like grabbing a fistful of wire wrapped in leather. "My name is Mag . . . *Ford*!" I said. "Ford Falcon."

"So I hear," said Toad, and although I had felt a little silly saying my new name, and even sillier knowing he'd just watched me talking to myself on the hood of a car, he didn't act like it was a silly name at all.

"I'm yer neighbor," said Toad, pointing back over one shoulder with his thumb. "Live on the other side of the ridge. Down there in Hoot Holler."

"Hoot? Holler?"

"Yah, folks used to call it Owl Hollow, but that's hard to say. Like y'got ball bearings in yer yapper. Mainly though, I figured Hoot Holler was a lot funnier." At this point he giggled like a little kid. Later I learned that he came up with the name Skullduggery Ridge, too, because in all the cowboy books he read when he was a boy, the bad guys ("skullduggerers" Toad called them) always snuck in over a ridge. Arlinda told me once that she still catches Toad sometimes trying to hitch his pants and squint like a gun-slinging cowpuncher.

"You own a rooster?" I thought I might as well ask.

"Hatchet!" he said. "Named him that 'cause his crows are all hacked off!"

"That would be the one," I said.

He giggled again. Then his face turned serious.

"I've been keeping an eye on you and your family since you arrived. Smelled your campfire smoke one day and tracked you up here. I figure you're good people. And I figure . . ."

Here he paused and looked up toward our ragged tarp-shack.

" . . . I figure you could use some help."

I just looked at him.

"I figure," he said, "you could use a *neighbor*."

I led the old man uphill to meet Ma and Dad. Ma was cooking over a smoky fire, but Dad didn't show up for a minute or two, and when he did, he came out from behind a tree and I thought he looked pale and nervous. But in five minutes Toad had them chattering like old friends. Toad had that way about him. And I think they were relieved to talk to a grown-up for a change. Later I heard Dad talking quietly to Ma, and Ma said, "If he was trouble, there'd have already been trouble."

Toad told Ma and Dad that back when he was a boy, the spot we were living on was located where the property lines of four farms came together. In those days, he said, before garbage trucks and landfills, every farm had its own "back forty" junk dump, and since ours had served four families for several generations, we'd find plenty of good stuff in there if we kept digging.

He also said he made regular trading trips to a nearby village named Nobbern, and if we scavenged up any iron or other useful items in Goldmine Gully he could trade them for nails, or flour, or sugar, or other things we might need. Later, when we learned that Toad had an entire junkyard of his own full of things to trade, we realized he certainly didn't need to lug ours to town. But at a time when we barely had two sticks to rub together, it was a big deal.

Over the next few months, Toad changed our lives completely. He lent us tools and gave us lumber and helped us build a real shack, dragging everything up the long ridge behind his twin oxen Frank and Spank. He gave us rain barrels so we didn't have to carry water or collect it in slimy plastic jugs, he brought up some cast iron pots and pans, he gave us an ax for splitting firewood, and after helping us build a coop, he gave us half a dozen chickens.

He also introduced us to his wife, Arlinda. She taught Ma and me about foraging for herbs and edible plants, and helped get us started with a garden. She even gave us garlic bulbs, so Dad would never run out. And about every other week she gave us one of her homemade pies, which are so big you could use one for a pillow.

Before long it seemed like we'd always known Toad and Arlinda. Like they were part of the family. One or two days a week I hiked down to help Toad—sometimes we'd sort junk and old steel for his trips to Nobbern; sometimes I'd help him clean his pigpens and chicken coop, or use an old scythe to cut and gather hay from the small meadow tucked up in Hoot Holler. In return, he and Arlinda gave us some of the ham and bacon they smoked, or seeds for our garden. Working with Toad was like going to school—he taught me all kinds of things, like how to use tools and repair leather, how to butcher pigs and chickens, and how to weave a rope from grass.

I even got to where I could understand more and more of Toad's silly talk.

Pig latin, he taught me, is where you move the first letter or couple of letters to the back of the word and then add -ay—as in "ig-pay atin-lay." And Reverend William Archibald Spooner was a preacher who lived in the 1800s and was known for flipping the front end of his words around in a way that wound up making them funnier, like the time he called a "well-oiled bicycle" a "well-boiled icicle."

And then sometimes Toad just invents his own rules. Like saying "flop-flip" instead of "flip-flop." Or describing Reverend Spooner as "door as a deadnail for bass-not-tenor a penny-ury or embroider but still a-lip in our lives!" If you study it out, you will see he is using "bass-not-tenor" instead of "low," which sounds the same as "lo," or "*penny*-ury" instead of "*cent*ury" and "a-lip in our lives" instead of "alive in our lips." Oh, and "embroider" is a synonym for "sew," which is a homonym for "so." In other (normal) words: "The Reverend William Archibald Spooner, dead as a doornail for lo, a century or so, but still alive in our lips!"

"Mr. Toad," I said, one day when I got to know him better, "you talk weird."

"I just lang love-uage!" said Toad, grinning like Christmas.

"Hmmm," I said. "Wouldn't know it the way you treat it."

He laughed and laughed.

5

"COCK-A-DOODLE . . . *AAACK-KACK-KACK-KACK*!"

Breakfast is finished. Dad and I are down in Goldmine Gully, digging in the damp, mossy earth. Hatchet is still at it.

"Admit it, you miss that bird," says Dad.

I roll my eyes, and Dad grins. Hatchet the Rooster and I do not get along. The last time I went down to help Toad clean his pig shed, *that bird* came after me like I'd been dipped in lard and rolled in seeds. Those peck marks on my kneecaps? Hatchet. The claw scratches on my forearms? Hatchet.

I pat the SpitStick slung over my shoulder. "The only way I'd miss that rooster is if I didn't aim straight," I say. Dad chuckles and goes back to digging. After his slow start, Dad is having a good day. It's good when Dad's happy, and I've learned to enjoy it, because I know eventually he'll get hollow-eyed and cranky, and then he'll disappear again.

I asked him about it once. "Now and then I just need some time alone," he said. And then he turned and walked away, like he didn't want to talk about it.

Like he needed some time alone.

Today though, the sun is shining and it matches our mood. Even though we're basically digging through trash, it still feels like a treasure hunt. You never know what you'll find. Mostly it's pretty unexciting—rotten wood, rusty soup cans, worthless plastic. But sometimes you find a pail with only a tiny hole in it, or a spoon that isn't bent, or maybe a chunk of iron Toad can trade for bags of oatmeal and brown sugar. One time I unearthed a cast iron wheel still attached to its axle. Toad said it was from an old hay stacker. Rather than trade it in Nobbern, Toad used it to rig up a device that allows Ma to adjust the heat on her cooking cauldron by turning the wheel to raise and lower it over the fire. Another time I discovered a faded red plastic dinner plate that was rounded on the bottom and wouldn't really sit flat. Dad saw me puzzling over it and grinned. "Go stand up by the shack," he said, taking it from my hand. Then he flipped it over and sailed it through the air right into my hands, and that was the day I learned to play Frisbee.

The first thing I dug up today was some clear plastic sheeting. It's still carefully folded, in its original wrapper. This is a big discovery because we can use the plastic to build miniature greenhouses—we call them hoop houses—for the garden. We don't get winter like we used to, but there are enough snap-blizzards and freeze-blasts to put the earth through herky-jerky seasons that can catch us by surprise, so much of the garden has to be kept under plastic. Also, until Dad finds more windowpanes, our shack windows are made of plastic sheeting just like this. They're nothing like glass, but they keep out most of the rain and let in some of the light.

We could survive without scavenging in Goldmine Gully, but we would be a lot skinnier and a lot more miserable. The things we dig up help us fill the gaps when we trade them for things we can't grow or make ourselves . . . and sometimes, for things just to put a little brightness in our lives.

"Hey!" says Dad. He's been working very carefully, scraping at the dirt and brushing it away with an old paintbrush, like he's an archaeologist looking for fossils.

His careful work has paid off, because there before him is a complete pane of glass—dirty, but without a single chip or crack. We find a lot of glass, but most of it is broken. In fact, as a scavenger, you learn pretty early never just to paw around in the dirt. Besides broken glass, we uncover a lot of sharp tin and old nails. One careless move and you're missing half a finger. And you can't just trot off to a hospital to get it fixed.

That glass pane would be valuable in Nobbern. But I know Dad won't give it up. He's been collecting them ever since we started digging, all in hopes of giving Ma her reading window.

"Only six more to go!" he says, with a big lopsided smile. Dad carefully wraps the pane in some rags and tucks it into his work pack. He's still smiling as I turn back to dig again.

But just as I'm reaching out with my digging stick I spy what looks like a tiny pink mouse ear protruding from the hillside. I brush the dirt away, and there looking right back at me is a small, round pig face. His eyes are wide and his mouth is open, and I can see the pale blue bill of a cap set back on his round head, which is about the size of a crab apple. "Oh!" I say, like a kid who sees a pretty rock, and forgetting everything I've learned, drive my hand straight into the dirt. Immediately a sharp pain shoots up the side of one finger. Sure enough, I've sliced it on a splinter of glass. I flex my finger quickly to make sure it still works, and it does, but it's bleeding pretty good. Now just to be safe I'll have to go back to the shack to wash it out and wrap some of Ma's poultice strips around it. First though—more carefully now, and using my digging stick instead of my fingers—I pry the pig free and hold it up so Dad can see it.

"Wow!" says Dad. "Porky Pig!"

I just look at him. I have no idea what he's talking about.

"From the cartoons!" he says. Sometimes Dad forgets I wasn't raised in his world. The last time I saw a cartoon I was tiny, and I certainly don't remember this pig being in any of them. I hand him the statue. He grabs it carefully because some of my blood has dripped on it, then brushes away some of the dirt and turns the pig faceup again. "Porky changed a lot over the years. This version looks like the Porky who was popular when my parents were children. You'll get a pretty penny for this in Nobbern. And speaking of pennies, look here." Dad points to a slot in the back of the pig's head. "It's a piggy bank. Some little child used to put coins in here." He shakes the pig, but there is no jingle.

"Guess this account's closed. Still, the pig will be worth more than any old money."

Dad's right. There is a man in Nobbern named Mad Mike who buys old things and odd things, but he especially loves old, odd things. Once Dad dug up an old toy truck with steel wheels, and when Toad and I took it to Mad Mike his eyes got wide and he gave us enough BarterBucks to buy flour for a year plus a new jackknife and a box of chocolate bars. When I asked Mad Mike who in the world would want an old toy dump truck that had been buried in dirt, he grinned and winked and said, "If I told you that, I'd be out of business!"

As we walk back to the shack, Ma stands up from weeding the garden. Dad unwraps the pane of glass and holds it up like it's treasure from an Egyptian pyramid. "One pane closer to your reading window, Marlene," he says.

Ma starts to smile, but then she sees my bloody hand. "Maggie! What happened?"

"Oh, I was digging up this pig . . ." I hold up the bloody Porky with my good hand, but Ma ignores the painted piggy, instead taking up my injured hand. "We need to get this cleaned up," she says, and marches me into the shack.

6

AFTER THE CUT IS CLEANED AND BANDAGED, AND WE HAVE EATEN lunch, I take Porky Pig out beneath the Shelter Tree. The Shelter Tree is a gigantic twisted oak with a trunk so massive, Dad, Ma, Dookie, and I can join hands and we still can't make a complete circle around it. Every year the rains work a little more dirt loose from the roots, and the ones that hang out in the open look like crazy knotted fingers. They make a nice footrest when I sit with my back against the trunk to begin cleaning up Porky Pig.

Using a rag and some water, I dab at the dirt and my own bloody fingerprints. I dab rather than scrub, because I don't want to rub off any of the paint, which is already chipped in places. Mad Mike taught me a long time ago that some old things lose their value if you clean them up too much. Still, I figure nobody wants a pig covered in my blood, so I pat away as much of it as I can. As the blood and dirt come away, I discover that the pig is made of two halves held together by a screw in Porky's back. If there ever was any money in him, someone unscrewed those halves and removed it long ago. Some of the blood seeped into the coin slot and dried in the seam where the two halves of the pig screw together. I pick at it with my fingernail and a twig, but a little piece of paint comes away, so I give the pig a final wipe with the rag and call it good. I'll let Mad Mike decide how much he wants to polish this pig.

I prop Porky up against a root and study him. He's standing on his hind legs like a human. He's wearing a bow tie, a red jacket, and that blue-and-white cap. I think he's supposed to be smiling but his eyes and mouth are open so wide it looks more like he just spied the Big Bad Wolf sneaking into the pigsty. There is a rust spot right where his belly button should be. On the square base of the sculpture a crooked set of raised letters spell out "PORKY."

I am too old to care much about toys these days, but I am excited about this pig, because I know it's worth more than any old broken gear or piece of steel.

I pick Porky up again and feel how heavy he is. I imagine how he looked on a toy store shelf when he was brand-new. How his little red jacket must have shined that day! Maybe he was a present for some little girl, and when she unwrapped him she giggled. Maybe she kept Porky on a bookshelf all the

way until she was an old lady and then after she died someone cleaned out her house and Porky wound up in a box of
junk that got dumped into Goldmine Gully. Then I think of
him buried in the dark dirt, packed still and silent in the soil
for years and years while the world spun and bubbled with
trouble, and suddenly I realize I am clenching Porky tightly
in both hands and my whole body feels light and mysterious,
as if I have just returned from a trip through time.

I open my hands and look at Porky resting wide-eyed on
my palms. *A time machine*, I think. Not a real time machine,
of course, but an object that allows me to travel in my head
back to a time I never even knew. To a time when things
weren't as tough as they are now. To a time when there was
time. Time to sit beside a window and read a book in the
sunlight, or daydream, or drop pennies one by one into a
piggy bank.

And that's when I realize: maybe that is exactly why Mad
Mike is able to sell things like this.

Ma sticks her head out the shack door.

"Tea, Maggie?"

"Yah, sure."

Ma's face lights up. "I'll put the kettle on!"

I walk down to hide the pig in the Ford Falcon. "Meet you
at the Shelter Tree!" I holler back at Ma.

"I'll bring Emily!" she says.

7

ONE DAY WHEN I ASKED MA TO READ *LITTLE HOUSE ON THE Prairie* to me for probably the forty-seventh time, she reached deep into her pack and drew out a rectangular object wrapped in cloth, which she carefully unwrapped until I saw it was another book. On the cover was the silhouette of a lady's head. Ma ran her finger along the spine, where I read the title: *The Complete Poems of Emily Dickinson.* Ma sat down, pulled me close, and murmured, "Now you're going to learn why I love to read."

It sounded like she meant it more as a wish and a hope than a command.

Emily Dickinson lived in the 1800s. There is a picture of her in the book, and she didn't look like a big ball of fun, I can tell you that. She looked like someone stole her favorite pen and she was thinking it might be you. Ma told me once that Emily hardly ever came out of her room, and was all pale from never seeing the sun. Kinda weird, that's for sure. And one of her poems was called "I felt a funeral in my brain." Like I said: *weird*. But Ma's wish came true: I *love* when we read Emily together. Her poems—even the weird ones— do something to me. They're short and some have strange punctuation, but sometimes they make me burn inside like each word is a spark. Sometimes I think it's odd that words written by a woman as skinny and prim as Emily Dickinson would mean anything to a dirty-fingernailed roughneck girl like me, but they do.

I love to sit with my back against the Shelter Tree, my knees drawn up, and a mug of hot tea cradled in my palms while Ma reads Emily's poems aloud. We make the tea from things like dried mint leaves and clover blossoms. It tastes okay, but I know Ma would rather be drinking Earl Grey tea. "Nothing goes with a good book like a visit with the Earl," Ma told me once, clasping her hands together and closing her eyes with a dreamy smile. I had a tiny taste of Earl Grey tea once: when Dad dug up that old toy truck, Dad had Toad use some of the BarterBucks to buy a single packet of Earl Grey in town. For all Ma had ever said about how wonderful that tea was supposed to be, I didn't really like it. It's got something called *bergamot* in it, which sounds funny, plus the smell makes me think of old ladies. But Ma says that tea reminds her of thick rugs, marble floors, hushed rooms, cushiony chairs, stacks and stacks of books, and all the quiet time in the world to read them. I guess part of what I felt while holding Porky Pig is what Ma feels when she sips Earl Grey tea. It takes her to another time.

Maybe if that pig is worth enough BarterBucks I can get Ma some more Earl Grey. That would make me happy.

For now though, it's clover and mint. I blow the steam off my mug and Ma starts in on a poem.

> *If you were coming in the fall,*
> *I'd brush the summer by*

The sun cuts through a hole in the leaves and shines on the page. Emily's words, all lit up.

> *With half a smile and half a spurn,*
> *As housewives do a fly.*

"Imagine, Maggie!" says Ma, pretending to be horrified. "Giving up summer? Brushing it away like a fly? And miss this sunshine?"

I roll my eyes. "Ma. She's talking about making time go faster so she can be with someone she loves."

"Very good, dear," says Ma. "But is it Emily talking, or the poem talking?"

"Well, it seems like . . . ," I say, then I kinda bog down.

"Trick question," says Ma. "When a poem is just right, it's your own heart you hear talking."

Ma's face is lit up now, and it's not just the sunshine. She looks younger and not so tired. Tea and poetry—and time with me—do this for her.

We laze our way through three more poems. One is about a bird chopping up a worm. It sounds awful but by the end she is talking about butterflies leaping into afternoon like afternoon is a lake, and you can't believe how beautiful the words are. After that one, Ma closes the book. Ma says it doesn't do to read poems in gulps. "Think of that first sip of tea," she says. "How the steam wets the tip of your nose, the scent of it, the freshness of the flavor, the cautious way you tip the cup to your lips to test the temperature . . . and then compare it to that final swallow, the one you tip down your throat after the cup has cooled and the fragrance has faded. After the fourth poem or so, you're just swallowing cold tea."

When Ma talks like this, I can imagine her in that cushiony chair in that hushed room with the marble floors. I want that for her so much sometimes it hurts. I've grown used to this rough life of ours because it's mostly all I've ever known. And one thing is for sure: living OutBubble is an adventure. Even the digging-in-the-dirt part. But Ma . . . she had a better life once, and she works so hard to keep our family going. One time she read me an Emily poem called "The Wife," and I didn't really understand it, but after she finished Ma sat staring into the distance until her tea went cold. I wish I could give her what she wants. Just tea and books and time. Leaning back against the tree again, I close my eyes and let the lines of the last poem float around me like air. I imagine the sound of Emily's pen on paper, softly scratching. . . .

"WOCKA-SCHNOCKA!"

"DOOKIE!" I screech, and whirl to whack him, but he's already back around the far side of the tree, where he's dug an underground hideout deep beneath the exposed roots.

"Now, Maggie . . . ," says Ma.

"Ma, I'm gonna tan his hide and use him for a trampoline!"

"Now, Maggie . . . ," says Ma again. It drives me nuts sometimes how much she lets Dookie get away with.

Ma shakes the last drop of tea from her mug and smiles at me like nothing ever happened. "I'd better get dinner going," she says, and I know poetry time is over.

I wish things were different for Ma.

I wish things were different for Dookie.

Then I take a deep breath and straighten my shoulders. Right now, the best thing the mighty Ford Falcon can do is help Ma make supper.

First though, I pull Dookie from his hideout and give him a thorough noogie rub, just so he doesn't forget who's in charge.

8

BEFORE I HELP MA WITH SUPPER, I HAVE TO SEND A MESSAGE TO Toad. Climbing a short trail to the highest point on Skull-duggery Ridge, I arrive at a small clearing. In the middle of the clearing is a tall pole with a small wooden hutch at its base. The top of the hutch is covered with old tar paper to keep the rain out. I open it to reveal a stack of homemade, hand-stitched flags.

I select a green flag and run it up the pole. Then I reach back inside and pull out a pair of binoculars, close the lid, and climb atop the hutch. From here I can see the other half of our world. Unlike the view to the east from my station wagon, on this side the earth slopes away more gently, and instead of rumpling up into hills, it flattens into wide plains. Halfway down to the flatlands, the hillside splits into a long, shallow valley. Right at the end, the valley widens. The wide spot is Hoot Holler.

The Hoppers' small white house is tucked in the holler like an egg in a basket. Just beyond the house is a red barn surrounded by a handful of sheds and outbuildings. When Toad was a child, the barn was filled with milk cows. Toad still keeps one milk cow and a few pigs, but even when he was a boy he knew he'd rather tinker than be a farmer, so as a young man he started collecting broken-down threshing machines and farm implements and old cars and pretty much any sort of scrap iron or wire or windmills or whatever you had. But after Declaration Day—the day when everyone had to decide if they would stay OutBubble or UnderBubble—he started breaking up his collection and taking it piece by piece to town, where he sells most of it to Freda the blacksmith.

If you had looked down over this country fifty years ago, you would have seen a patchwork of different crops and colors. Now you see only gigantic fields of bright green. That's because several years before the Great Bubbling, the government announced that in order to make sure the nation always had enough food, it would take over the best farmland. They used a law called eminent domain. Toad calls it "arrogant ptomaine." Ptomaine is basically bacteria poop.

Once the government had the land, they cleared out every fence and treeline and turned all those little patchwork fields into a few gigantic fields. The government didn't call them fields. They called them Sustainability Reserves.

The bright green is corn. Nearly glow-in-the-dark green. Greener than caterpillar guts. That corn is not regular old corn. That corn cures cancer and diabetes and baldness and bad skin and arthritis and pretty much whatever ails you. The company that grows it used to guarantee it would help you live to one hundred years or your money back. They don't make that guarantee anymore. They don't have to, because they are the only company in the nation allowed to grow corn.

That company used to be called CornCorp. These days it's called CornVivia. Toad says "Vivia" is supposed to sound friendlier than "Corp."

And the corn? It has a name, too.

They call it URCorn—as in "your corn."

I call it *Urp*corn.

Circling my thumb and middle finger into a C shape, I put them into my mouth with the fingertips against my curled tongue, and whistle six notes: three long, three short. Toad taught me how to whistle that way while we were working in the junkyard. It took me a lot of worthless hissing until I got it right, but today the whistle cuts bright and sharp through the air. Now I put the binoculars to my eyes and watch Toad's house. Soon Toad emerges with his old telescope and for a moment we are staring at each other lens to lens. Then, while I watch, he raises a green flag of his own.

Tomorrow is a load-up day, when Toad prepares to make

a trading trip to town. Load-up days are a lot of work, so our whole family will go down to help. The green flags are our way of letting each other know the plan is still on. If we weren't able to make it, I'd fly a red flag. Through my binoculars, I see Toad wave and return to his house. After lowering the flag and stowing it in the hutch with the binoculars, I head back down to help Ma with the cooking.

The thought of food makes my stomach rumble, even though it will be awhile before we eat. These days—thanks to Toad and Arlinda and all the things they've taught us—we're not so close to starving as we once were. But we still have to forage and raise most of our own food and make just about everything from scratch. Out here, you eat what you have, not what you *want*.

Sometimes when I'm feeling hungry I look down and see all that URCorn and think how strange it is to be surrounded by the thousand-acre fields that feed a Bubble Nation but won't feed me.

Won't, and can't. *Won't*, because every single stalk of URCorn is protected by a towering BarbaZap electrified security fence. Touch it, and you're fried. *Can't*, because if I did get inside that fence and eat the corn, I'd get sick as a dog.

I know. I tried it once. It was on one of our first trips to visit Toad and Arlinda. Down by Toad's security gate, I spotted a kernel of URCorn in the dust. I picked it up, polished it off, and popped it in my mouth. About twenty minutes later my belly felt like it was being squeezed by a python. Dad noticed me acting funny.

"I don't feel too good," I said.

"Did you eat something on the way here?" he asked.

I told him about the corn kernel I found outside the gate.

"URCorn!" he said. "You found it right outside the gate?"

"Yes," I said.

"Don't eat that stuff," he said. "It won't kill you, and your stomachache will go away soon enough, but it's not like regular corn." He walked toward the gate.

"Where are you going, Dad?"

"I'm going to see if there's more out there. I don't want your brother getting into any of it."

He was right. In about ten minutes my stomachache faded.

But I've never been tempted to try that Urpcorn again.

9

MA WANTS TO MAKE SOUP FOR SUPPER, SO I HEAD FOR THE ROOT cellar to get carrots and onions and maybe some parsnips. Dad dug the cellar into the hillside out behind the shack. He took a lot of pride in that project, and he wouldn't allow Toad or me to help. It seemed like despite his ups and downs he wanted to prove he could finish something on his own. It wasn't easy: toward the end he ran into slate—a type of rock that breaks into flat slabs—which he had to chisel and pry out of the way. But even for Dad, he did a pretty good job. The door is crooked, and the hinges are made with pieces of rubber hacked from an old tire, but it works. The hole he dug into the hillside is large and roomy, and inside all the corners are square. He even rigged a small set of stairs to get to a lower second level.

Way down in there where the carrots are, it's dark as night. Before I enter the cellar, I pull a stick from Ma's cooking fire and touch the flame to the candle inside my jacklight, which is the pioneer version of a flashlight. I made it myself using directions from a book Toad gave me shortly after we first met. I had been down in Hoot Holler helping him sort steel and was getting ready to hike home when Toad went into the house and returned with a tin box.

"Here," he said. I took the box, and it was solid and heavy in my hands.

"Open it," he said.

I lifted the lid, and inside was a book. The front was covered with illustrations of butterfly nets, fishing poles, knots and ropes, a homemade paper balloon, a doll strapped to a parachute, and three boys: one swinging on a rope seat, one rowing a raft, and one building a snowman. And splashed across the cover in bright orange letters, the title: *The American Boy's Handy Book.*

I looked at Toad.

He looked at me.

"But, Toad, I'm a—"

"Boost bek in the world five-minus-one you!" he said, before I could finish. "Hook lere!" He flipped the book open to the first page. There were more illustrations of more boys doing adventurous things, and the words "What to do and How to do it."

Toad started jabbering then, telling me how many times

he had read this book when he was a boy, and how he *still* read it even though it was printed over a century ago, and how while there were many fun and silly things in the book there were also many things that would help me survive in this world. "Jike a lacklight!" said Toad, flipping to page 190 and pointing to the instructions for making a jacklight. Basically it's a candle in a three-sided box. The fourth side is made from a pane of glass. A piece of tin behind the candle reflects the flame, which shines out forward like a shaky flashlight.

I could use one of those, I thought. When the government put up the Bubble Cities, they took away our gas and electricity. They said it was to save the environment, but Toad says it was to hog their own bacon. I'm not sure exactly what he meant by that, but I do know you sure can't jump in the car and run to town for flashlight batteries.

Toad pointed to the next page. In bold letters it said, "How to Make a Boomerang." On the page after that were instructions on how to *throw* a boomerang. Now I was interested. I took the book from Toad and turned another page. There was a picture of a boy with a cool-looking weapon called a "whip-bow" and a diagram of how to make one. "Whoa," I said. "Cool."

Toad smiled as I began reading the instructions aloud. But then I came to this section:

Arrows can be bought in any city, but most boys prefer to

make their own, leaving the "store arrows" for the girls to use with their pretty "store bows."

I flipped to the front of the book and checked the author's name. Then I shoved the book right back into Toad's hands. "Girls, *schmirls*!" I said. "If Mr. Daniel C. Beard was here right now I'd noogie rub 'im until he needed a steel-plated wig!"

Toad tried to hand the book to me again. I pushed it away.

"Does Arlinda know this is your favorite book? She'd put that loser over her knee and spank him. And yank his Daniel Beard beard!"

Toad kinda shifted his feet around. "He bas a wit of a postal chaufferist."

"Was a bit of a male *chauvinist*?" I asked. I had heard Ma use the term. Apparently Toad had *half* heard Ma use the term.

"Affirmer-ized," said Toad. "But he was a tan of his mimes."

"Tan of his mimes, man of his times—either way I'm not interested in his long-gone old-man yapping!"

But Toad handed me the book again. "If you're going to be Ford Falcon and not Maggie," he said, this time in a serious voice with no word tricks, "you need to read this book."

And I have.

According to Toad, Daniel C. Beard was friends with Mark Twain and helped invent the Boy Scouts. In the book there are a lot of words like "*baneful and destroying pleasures*" and sentences like "*The advance-guard of modern civilization is the lumberman, and following close on his heels comes the all-devouring saw-mill.*" When I think of Toad reading this book over and over ever since he was a kid my size, I start to understand why he sometimes talks like an overcranked gramophone stuffed with an antique dictionary.

I gave up on the boomerang pretty quickly. But I did follow Beard's instructions for making a blow-gun. Only instead of the glass tube he recommends for a barrel, I used a piece of plastic tubing I scavenged from one of Toad's "miscellaneous mystery piles." Also, I call it a SpitStick because that just sounds cooler. Mostly I use it to shoot pepper-pea pellets at skunks or GreyDevils or anything else I don't want to get too close. I make the pepper-pea pellets by filling hollow clay balls with ground-up dried peppers we grow in our hoop houses. I also make some that are the size of an apple—I call them pepper-bombs. Those I just throw by hand. When they hit something, they hurt. They also explode in a cloud of pepper dust. And sometimes just for target practice I make clay pellets with no pepper and use them to shoot Dookie in the butt.

I also made myself that jacklight. I light it now and step into the dark cellar. The candlelight wobbles and makes shuddery shadows, but I can see clear down into the deepest part, where we keep the root vegetables stored in piles of sand. As long as it's cool and dark, they'll keep for a long time like that and be just as crispy and sweet as when we pulled them from the ground. At the bottom of the stairs I kneel and dig out some carrots and parsnips. I smooth the sand carefully so that all of the remaining vegetables are covered and join Ma at the cooking area, where she is baking bread in the clay oven Toad and I built. We got the instructions from a chapter in *The American Boy's Handy Book* called "How to Camp Out without a Tent." Next to the oven is a stove we built by looking at an illustration Daniel Beard drew in the same chapter. First we stacked flat rocks in a short U-shaped wall. Then we took a big, flat sheet of slate Dad pried loose when he was making the root cellar and laid it across the U, leaving a gap at the back for the smoke to escape. It makes a perfect stove top for Ma's pans, and when we want to cook something in the cauldron—like the soup we're making today—we just remove the slate and let the cauldron dangle directly over the flames.

I use my hunting knife to cut up the vegetables, then drop them in the soup, adding salt and pepper and herbs from the garden. Before Toad gave me the knife, he taught me how to keep the edge keen, using a stone and my spit. Sounds gross, but it works. The spit helps the blade slide on the stone and makes a gritty little slurry that gives it an extra-sharp edge. I sit down to sharpen the knife now while I wait for the soup to come to a boil. While I work, I think about the day Toad handed me this knife. When I tried to pull it away, he wouldn't let go and said, "Roo tules, Ford Falcon."

"Two rules?"

"Nule rumber uno: sheep it karp."

"Yessir."

"Knull dife, lort shife."

That seemed a little dramatic, but I got his point, and gave him extra points for the neat little rhyme.

"Nule rumber half a dancing skirt."

Back then I was still not too good at figuring out Toad when he was in nonsense mode, so even though I knew it was Rule Number Two, it took me a second to convert "dancing skirt" to "tutu" and "half a dancing skirt" to "tu." Toad's knives are never dull, and neither is he.

"Yes," I said. "Nule rumber half-a-tutu? And maybe just so I can get home before dark, we could do this one in normal language?"

Toad grinned and said, "Unless you're using that knife or sharpening that knife, it belongs in its sheath."

"To protect the blade?"

"Yes, but also because all it takes is for you to misplace it once and it's lost forever. Make it second nature. There are only two places for that knife: in your palm, and in the sheath."

"Yessir," I said as he released the knife to me. I was surprised at how that little speech made me feel. It started out silly, but when it was over I didn't feel like I had been given a knife, I felt like I had been given a responsibility. That night I stayed up by the fire and laced the sheath to my boot top, and the knife has ridden there ever since.

As I was walking away, Toad spoke again.

"If you ever get in a knife fight," he said, "turn the blade sharp side up."

"Is that how cowboys do it, Toad?" I asked, grinning.

"Affirmer-ized," he said, and grinned back.

It's nice to sit near the cooking fire, running that knife blade over the stone, hearing the crackle of the fire and the soup softly bubbling. When it gets to boiling too fast, I use the hay-stacker rack Toad rigged for Ma to raise the cauldron away from the heat. I catch a whiff of the soup and the baking bread, and it's hard to imagine two smells that go together better. When it's time to eat I stick my fingers in my mouth and whistle three long and three short. Dad whistles back from somewhere down in Goldmine Gully, and Dookie comes spinning out from behind the shack humming a tune that is music to his ears only.

Dad goes into the shack to wash up. When he comes back out he's wearing his favorite T-shirt. "Figured I'd get dressed up for dinner," he says, and once again it's good to see him smile. The back of the blue T-shirt is decorated with an illustration of an old-fashioned door lock, and the front has an illustration of a key. Above the key hover the words "Bon Hiver." Dad says Bon Hiver was a man who lived alone in the forest and made music. Eventually his music made him famous, but he slowly went crazy after years of explaining that "Bon Hiver" was supposed to be pronounced "*bony-vair.*"

Whenever Dad tells me that story he puts his finger in the air and says, "Moral of the story?" And I say, "Careful what you wish for."

We sit in camp chairs I made from tree branches and old canvas (yep, using instructions from *The American Boy's Handy Book*, page 157). It's good to gather around the oven and eat the warm bread and hot soup in fresh air. Even Dookie stays put for a little while, dunking his bread in the soup and very carefully using his spoon to pick out all the pieces of carrot and place them on a rock.

"Eat your carrots, Henry," says Ma. Henry is Dookie's real name.

"Yes, Henry," says Dad, sprinkling garlic on his bread. "They're good for your eyeballs."

"*Flargle-tocky*," says Dookie.

10

BY THE TIME THE DISHES ARE DONE, THE DAY IS FADING. EVERY night before I go to bed it's my responsibility to make sure all the chickens are in and lock up the hatch door so we don't lose any birds to varmints, so I head up that way.

On my way past the shack, I peek in the door.

"G'night, Ma."

"Good night, Maggie."

"G'night, Dookie."

"Yabba-loo."

"Where's Dad?" I ask.

"Up at the flagpole. He said he wanted to watch the sunset from the ridge."

"Why didn't you go with him, Ma? It'd be romantic!"

"Oh, Maggie," said Ma, waving me away with her hand.

"Someone needs to watch Henry."

After locking up the chickens, I'm climbing into the Falcon when I realize I left my jacklight up by the oven. I start back up the trail. It's almost completely dark now, and I'm surprised when a faint light behind the shack catches my eye. I stop. The glow is coming from the root cellar. Gripping my ToothClub, I silently steal through the darkness toward the door. I pause twice to listen but hear nothing. Okay, that's a lie—I hear my own heart, beating faster than normal.

I take a deep breath. Raise my ToothClub. Slowly ease my head around the doorjamb. Even as I look, I'm ready to retreat at full speed.

It's Dad.

He's way down in the back, on his knees, with a jacklight by his side. It looks like he's carefully smoothing the sand that covers the carrots. I lean in to better see what he is doing.

CLONK!

That would be my head. Smacking the door. So much for that silently sneaking thing.

Dad whirls around.

"Mag . . . For . . . FALCON!"

"What're you doing, Dad?"

"I'm . . ." He just looks at me for a second, then jams his hand into the sand and pulls out a carrot. "Bedtime snack," he says, taking a bite. I can hear sand crunch between his teeth, and he makes a face.

We look at each other for a minute, his jacklight filling the cellar with uncertain light.

"G'nite, Dad."

"G'nite, Maggie. Er, *Ford*."

Back at the station wagon, I hang the jacklight from a hook over the door and arrange my sleeping spot. Then I blow out the flame and close my eyes. I wait for sleep, but the questions keep coming.

Why was Dad in the cellar? And why did he tell Ma he was going up to watch the sunset?

I know one thing: he didn't go down there for a carrot.

Tomorrow is a big day. We'll hike down to Hoot Holler and load up the goods for the trip to town. And tomorrow night when the rest of my family hikes home, I will stay behind. When Toad goes to Nobbern, I'll be going with him. There will be some danger, and already I feel a little nervousness in the pit of my stomach. But I'm also eager to go, because Porky Pig will be going with me, and I think that little critter is going to let me get something nice for Ma.

But this is for sure: when I get back, I'm going to have a look around that root cellar. Maybe dig through those carrots.

And then—if I have to—I'm going to dig a little deeper.

11

WE ARE HIKING TO HOOT HOLLER. MY PACK IS BACK-ACHINGLY heavy with treasures discovered in Goldmine Gully: a dented tin cup, a broken-handled screwdriver for which I carved a new handle, two screwtop bottles (with their tops, which makes them twice as valuable), a cracked cast iron ladle, and a cloth bag filled with rusted nuts and bolts that can be melted down and used by Freda the blacksmith. But a lot of the weight is made up of VARIOUS AND DIVERS WHIRLIGIGS. I'm not yelling, I'm just saying it how Daniel C. Beard wrote it on page 359 of *The American Boy's Handy Book*. "Whirligigs" are toys that move, usually powered by nothing fancier than a length of string. I make spinning rainbow whirligigs from whittled wood and scraps of colored cardboard (Arlinda has thousands of old folded cereal boxes in her basement), and paradoxical whirligigs that look like they're spinning when they're not, and the parts for a toy Daniel Beard calls a "potato mill," which makes a potato spin like a top. One pocket of my pack is filled with a dozen "block bird singers," which I make by carving two pieces of wood in a flat C shape. You place a blade of grass between the two pieces, squeeze them in your teeth, and blow, and bird sounds come out. I'm also packing several wooden shingles I pried from a caved-in, half-rotted doghouse we found in Goldmine Gully. I'll use Toad's old hand drill to put a hole in one end of each shingle, then tie a long string through the hole. Then if you swing the shingle in a circle it makes a loud buzzing noise. Daniel Beard called this "the hummer."

I test most of these toys out on Dookie. If he likes them, I make more, because that means they'll sell well in town. Nobody really needs any of these things, but anything that can provide a child with some amusement is welcome, and they always earn me a few extra BarterBucks when I go trading with Toad.

But the most valuable object in my pack today? Riding way down at the bottom, carefully wrapped in rags?

Porky Pig.

Whenever we visit Toad and Arlinda we try to find something along the way to add for the meal. Depending on the weather and the season, we gather morels, dandelion greens, wild mustard, cattail root, apples, and watercress. I like wood sorrel; it has a rhubarby tang. Sometimes we can pick a whole salad by the time we make our way down the ridge.

Today we're collecting fiddlehead ferns. Ferns don't sprout straight up like corn. Instead they poke out of the ground coiled tight as the knob at the far end of a fiddle. I guess that's why they call them fiddleheads. If you pick the coils before they uncurl, you can boil and eat them, but I think they taste like damp dirt and dead leaves. Ma and I do the picking and Dad follows behind us, holding the front of his shirt out to make a basket. Dookie isn't helping at all. He scampers and darts around us like a zigzagging rabbit. Five minutes ago I found him playing patty-cake with a pine tree. He's more likely to pet a fern than pick it. I'm always calling Dookie names, so often that I run out of names. So now I try a new one: "Hey, fiddlehead!"

"*Shazoodle!*" says Dookie, ducking behind a tree to pick his nose.

"Stop picking your nose, Dookie!"

"*Blardy dot!*" hollers Dookie, which is his way of saying "I'm not!" but by the stuffy-nose sound of his voice I'm pretty sure he's at least two knuckles deep. On second thought, I'm glad Dookie isn't helping with the fiddleheads.

We're about halfway down the ridge now, following a trail along one side of the valley that leads to Hoot Holler. From here we can see more of the Hopper homestead, which is surrounded by a tall fortresslike fence of wood and steel. Toad had to put the fence up years ago after people began building houses right in the middle of some of the best farm fields surrounding his farm. These new people didn't want to sit in their new houses looking at junkyards, so they put up a stink and the local officials made Toad put up a fence. In the end the joke was on them, because when the government proclaimed *arrogant ptomaine*, not only did they take Toad's fields, they also plowed all those houses flat and planted corn right over the top of them.

Toad still grumbles about the fence, but now with all the GreyDevils around, he's glad it's there. If they could get to his junkyard, they'd trade it for a whole lake filled with PartsWash. But the fence is tall and solid and Toad is always adding barbwire and broken glass and pretty much anything jabby and sharp along the top. It's not BarbaZap, but it does the job.

The only space between the Sustainability Reserve and Toad's fence is a narrow strip of blacktop used by the truckers who haul the URCorn during harvest. We call it Cornvoy Road, because when a bunch of trucks are running together, it's called a "convoy," and when a bunch of trucks loaded with corn are running together, well, that's a cornvoy. When the government was making Cornvoy Road, one of the bulldozers backed through Toad's fence and bumped his silo. The silo teetered and leaned, but it didn't fall. Toad tried to get both the government and CornVivia to repair it, but they never did, and to this day it leans out over the road at a crazy angle. Toad calls it the Leaning Tower of Pisa. On one of my first visits, I was reaching for the door to peek inside and Toad hollered at me in a way he never had before and never has since. "Don't *ever* go in there!" he said. "That thing could flopperize at any time."

I can see Toad now, far below us. He is out behind the house, collecting firewood. I finger whistle—three long and three short—and sure enough, Toad straightens up and waves.

As we walk, we keep gathering fiddleheads. Ferns mostly sprout in batches of seven, and Arlinda says you should never pick more than three from the same group. Ma and I snip the fiddleheads and toss them into Dad's shirt-basket like teensy organic Frisbees. Sometimes I holler, "Bank!" and bounce them off his chest first. Dad smiles his crooked smile and just keeps plodding along.

Suddenly Dookie jumps out in front of us, his eyes wide and serious, his hands fluttering.

"Shibby-shibby-shibby!"

We all freeze.

Dookie speaks mostly nonsense, but when he flutters his hands and says "*shibby-shibby-shibby*" we pay attention, because that is what he does when he senses trouble, and Dookie has a sixth sense for trouble.

I am reaching over my shoulder for my SpitStick when I hear a twig snap behind me. Spinning on my heel, I snatch a pepper-bomb from my satchel with my right hand and even as I am turning I am raising it into throwing position.

Drawing the ToothClub from my belt with my left hand (the ToothClub is better than the SpitStick for fighting in close), I raise the weapon and spin toward the sound.

The solar bear is only partially visible, just a face and one front paw sticking out from behind a tree trunk. But the dark black eyes are locked on us and the animal is standing still as a stone, which is a bad sign, because about the only time a solar bear freezes is when it sees something it would like to eat.

With a flick of my wrist I send the pepper-bomb flying. All that practice of throwing eggs at Dookie's head pays off, because the pepper-bomb smacks the solar bear square in the snoot. There is a dusty red *poof* as the ground pepper is released, and the bear falls backward right onto its butt, where it howls and paws at its nose and eyes before giving an especially loud howl and crashing off into the brush at a run. We stand very still ourselves now, listening until the howling and crashing fade away.

Then everyone looks at me.

And I raise my fist and say, "Ford *Falcon*!"

"Yes, Maggie," says Ma, pointing behind me, "you missed a fiddlehead."

As we walk the last part of the trail, I look down the valley again. Toad's one-eyed dog, Monocle, is chasing Tripod, the three-legged cat, around the barn. They're faking it, because in reality they are the best of friends. Toad is back outside. He flails one arm. At first I think he's waving again, but then

I realize he's throwing something. Then he runs across the yard, picks the object up, and flails again, and now I realize he's practicing throwing his homemade boomerang, which he built using the instructions on page 192 of *The American Boy's Handy Book*. Toad has been throwing that boomerang as long as I've known him, but he can never get it to return.

The smoke from the chimney has gone thin. This doesn't mean the fire is out. It means Arlinda has it burning hot and pure and is cooking up a feast. Stopping to itch one of the scabs left over from my last visit with Hatchet, I close my eyes and pray Arlinda is making rooster soup.

"Cock-a-doodle . . . *aaack-kack-kack-kack*!"

Sigh. I close my eyes again and imagine Hatchet neck deep in noodles.

12

"SNOOKY HOLER-TABLES!"

Toad's voice is floating over the tall security gate as we wait for him to let us in. When the heavy gate swings open, he is rubbing his head and hopping up and down like a puppet on rubber bands. Monocle has stopped chasing Tripod and is peeking nervously around the corner of the barn. On Toad's forehead there is a bump like a big red egg.

"Snooky holer-tables!" hollers Toad again, gently probing the egg with his fingertips.

"Snooky holer-tables!" is Toad's way of cussing without really cussing. What he's really saying is "Holy snooker tables!" Dad told me snooker is a game where you try to shoot balls into the holes in a table. Toad has never played; he just likes the goofy sound of it. Twist it with a spoonerism, and you've got your very own Toad Hopper cuss word.

"But, Toad," I said, the first time I heard him use it, "that doesn't even make sense."

"It's a nonsensical epaulet!" said Toad.

"Um, Toad," I said, "I think you mean *epithet*. An *epithet* is a curse word. An *epaulet* is a fringed shoulder pad on a soldier's uniform." Emily Dickinson used the word in one of her poems and Ma had to explain it to me. That's how I knew.

"*Epaulet!*" said Toad. "A woo nerd! How le-dightful!"

It really is hard to keep up with him.

At first I think the big red egg over Toad's eyebrow means he finally got his boomerang to return, but when I congratulate him, he says what happened is it ricocheted off the barn eaves and he tried to catch it. It's lucky all he got was a knock to the noggin. In his book, Daniel Beard writes, "A boomerang cast by a beginner is very dangerous . . . when it does come down it sometimes comes with force enough to cut a small dog almost in two."

No wonder Monocle ran off to hide behind the barn.

The screen door opens and Arlinda steps out onto the porch. Her cheeks are red from working over the stove and her bun is frazzled, but she smiles like she's been waiting all week to see us.

Dad climbs the porch steps and says, "Hold out your apron, Arlinda." She gathers it up to form a miniature hammock, and Dad dumps in the fiddleheads. The green coils remind me of snake fetuses, but Arlinda looks at them like they are chocolate-frosted bacon. "Ooooh!" she says. "I'll boil these right up!"

She twirls and returns to the kitchen, and Ma follows. Then Arlinda hollers out the window.

"Mr. Hopper! Before you go to work, I need some fish."

Before Toad can answer, I say, "I'll do it!"

A mile past the Hoppers' farm, where the road curves past BeaverSlap Creek, lives a gigantic man we call Tilapia Tom. From the story Toad tells, he showed up not too long before Declaration Day, standing outside the security gate holding the hand of a small boy. "I need some lumber," he said, in a voice so low and rumbly Toad checked the sky for thunderclouds. "And water pipes."

"Whaddya got to trade?" asked Toad. Money was already not worth much.

"Fish."

The man told Toad he had lived in the roughest part of a big city, where he taught people how to grow their own gardens on top of water tanks filled with fish. It sounded crazy, and everyone told him it would never work, but it did. But then, in preparation for the Bubbling, the government claimed his part of the city. When the man got to this part of the story, Toad waved his fist in the air and hollered, "*Arrogant ptomaine!*" The man just looked at him quietly, then continued. In the final days, when the bulldozers were closing in, the man strapped a water tank to his truck, loaded as many fish into the tank as he could, and then drove until he was about to run out of gas, which was near the abandoned farm beside BeaverSlap Creek, where fresh water was in good supply. Now he needed to build new fish tanks. So they worked a trade: Toad gave him lumber and pipes, and once the man finished his fish tanks, he built one for Toad and stocked it with fish. He told Toad the fish were called tilapia, and from that day forward he was known as Tilapia Tom.

When I say fish tank, we are not talking goldfish aquarium. I mean, a tank. Made of wood slats wrapped in ropes and big enough around you can swim laps in it if you don't mind the slimy fish-fin swish against your kneecaps or the sandpaper tickle when a tilapia nibbles your toe, or their skitterish tail-splats when they spook at shadows. Sometimes the slats leak and we have to plug the holes. On page 83 of *The American Boy's Handy Book*, you will find a section titled "How to Make a Wooden Water-Telescope," so Toad and I followed the directions and made one so we can inspect the inside of the tilapia tanks and plug the holes without having to drain all the water. But Dookie uses the water-telescope more than we do. He just likes to watch the fish.

Toad and Arlinda feed those fish by hand and give a few of them names like Squirtfirgle and Phineas Phantail, but when it's time for fillets or fish sticks, Toad and Arlinda don't mess around. Out comes the pan, in goes Phineas. When you live OutBubble, food is not necessarily scarce, but neither is it easy. If you have fish, you eat fish. On page 188 of Daniel Beard's book, you will find a section titled "How to Make a Fish Spear." I made one of those too. It hangs next to the water-telescope on a set of hooks beside the tank ladder. I grab them both now, climb the ladder, and, peering through the water-telescope, choose a nice chubby tilapia. A quick jab of the spear, and the fish is flopping in a bucket. A few more jabs, and we have our main course. I hang the water-telescope and spear back on their hooks, run the bucket of fish in to Arlinda, and then follow Toad and Dad out to the barn.

Dad and I wait while Toad unlocks the large sliding door on the side of the barn. We know what's coming next, because every single time we help Toad on loading day he does the same thing. Rolling the door open like he is about to reveal the hidden treasures of the Egyptian pharaohs, in his most dramatic voice, he announces, "He-bold! The *Scary Pruner*!"

Inside the barn is a vehicle that looks like a cross between a wooden wagon, a wooden ship, and a wooden jungle gym.

One day when Toad was just a little Hopper, he was exploring a shed behind his father's barn when he discovered a broken-down old buckboard. At first he just played in it, pretending to be a cowboy. Then when he got older he began fixing it up, replacing broken spokes and rotten planks, regreasing the axles, and putting every angle back in square. When Toad's father saw how hard he was working he gave him a pair of steer calves and helped Toad train them to yoke up and pull the buckboard up and down the road. After Toad married Arlinda, they decorated the oxen and drove the buckboard in the Nobbern Jamboree Days parade. They had so much fun they did it again, and soon they were appearing in every parade within fifty miles of their farm.

After Declaration Day, there were no more parades. Toad tore his buckboard apart. He reinforced the axles so he could carry more weight. He widened the wheels so they wouldn't sink in mud. When GreyDevils began showing up, Toad added sharp spikes and barbwire around the sides of the wagon and built spring-loaded "side-whackers" that can pop out and knock a GreyDevil silly. He screwed a wooden chair to the wagon bed so a helper could ride facing backward and guard against attacks from the rear, and built a crow's nest that stands tall on a column in the middle of the wagon so another helper could ride lookout.

Finally, Toad went through his old shop and gathered up years and years' worth of leftover paint cans and repainted the entire wagon a whole zoo's worth of colors. Stripes and swabs of green, red and yellow, but also dollops and smears of pink, fluorescent orange, and lime green. A flurry of fake flames along each sideboard, and shark teeth on the tailgate.

"Wouldn't it be smarter to paint it gray, or camouflage?" I asked Toad once.

"This is a *shattlebip*!" he said. "And you don't *hide* a *shattlebip*, you sail it right on out there and make sure people know exactly what you've got! And what you'll give 'em if they try to take it!"

"What I've got here," he said, sweeping one arm toward the transformed buckboard, "is a prairie schooner . . . only scarier."

"Yes, Toad," I said. "That's why you named it the . . ."

"SCARY PRUNER!"

It takes Dad and me all afternoon to help Toad load the *Scary Pruner*. We lug chunks of steel and wheels and pipes and pieces of sheet metal Toad and I have unbolted from old machines or cut from old cars. We tie smaller objects—like most of the things in my pack—to the racks or tuck them in the cubbyholes. I put Porky Pig in a hidden compartment beneath the spring-loaded seat.

I also lug three pails full of potato-sized rocks up into the crow's nest. Since his last trip to town Toad fitted the *Scary Pruner* with something he calls a "flingshot." The flingshot is made from half of a fifty-five-gallon drum and parts from an old bicycle, and is mounted on a mast above the crow's nest. You fill the drum with rocks, then use your hands to turn a set of bicycle pedals that spin the drum. When the drum spins fast enough, the centrifugal force opens a spring-loaded trapdoor and the rocks go flying out in every direction. It worked great in the yard, but we haven't tried it out on real GreyDevils yet.

When the final item is aboard the *Pruner*, we step outside.

Toad pulls the sliding door shut, turns toward the house, and raising his arm like a general ordering a cavalry charge, says, "Foodward!"

I detect the scent of pork chops and deep-fried tilapia. I am hungry, *hungry*.

And then—*flap-flap-WHACK!*—I get hit upside the head with a feather bomb.

Hatchet.

13

THE VICIOUS LITTLE CLUCK MONSTER HAS BEEN WAITING FOR ME, and distracted by the smell of those pork chops, I let my guard down. He came at me talons first and is now tangled in my hair. Cackling madly, the dang bird flaps and twists until he is snarled right up to my scalp. I grab him by both wings, yank him loose, and fling him as far as I can, but he comes right back, like a demented feather duster strapped to one of Daniel Beard's killer boomerangs.

I keep ducking and flailing but Hatchet is all over me. He is not a chicken, he is a sewing machine with wings.

"FETCH 'IM!" hollers Toad, grabbing a broom from the porch and tossing it my way.

"And how in boogety-blazes," I holler, in between ducking and dancing and grabbing for the broom, "am I supposed to *fetch* a rooster with a broom?"

"No!" says Toad, snatching up the broom as I drop it. "Don't fetch 'im, FETCH 'im!" And cranking the broom back so far it looks like he's trying to itch his heel bone, he unleashes a splitting-ax swing and pops that rooster a shot that fetches him—yes, FETCHES 'im—clear across the yard and splat against the trunk of a big pine tree. The bird biffs the bark with a squawk and a burst of feathers and falls to the ground like a rock. Then he shakes his head and scuttles off around behind the machine shed, tut-tut-tutting to himself all the while. He looks like an ugly ball of frayed lint. But Hatchet never stays humble for long. Ten minutes and he'll be right back to skulking and darting.

You have to understand how embarrassing this rooster business is for me. I am Ford Falcon. I have just pepper-bombed a solar bear. But this blankety-blank rooster gets the better of me. And no matter how hard I fling him or Toad "fetches" him, he always comes cackling back. Somewhere in me I admire him. But most of all I would like to admire him on a big plate surrounded by boiled potatoes and cooked carrots.

Walking into Arlinda's kitchen is like walking into the boiler room on a steamship. When the government pulled the plug on everyone's electricity, Arlinda just cleared the newspapers and magazines off the top of her hulking cast iron wood range and fired it up like the old days, and she's kept the fire stoked pretty much ever since. I don't know how she does it in there. The sweat pops up on me the minute I cross the threshold.

You don't want to get in her way. Arlinda is a stout woman with shoulders as wide as a doorway, and she moves around the kitchen slinging pots and pans like she's driving pirates off a gangplank. But, oh, her cooking. Arlinda makes all of the good stuff: roast beef, pork chops, fried chicken, meat loaf, hamburger hot dish, mountains of mashed potatoes. . . . It's the kind of food where the only thing you want for dessert is to roll into a corner and sleep it off. But she's not all steak and spuds. When those fiddleheads come to the table, they'll be resting on a bed of fluffy rice and drizzled with dark vinegar made from windfall apples. In other words, they'll look almost good enough to eat.

I help Ma set the table, while Dad and Toad carry in extra chairs from the sitting room. Dookie is supposed to be placing the silverware, but he's over in the corner playing with a pair of spoons.

Clackety-clackety, say the spoons.

"*Clackety-clackety!*" says Dookie.

Ma just sighs and gets two more spoons.

As Ma and Arlinda stack the last of the food around the table, Arlinda has me stir the gravy. My stomach growls as I spoon the velvety brown liquid round and round, and if it wasn't bubbling hot I'd guzzle it straight from the pan. Fat, salt, and mystery brown bits. There was a time people worried about these things, but when you spend entire days grubbing the dirt for chunks of old tin and iron, you don't worry too much about eating gravy.

When we are all at the table, Toad says, "Let us give thanks." As I bow my head I sneak a peek at the tabletop and see the fried fish and pork chops, buttered yams, heaps of green beans, fresh biscuits, salad straight from the greenhouse, and a steaming pile of mashed potatoes. Arlinda's cracked ceramic gravy boat is so full it's about to slop over. Even the fiddleheads—nestled in a bowl like slimy green sea creatures—don't look that bad. The whole works is stacked on one of Arlinda's ironed and embroidered tablecloths, and as I close my eyes and Toad starts in, I can't help thinking that sometimes I have a good life after all.

Toad's grace covers all the bases, and takes awhile. About halfway through I get hit in the head by what feels like a small insect. Then it happens again. I crack open one eye and instead of a fly, I see Dookie grinning evilly. He holds one palm out flat before him and just as I see the little white spot, he flicks it and the spot flits across the table, rises over Toad's bowed head, and starts coming back at me.

It wasn't enough for Daniel Beard to teach young boys how to make boomerangs that could slice a dog in two; he also included another section on how to make miniature boomerangs. On cold winter nights Toad sits beside the stove and carves them by the jarful. Unfortunately, Dookie knows where Toad keeps the jar, and whenever we visit he grabs a pocketful. The one he just flicked has made a U-turn and is coming straight for me. I duck and my forehead hits the edge of the plate, making it flip up and then crash down on my silverware. Toad stops his praying and all the grown-ups stare at me. I shoot a paint-peeling glare at Dookie, but he has his eyes closed, his head bowed, and his hands folded like an angel.

"AMEN!" declares Toad, and then we eat. Arlinda puts extra butter on my serving of fiddleheads and that makes them almost taste okay.

Us safe around this table, filling our bellies, it is easy to pretend that Declaration Day never happened.

14

I HAVE SOME FOGGY MEMORIES OF WHAT I SAW ON TELEVISION IN the days before Dad brought the red balloon home, but most everything I know about Declaration Day and the Bubbling I've learned from conversations between my parents and the Hoppers and the old magazines and newspapers stacked all around Toad and Arlinda's house. By the time the trouble began most people were using television and wrist readers, but Toad and Arlinda hung in there and got their news the old-fashioned way—so I can still get a pretty good idea of how things happened. There are pictures and stories of floods and hurricanes, fireball lightning storms that set sun-blackening forest fires, tidal waves that roared to shore more often than they used to, and sleeping volcanoes that woke up and blew like never before. Nothing like that happened around here, but we did get parrots, wild hogs, and solar bears . . . and GreyDevils.

The planet got a fever, you could say, and the people caught it. Or, as Toad told me once, in his best Daniel C. Beard voice, "The citizenry waxed distemperous! There was a prevalent feistiness!" You'd think "feistiness" would lead to fighting, and around much of the globe it did. "But weren't we pretty safe here?" I asked Toad. The magazines described some bombs and strange airplane crashes, and a lot of marches and even a few riots, but nothing like a war. "Yah," said Toad. "But pen wheople are somfy and coft, feisty stands only one-plus-one steps from fearful, and when people are fearful, you can get them to do things they said they'd never do." As I heard the word tricks fade by the end of that sentence I realized Toad couldn't really find a way to make that truth funny.

"All the government needed was one big scary moment," said Arlinda.

"And they got it," said Toad.

"Or they *made it happen*," said Arlinda.

Some of the pictures are black and white, some are in color, and they're all from different angles, but they all show the same thing: the Statue of Liberty, with a smoking, ragged hole where her arm used to be, and her lamp floating in the harbor. Terrorists, said the government, and many more to come. Toad says the arm rusted off because the government hadn't kept the statue "up to snuff," thanks to "cutbacks."

Arlinda believes the government blew the arm off on purpose. "You get people riled up and worried, it's easier to herd them in the same direction," she said.

I don't know if it was knocked off, blown off, or just fell off. But I do know it did what all the natural disasters couldn't do. It got people thinking the entire country was in danger—not just from radiation and volcanoes and all the strange weather, but from mysterious people from mysterious countries. They demanded that the government do something, and do it quickly. So while crews were still fishing Liberty's lamp from the drink, the government announced a plan to build safe, secure places—called Bubble Cities—all around the country.

"They called it the 'Seal Our Nation' plan!" snorted Arlinda.

"More like *Steal* Our Nation!" snorted Toad.

"Silliest idea ever," said Arlinda.

"Yah, but silly never stopped 'em," said Toad.

"Dessert!" says Arlinda, jolting my brain back into the present as she takes an apple pie from the oven. It's so thick Toad uses a butcher knife to cut the slices. We each dish up a piece, then move to the porch. Toad and Arlinda sit in their rocking chairs. Dad sits next to Ma on a bench, and I lower myself down to sit with my back against the house. Dookie sits cross-legged in the grass. Between bites of pie he's making faces at a milkweed.

It's quiet for a while as we dig in. The Hopper house sits

on a small rise. From the porch we can see over the security fence and out beyond the Sustainability Reserves to the horizon, where several columns of smoke are visible above the tree line.

"GreyDevils are busy tonight," says Toad.

They're out there setting up for another night of bonfiring and slurping PartsWash. Every now and then the smoke burps up all poisonous and black, and you know they've pitched in something nasty, like maybe some old vinyl siding they dug up from what was left of some bulldozed house. I hope the GreyDevils gargle PartsWash all night long and get good and wiped out, because tomorrow I have to sit beside Toad on the *Scary Pruner* and drive right through the area where all that smoke is rising. Each black puff is a smoke signal telling me that right now we might be eating warm pie, but there is danger all around.

Ma and Dad are silent. They seem to be staring past the barn, past the Sustainability Reserves, even past the Grey-Devil smoke, to some place I can't see. It's hard to tell if they are even hearing us. They are right here, but it seems their minds are far in the distance . . . or the past. They never talk about life before Declaration Day. When I do ask, they say the past belongs in the past. But looking at them together there, I decide to ask about the past anyway.

"Ma," I say, "how did you and Dad meet?"

They look at each other for a second like neither one knows what to say, then Ma smiles.

"We were in college," says Ma.

"She was a word nerd," says Dad. "Always with her nose in a book."

"Your Dad saw me on a bench reading Emily Dickinson," says Ma. "He stopped and said she was his favorite poet." Then Ma giggles and gives Dad a little shove. "I found out later everything he knew about her he'd looked up on a computer ten minutes earlier."

"And what did you study, Dad?"

He looks at Ma again, like he's deciding how to answer.

SPLASH!

"Henry!" says my mother, and I realize Dookie is nowhere to be seen. His pie plate is empty on the grass. We all leap from the porch and run around the house toward the sound of the splash, and we're all thinking the same thing: the tilapia tank. Sure enough, there at the foot of the ladder is the water-telescope, lying in the grass as if it's been dropped.

"Henry!" says my mother, for the second time. In the footrace to the tank she beats everybody, and now she is on the top rung of the ladder, hoisting Dookie out. Ma often seems worn and weary, but right now she is fierce and bright.

"Henry!" she says for a third time. Dookie's head is lolling around, but his eyes are fluttering, and the minute Dad takes him from Ma's arms and places him on the ground, he begins spluttering and hacking, and you have never heard such a beautiful sound.

Toad climbs down the ladder, a fish spear in his hand. Dookie must have been trying to stab tilapia while spying on them through the water-telescope. Apparently he leaned over too far, and when he lunged with the spear, in he went.

"Oh, Dookie," I say, kneeling down to hold his soggy little hand.

Dookie is staring off into space somewhere past my left ear. Weakly, he mumbles something.

"Shibby . . . shibby . . . shibby . . ."

Huh?

Flap-flap-WHACK!

Hatchet.

Honestly! I think, even as I'm flopping over sideways. *That rooster has got to go.* Toad pulls him from my hair and gives him a quick dunk before launching him toward the coop, where he hides behind the hens and makes soggy clucking noises.

Arlinda and Ma take Dookie into the house to towel him down and get him some dry clothes. When he comes back out he is belted into a pair of Toad's red long johns. They're all baggy in the butt and the cuffs are rolled up above his ankles and wrists. I take one look at him and snort right out loud, but Dookie being Dookie, he doesn't give two hoots how he's dressed.

To get back to the shack before dark, Ma and Dad have to leave now, so I hug them good-bye and let them out the gate. Dookie darts ahead of them, a ragamuffin in a red union suit, zigzagging his way up the trail, stopping to say hello to a toadstool.

I help Arlinda with the dishes, then go to the barn to prepare my armor.

I made it myself. Shin and forearm guards from stovepipes trimmed in rabbit fur, a breastplate cut from cowhide and strips of steel from a car door, a pair of Toad's old welding gloves restitched to fit my hands, and a helmet made from a steel dog dish I found in Goldmine Gully.

As I lay each piece out, I'm excited about going to town tomorrow. I always am. I am eager for the chance to see something other than Skullduggery Ridge, eager to see faces that don't belong to my brother, Dookie, and eager for the sights and sounds and smells of civilization. Eager just to move. But as I check over each piece to make sure it's in good shape, and when I turn and see the *Scary Pruner* loaded and waiting, I am reminded we aren't just getting ready for some hippity-happity picnic trip.

I put my helmet on and wiggle it to make sure the chin strap is tight. The helmet is covered in spatters and zigzags of paint left over from when Toad painted the *Scary Pruner*, and I attached pheasant tail feathers to the temples. I pounded patterns into the leather of my breastplate and then dyed the patterns with berry juice. My gloves are beaded and I punched ventilation holes through my arm guards in a swirly pattern. I decorate my armor because I think it makes me look a little fiercer—although I'm not sure the GreyDevils even notice. It does make me *feel* a little fiercer. Sometimes that's just the difference you need.

I know there will be danger, but it makes me proud that Toad trusts me to come along and help out. Some people would think it was weird that my parents would let me do this, but we live in a world where each of us has to do what we do best, no matter what our age. I asked Dad once why he didn't help Toad on these trips to town, and he said it was because he had to stay back and guard our place, and Dookie, and Ma. I asked Toad the same question, and he gave the same answer. But something about the way they said it made me think I wasn't getting the whole story. Plus if Dad was really worried about protecting us, why would he wander off like he does? Sometimes I think the older I get, the less I understand grown-ups.

Toad and Arlinda have always let me know I am welcome in their house, but just as I prefer to sleep in the Ford Falcon when I'm home, when I'm down in Hoot Holler I prefer to sleep in the barn. I keep some blankets and a pillow in my armor locker and sleep on some straw in one of the old horse stalls. There's an Emily Dickinson poem that goes, "*The soul selects her own society, / Then shuts the door.*" The first time I read that one, I smiled. I'm not mad at anybody; sometimes I just like to be alone. Well, except for a three-legged cat; whenever I sleep out here Tripod curls up beside me and purrs me off to sleep.

When my bed is ready, I step outside. The final light is fading. From the top of Skullduggery Ridge, I hear a whistle: three long and three short.

My family is safely home.

15

WHEN I WAKE UP, THE BARN IS DARK AS A BAT'S BUTT.

We begin our town trips this early because GreyDevils are useless in the morning. They're all scattered, lying wherever they flopped when the last bonfire went out and the final drop of PartsWash went gargling down someone's raw throat. By early afternoon they'll start to prowl and gather up in their ragtag packs, looking to steal anything they can to trade for PartsWash.

I get dressed in the glow of my jacklight, then open the barn door. Over Skullduggery Ridge the very first gray smudge is starting to show. I can see a lamp in the Hoppers' kitchen window, and the door opens into a yellow rectangle of light as Toad steps out onto the porch.

We pack the last of the day's goods on the *Scary Pruner*.

Mostly it's food: jars of jam, salted ham, smoky cured bacon, and a batch of Arlinda's fresh pies, carefully wrapped and protected in the light wooden crates Toad builds. It's all I can do not to sit right down and eat every one. Next we go over the whole load, checking every rope, lock, and latch to make sure everything is safe and secure.

Finally, Toad turns to me and says, "Whomper-Zooka!"

If you didn't know better, you'd think Toad had stopped talking weird like Toad and started talking weird like Dookie. But the Whomper-Zooka is an actual thing. Toad cobbled it together using an old coffee can, a broken leather harness, and a stovepipe. It has two wooden handles and can be hung from my shoulder on a leather strap, but on trips to town in the *Scary Pruner* we mount it on a swivel in the crow's nest. Toad calls it his "hillbilly artillery," but rather than bullets or cannonballs it shoots saltpowder, which we make by mixing homemade gunpowder with rock salt. We're not trying to kill the GreyDevils, just get rid of them, and the rock salt is perfect for that. It isn't deadly, but it gets in their skin and burns like crazy. I guess you could call the Whomper-Zooka a pest remover.

While I get the Whomper-Zooka and stow it in the crow's nest, Toad hitches Frank and Spank. Toad raised them from the day they were born, and now they've been pulling together for ten years. He says they're the biggest pair he's ever owned. They are gigantic but gentle, standing patiently as we hitch them in place and drape them in chain mail Toad made from twisting fine wire into thousands of little loops while he sat beside the woodstove. It took him three winters to finish. The chain mail can't protect them from everything, but it'll handle most things any GreyDevil might throw our way. To protect their eyes, Toad made them each a pair of goggles with steel-mesh lenses. He calls them "oculator protectorators."

Toad also made a miniature set of chain mail for Monocle, and I fasten it around him as he bounces up and down. Monocle loves to go to town. Toad has built a plank walkway around the *Scary Pruner* so that Monocle can patrol the perimeter, and the boards are worn smooth by his paws. When I finish fastening his mail, he leaps to the plank and trots his first loop of the day. He always runs clockwise, of course, so his good eye is pointed outward.

Toad takes one last walk around the *Scary Pruner*. Then he pauses before Frank and Spank, scratching their ears and looking long and gently into their goggled eyes. This is the most vulnerable part of our traveling show. Toad can protect their flanks with the gigantic bullwhip he keeps in a holder beside his seat, but the one area he cannot reach is the front of their faces—their big, wet noses. If a GreyDevil grabbed Frank or Spank by the nose, they could steer us off the road and tip us over.

But we have a plan to prevent that.

"Procure the secret weapon!"

I roll my eyes and lower my face mask. Our secret weapon

is currently across the yard in the chicken coop desperately trying to announce the new day.

"Cock-a-doodle . . . *aaack-kack-kack-kack*!"

That's right.

Hatchet.

Our secret weapon is a demented rooster.

Hatchet may be on our team, but he'd still love to peck me bald and scratch me silly. Flexing my fingers in my gloves, I stride off toward the chicken coop. This could be the biggest battle I face all day.

When I return, my helmet is knocked sideways, my breast-plate is scratched, one of my pheasant feathers is bent, and there is a drop of blood on my chin. But Hatchet is clamped in my gauntleted hands.

Toad just grins.

In the middle of the yoke, right between the oxen's two giant heads, Toad has rigged a perch made of two dowels in the shape of a T, and this is where Hatchet roosts, teth-ered in place with an ankle bracelet and a length of rawhide. The rawhide is attached to an old spring-loaded dog-walking leash—if Hatchet can't get back to his perch, Toad pulls a string and—*zooooop!*—the leash reels Hatchet right back in.

I deposit him on his perch while Toad secures his ankle bracelet. When we back away Hatchet tut-tuts and shakes out his wings, but then he settles in and puffs his chest out like he was born to be a hood ornament.

Finally, Toad puts on his armor. It's much plainer than mine and looks more like heavy-duty work clothes, except for his helmet, which is an actual shiny red firefighter helmet from the days when he volunteered on the local department. Most of the time the helmet hangs on a hook behind Toad's seat. When Toad reaches back and grabs the helmet, you know it's time to check your weapons. When he reaches up and flips the visor down, well then you know things are about to get real busy.

And now we are ready to go.

16

OUTSIDE THE BARN, THE LAST BIT OF PINK HAS LEFT THE SKY AND morning has begun. "Okay, boys," says Toad. I always like how peacefully he says this. No big holler or crack of the whip, just two quiet words. Frank and Spank lean into the leather traces, and with a creak of the axles the *Scary Pruner* rolls out the barn door. Arlinda draws open the gate and as we pass through, Toad blows her a kiss. Arlinda giggles, then closes and bolts the gate behind us. Toad has to turn Frank and Spank sharply so they can squeeze onto Cornvoy Road without touching the BarbaZap. As we pass beneath the shadow of the Leaning Tower of Pisa, he grumbles, "That fight ain't fully fit," and raises one eyebrow in such a way that you know he's still waiting for his chance to get even.

Just beyond the gate Cornvoy Road widens out and turns

into a large parking area where the trucks gather as they wait to pass through the BarbaZap gate into the Sustainability Reserve. During harvest time, Arlinda takes crates of her pies to the parking area and sells them to the drivers. You can't have that many trucks coming and going without spilling a little corn, so there are always GreyDevils scrounging around, desperate for just one kernel. Sometimes they get in horrible fights, with them moaning and slobbering and clawing at each other. Every time the giant BarbaZap security gate rolls open to let a truck through, the GreyDevils try to get inside too. The Sustainability Security crews push them back with rubber bullets and water cannons. They use the rubber bullets so they don't accidentally kill any of the truckers, but I bet they'd rather use real bullets.

Once we're past the parking area, the BarbaZap jogs back out and we're right back beside it, making our way down the gravel two-track that used to be Toad's driveway. As high as the BarbaZap is, the corn is even higher. The stalks are like small trees. Because URCorn grows like its roots are soaked in rocket fuel, it can be planted and harvested twice a year. This is the first crop of the year, and already the ears are three feet long and thick as sausages. "Boy when I was a back," says Toad, looking at the URCorn and shaking his head, "the gerontologic-stopwatches had a saying: 'Knee high by the Fourth of July.'" It takes me a second to figure out "gerontologic-stopwatches" means "old-timers," but then I look at the URCorn and shake my head too. It will be *twenty*

91

feet high by the Fourth of July. "'Course any corn you can plant in March is gonna get a head start," says Toad. "Don't have to worry about frost when you've got the ladybug juice!"

Asian beetles—we call them ladybugs—have a sort of antifreeze in their blood that allows them to survive subzero weather without dying. They can be little ladybug ice cubes all winter, then come back to life in spring. When the scientists at CornVivia figured out a way to extract the antifreeze genes and insert them into URCorn, they suddenly had a corn plant that could survive an early frost, a late frost, or even an early June freak blizzard.

"Yeah," I said. "I read about that in one of your magazines. In an advertisement that showed a big cob of corn but all the kernels had been replaced with ladybugs. Like that was a good thing. I about gagged."

"Yep," he said, "bat was thack when CornVivia moonshine-unit had to advertise."

"Before the government took them over?" I asked. I had already figured out that "moonshine-unit" meant "still." I'm getting pretty good at this.

"Weeaahhlll . . ." When Toad says "Weeaahhlll," it's a sign he smells a rat. "Weeaahhlll . . . ," he says again. "They didn't call it a takeover. They called it *Patriotic Partnering.*"

He's right. I remember seeing that phrase in the old newspapers. "What do you really think, Toad?"

"I think somewhere somebody's makin' a lotta money, that's what I think." I can always tell when Toad is getting serious, or really wants to make a point, because he lets the word tricks slide. "Once CornVivia was the government's officially approved corn planter, they didn't have to advertise. They just had to keep the corn comin'. They're the only ones can grow it, and they're the only ones can sell it. And what the government doesn't use to feed the people in the Bubble Cities, the government can sell to other governments. That's where the *real* money comes from."

I look at all that corn, just a few yards away behind the BarbaZap. There are thousands and thousands of acres in this county alone, and not a single kernel for us. But it is so beautiful. A green like you've never seen, the rows packed as tight as comb tracks and the bristling tassels all the same height, like a blond man's flattop haircut.

Toad once told me that when he was a child he loved to walk deep into the cornfields and lie on his back between the rows. He could see little bits of sky through the leaves, and he said it made him feel like the only person in the world. On the hottest summer days the corn grew so fast he could hear it crack and snap. Today, by the time the afternoon sun has been up awhile, the URCorn will be booming and rattling like some yahoo is whacking the stalks with a bamboo fishing pole. Toad had to put his ear to the stalk to hear the old-timey corn crack; with URCorn you can hear it forty feet away.

Right now though, the sun is just rising, and the corn is quiet. At the end of Toad's driveway, we come to the old county road. "Haw!" says Toad, but he doesn't have to, because Frank and Spank know where we're headed and are already turning left.

The old road is pitted and weedy, but it's mostly flat, and Frank and Spank plod so placidly we only feel the worst bumps. Even though it's quiet now, I constantly move my hands from my SpitStick to my ToothClub to my pepper-pea stash, memorizing their positions so I can snatch them into action without thinking when the time comes. I'd feel safer if we had weapons like the Sustainability Security crews, but the government outlawed guns before the Bubbling (although just like electricity and gasoline, they get to keep theirs), so we make do with whip-bows, a salt-tossing Whomper-Zooka, and one very cranky rooster. I asked Toad once what it was like to have to turn all of his guns over to the government. He raised one eyebrow and said he only knew how it felt to "surn *tome*" of them over. I suppose there's a reason he knows how to make gunpowder. But Toad has also told me many times we want to fight off the GreyDevils, not kill them off. It helps that the GreyDevils are rarely armed with anything more than rocks and sticks.

As we approach the curve that runs along the edge of BeaverSlap Creek, a solitary figure appears. Toad elbows me. "Friend or foe?"

I grin, because he says this every time we make this trip, and we both know the answer before I give it:

"Depends on whose side yer on!"

It's Toby. Son of Tilapia Tom. Toby isn't quite old enough

to grow a beard, but already he stands over six feet, and his arms are the size of a grown man's legs. He too is wearing homemade armor, but his is all flat black. When you're as big as Toby you don't need decorations and doodads to make yourself look fierce.

Toby is gigantic, but he is also graceful. He carries a fight-stick the size of a fence post, but he can flip and spin it like kindling, and he can fling a whip-bow arrow so accurately you'd think it was strung on a string. And if a GreyDevil comes in close, Toby can drop the graceful stuff and fight with nothing but muscle and fist. Toad once told me that before the Bubbling, Toby's father made his living as a fighter—sometimes in a cage, sometimes on the street. He taught Toby a lot about fighting, but you'd never guess because they're both so calm and quiet.

A second figure appears, hulking even larger than Toby: his father, Tilapia Tom.

"Mop o' the tornin' one-plus-one ya, Tobe and Tommy!" hollers Toad as he pulls the oxen to a stop.

"Mornin'," says Toby softly. And that may be all we hear from him for the rest of the day. For Toby, two words is a speech. I jump down and help load several wooden crates filled with dried, smoked, and salted fish. Then Toby climbs into the backward-facing chair at the rear of the *Scary Pruner*, where he will spend the day making sure we aren't attacked from behind.

The *Scary Pruner* rolls forward. Our next stop will be Nobbern. When I look back at Toby, I see his shoulders, ax-handle wide and thick as a buffalo hump, his body rocking gently to the roll of the road, his head swiveling left to right, as it will during the entire trip. Just the sight of him guarding the tailgate is enough to stop most GreyDevils.

A mile past Toby's place, Toad veers Frank and Spank off the road and up the ramp leading to the interstate. As we merge into the northbound lane, I think how weird it is to be clunking along at the speed of oxen over the cracked and weedy concrete where cars and trucks used to whizz back and forth.

The southbound lane is in much better shape, because the government maintains it for the cornvoys to use during harvest seasons. When harvest is in full swing, the cornvoys are really something to see—long lines of roaring trucks blasting black clouds of smoke into the sky through exhaust pipes that are made of shiny chrome. Many of the drivers decorate their trucks with flags and bright stripes and zigzags of paint—just like the *Scary Pruner*. The trucks also have big steel grates on the front to catch anything that gets in front of them. Toad says the grates are called "cow-catchers" or "brush-busters" but I call them "GreyDevil graters."

The cornvoy drivers are rough and cheery and almost all of them will give you a big grin and a wave if you wave first. Toad says the drivers get paid by the load, so as you can imagine they don't spend a lot of time worrying about safe driving. The government and CornVivia like the arrangement because the truckers are not working for either of them, and they are disposable. If one of them crashes, or if one of their trucks breaks down, there's always someone else ready to jump in because being a cornvoy driver is kind of like being a cowboy in one of the Wild West cowboy books Toad used to read. You can pretty much do what you want. They follow only two rules: haul as much URCorn as possible as fast as possible.

Frank and Spank plod along. I can hear songbirds in the weeds and parrots in the trees. The sun is warm, and I'm beginning to bake in my armor. My eyelids are getting heavy. I'm thinking how delicious it would be to let the *Scary Pruner* rock me to sleep. And then, just as my eyes are about to droop closed, behind a tree trunk I see movement.

A shabby figure, pulling itself up from the ground.

A GreyDevil. Just now waking from the previous night.

"Shise and rine, Washer-Slosher!" hollers Toad. The Grey-Devil is standing now, or at least holding itself upright by clinging with one hand to a sapling. With its other hand it is holding its forehead. It is in no shape to move, but from beneath the hand I can see its red and yellow-rimmed eyes following us.

By the time we're headed back home, that GreyDevil will be a lot more perky.

And it will have a lot more company.

For now though, we just roll along. We see a few more GreyDevils, but they just stare at us as we pass.

Two hours later, we arrive in Nobbern.

17

WHEN TOAD TURNS THE *SCARY PRUNER* UP MAIN STREET, I TRY
to imagine how different it must have looked when he and
Arlinda came to be in the parades. Nobbern isn't really
much of a "town" anymore. It's like a ghost town, only the
ghosts have been replaced with real people. On the outskirts,
a lot of the buildings have been burned, and the ones that
haven't burned have fallen in. All that remains has been torn
to bits by scavengers. Closer to the center of town, more of
the houses are still standing, although they look like they're
abandoned—until you see someone peeking out a window
and realize that house is still a home. Little things like that
make me think I have it pretty good out there on Skullduggery Ridge in my station wagon.

Nearer the center of town, the buildings start to look a

little better, and a little busier. Even without electricity or gasoline people find ways to trade and travel and survive. Here and there you'll see a steam engine vehicle, or an old car powered by a contraption called a gasifier, which uses wood for fuel. Some people have horses and mules, but most people walk. I asked Toad once why he didn't fix up one of his old steam engines.

"Don't wanna ride next to a giant hot water bomb," he said.

"Then why not get a horse?"

"A hay-burner?" he snorted. "Too jumpy, too spendy." Then he said, "Lottom bine? Peam stower or porse-hower, you'll wear yerself opposite-of-in keeping either one hed and fappy." He paused, and pointed at Frank and Spank. "Dem *dos* oxii is all the horsepower I like-dough-knead. Plus, any knucklehead can traise and rain an ox."

All along Main Street, people stop and stare at the *Scary Pruner*. We do make quite a sight, creaking along at top Frank-and-Spank speed, Monocle running his happy laps, Hatchet flapping his wings and squawking like a flea-bitten vulture with a lung disorder.

"Greetings and salutations!"

It's Al the blacksmith, his voice booming from up the street. His round belly is draped in a leather apron that reaches from his chest to his knees. A big hammer dangles from one hand while he waves at us with the other. Toad carefully pulls the *Scary Pruner* to the curb, and even before it comes to a stop Al is poking and pulling at the scrap iron. "Oh, I like that," he says, holding up a piece of angle iron. "Oh, that's a beauty," he says, patting a steel shaft we pulled from an old corn picker. But even as he's talking, I notice what I always notice about Al: his apron is clean, his hammer (which is now propped against a chair on the sidewalk) doesn't have a single nick or ding, and all the while he's talking he's having to raise his voice to be heard above all the clanging and banging back inside the blacksmith shop—where his wife, Freda, is doing all the work. Arlinda told me once she can't imagine what Al is good for "other than the fact that if the bellows go bust, he can blow hot air."

The clanging stops, and out through the shop door steps a woman with hands like hams and a blond braid thick as a ship's rope. Al scoots to her side.

"I've initiated the intake process," he announces, hooking his thumbs behind the straps of his spotless apron. He's trying to look and sound important, but beside Freda he just looks like a little boy playing dress-up. She doesn't even look at him. Instead she nods her head at Toad, reaches into the *Scary Pruner*, picks up a pair of trailer axles like they're tooth-picks, and carries them up the steps.

"There's some top-grade stuff here," says Al, scooting along behind her, his hands empty. "Regrettably, during my appraisal I did detect some rust pitting, so I am professionally compelled to recommend a small deduction." Toad looks at me and winks.

"Also, I—*ohf*!" Al is prattling right along on Freda's heels, and when she stops at the weighing scale, he rams his belly button right into one of the axle ends. While Al clutches his jelly belly and gasps for breath, Freda weighs each axle, scribbling the number in a grubby notebook. Leaving Toby to guard the *Scary Pruner*, Toad and I haul the rest of the scrap into the blacksmith shop. It's dark and black and hot in there, and smells like scorched metal. It always makes me think of Emily Dickinson's poem "The White Heat." There's a blacksmith in that one. Al has his breath again, and as we work he scurries back and forth with us, jabbering away and stopping once to fussily brush a cinder from his spotless leather apron. He never does actually touch anything made of iron.

Toad hands a sewing machine leg to Freda, and Al butts in. "Darling, as your beloved metallurgist, I must remind you that cast iron is prone to cracking."

"Al!" says Toad, clapping one hand to his chest like a fainting maiden and pretending he doesn't realize Al is talking to Freda. "You don't have to call me *darling*!"

Al splutters, and Freda smiles faintly as she weighs the sewing machine leg and moves on to the next item. The way she studies every piece, you can tell she's already imagining just how she might use it. When the final chunk of scrap is weighed and accounted for, she and Toad review the list together. Then Freda writes a number on a slip of paper, circles it, scribbles her initials beside the circle, and we go on our way. "Pleasure doing business with you," bubbles Al, following us out to the *Scary Pruner*. "We are honored to repurpose your recyclables." He shakes my hand, and his palm is as soft and pink as a piglet snoot. Back in the blacksmith shop, Freda is already hammering away.

Next we stop at the grocery. Toad and I carry in Arlinda's pies and preserves and the hams and bacon, and some of Tilapia Tom's crated fish. Then Toad produces a list put together by Arlinda and hands it to the grocer, who brings us salt, flour, and other basics we can't make ourselves. When we're finished, the grocer tallies all the things we brought in minus all the things we're taking, scribbles a number, circles and signs it the same as Freda did, and hands it to Toad.

We call these numbers BarterBucks. After the Bubbling, money was worthless. A lot of the banks were robbed and looted, but it didn't do the thieves any good because the money wasn't useful for much more than starting fires. For a while people just traded directly with each other. That works for some things, but the trouble is that Freda the blacksmith doesn't have the salt Toad needs, and the grocer isn't going to trade a bag of salt for the axle from an old manure spreader. Instead, Freda writes down how many BarterBucks she's willing to pay for our iron. Later today, Toad will take the paper to Banker Berniece, who works out of the old bank building. Banker Berniece will subtract the number from Freda's account and add it to Toad's account.

For keeping track of everyone's BarterBucks, Banker Berniece gets a percentage of everybody else's BarterBucks. Basically, Banker Berniece is a banker with no money. In a bigger, faster-moving world, this system would never work. But here in tiny Nobbern it works just fine because everybody knows everybody else—including Banker Berniece. If she doesn't play fair, word gets around, and no one will trust her or trade with her. Same goes for her customers.

After the grocery, we stop at the hardware shop for leather repair supplies, the tailor shop for thread, and the diner, where we unload more of Arlinda's pies and Tilapia Tom's fish. At each stop, we leave with another signed and circled number on a piece of paper. Toad folds each note and keeps it in his pocket.

Finally, Toad pulls the *Scary Pruner* to the curb before a three-story brick building with tall, narrow windows on each floor. A large hand-painted sign nailed above the door reads "MAGICAL MERCANTILE." We unload the whirligig crates and stack them on the sidewalk. When we're ready to carry them inside, I climb back aboard the *Scary Pruner*, open the hidden compartment beneath the seat, remove the bundle of rags hiding Porky Pig, and tuck him in the bottom of my pack.

Stepping inside Magical Mercantile is like stepping into a museum inside a circus inside an antique store. The floors are made of long, narrow boards that make creaky squeaks when I step on them. Each room is filled wall to wall with long wooden tables, and along the walls there are shelves that go clear to the ceiling and can only be reached by wooden ladders hung on rolling rails. The shelves and tables are stacked with everything you can imagine and even more things you can't imagine: one-armed dolls, patched rubber boots, plastic silverware, board games in beat-up boxes, books, mismatched dice, used paintbrushes, cans of half-used paint, thumbless mittens, jars of broken crayons, half-empty bags of balloons, colored drinking straws, and a thousand other odd things.

"Toad Hopper!"

I look up just in time to see a short, bright-eyed man leap from the top stair of the second floor and slide down the wooden banister. It's Mad Mike, the owner of Magical Mercantile. He is wearing a green eyeshade, a pair of bright orange coveralls, a polka-dotted bow tie, and ballet slippers. Toad says Mad Mike wears the ballet slippers because he's always running up and down those three sets of stairs from floor to floor, and heavy boots would add up. Other people say Mad Mike was once a circus acrobat. The way he leaps off the banister and lands lightly on his feet, it could be true.

"Whaddya got?" says Mad Mike, skipping around behind a long counter.

We arrange our crates and Mad Mike digs through them eagerly, commenting now and then. "These mini-boomerangs are real hot sellers! Kids love these kaleidoscopes!" After he inspects each new item, he scribbles on his list. But this time, just before he circles the final number, I cover it with my hand. "Hold on," I say. "I've got one more thing."

I reach into my pack and pull out my carefully wrapped treasure.

18

"PORKY PIG!" SAYS MAD MIKE, THE MOMENT I REMOVE THE RAGS. It's a race between his eyes and his grin to see which can go wider. "Oh-ho-ho! That's a *beauty*!"

I hand him the pig and he studies it from every angle. "Porky! I haven't seen him in *years*!"

Then he looks at me. "You just dug this up?"

"Yep," I say. "Just dug it up."

He places it on the counter and stares at it, cocking his head this way and that. Finally, he scribbles a number on a piece of paper and hands it to me.

The number is bigger than I could have dreamed.

But I am Ford Falcon. Falcons have clear vision and know when to go in for the kill. When I saw the excitement in Mad Mike's eyes, I knew I really had something. I stare at the number and suck slowly on one tooth so it makes a long, sad, squeaky sound. Toad taught me that move. It's a way to give yourself a little time to think, and also to make the other person worry about losing the deal. Finally I make a face like someone just offered me a dish of cold fiddleheads and shake my head.

"Who else you gonna sell it to?" says Mad Mike.

"Oh, I'm gonna sell it to *you*," I say, "but for twice that." I'm bluffing, because he's right, no one else will buy this pig, but I also know from the look on his face that he already has this pig sold.

"Hmm . . . ," says Mike, looking at the pig again. Now he has his poker face on, but it's too late. I guess maybe he thought he was dealing with some sweet little girl. Mad Mike, meet *Ford Falcon*.

"You need me, I need you," I say. "Give me a good number."

Mad Mike crosses out the old number and scribbles a new one. On the inside, my heart leaps. But on the outside I don't show a thing.

I suck my tooth again and make Mad Mike wait a little. Then I point to a red rubber ball on the shelf behind his head. "Throw in one of those for my little brother," I say, "and we have a deal."

Mad Mike takes the paper, circles the number, and signs his name. As he turns to get the rubber ball, Toad jabs me in the ribs and whispers, "Well played, Ford Falcon."

I grin, and sneak another peek at the number. Even

though there was a lot of luck in finding that pig, I feel proud, because if I hadn't been down there digging it wouldn't have happened. Now I will be able to buy extra supplies to help my family. Before we leave I will stop back at the grocery to buy salt and sugar and molasses. At the hardware store I'll get sulfur matches, a good soup ladle for Ma, and a pickax for Dad. I'll even buy a sack of hard candy for my snot flicker of a brother, Dookie. A little treat to go with the red rubber ball.

But first, there is something else.

"Mad Mike, I need to buy some tea."

I could just buy some tea at the grocery, but it's plain old stuff and usually stale. Not only does Mad Mike have tea that is fresh, he has tea in tins. Pretty tins, decorated with scrolls and designs and frilly letters, just like you'd want if you were going to brew up a batch and settle in with a book. Even in the hardest of times, you'd be amazed at what you can find if people want it bad enough. And if you want something odd or hard to get, Mad Mike is your man. The heavy steel-toed boots on my feet right now came from Magical Mercantile. The sulfur and saltpeter Toad uses to make his Whomper-Zooka powder come from Mad Mike. There are rumors that if you want guns, Mad Mike can get those, too. How Mad Mike gets ahold of some of these things is anybody's guess. He may be a tad shifty in his wheelings and dealings, but he's good at what he does.

"Whaddya have in mind?" says Mad Mike. All of a sudden

he's all perked up again, like a fox that spots a mouse. Or like *he's* the falcon.

"Earl Grey," I say. "For my ma."

"Oh boy," he says, heaving a sigh. "It'll cost ya." He speaks regretfully, shaking his head as if each word is breaking his heart. At least he doesn't suck his tooth.

"I know. But lucky me, I sold an overpriced pig earlier today, so I'm loaded." Toad grins and elbows me again. But Mad Mike is grinning too. The one thing a wheeler-dealer likes to do is wheel and deal.

Mad Mike disappears into the back room, returning with a small square container. It's deep black and trimmed in dark red and bright silver. He hands it to me, and the tin feels glossy smooth against my palm. On the front a scroll is unfurled like a banner, and inside the scroll, in golden letters that are pressed into the tin so I can feel them with my fingertips, are the words "Earl Grey Tea."

We dicker over the price a little, but I let Mad Mike off pretty easily. I can buy a lot of tea with what he paid me for that pig. He wraps the tin in a soft cloth, and then a paper bag. As I carry it out the door I think of Ma and how she'll smile when she sees it and I figure it's worth all the Porky Pigs in the world.

I do the last of my shopping, picking up the things for Ma and Dad and the candy for Dookie, then Toad and I take our BarterBucks to Banker Berniece. She's a small, quiet woman with her hair up in a tight bun who always wears a man's suit and tie and sits behind a huge wooden desk that makes her look even smaller. The desk sits squarely in front of the gigantic bank vault door with polished steel handles and big dials and thick brass hinges. This makes Banker Berniece look tinier still.

"Activate yer abacus, Miss Mathematicus!" says Toad as we enter the bank. Honestly, sometimes it'd be nice if he could just say hello like a normal person. Banker Berniece doesn't smile or frown, she just looks up and in a flat voice that is neither friendly nor unfriendly, says, "Good morning, Mr. Hopper," then reaches out to take the wad of Barter-Bucks slips Toad has dug out of his pocket.

One by one she smooths the crumpled papers and arranges them neatly on the desktop. Then she opens a desk drawer and takes out a fountain pen, a bottle of ink, an envelope, and a giant book that says "LEDGER" on the cover. She arranges them all on the desk, each in its place, as carefully as she arranged the BarterBucks slips. Then she goes through the slips one by one, entering them in the ledger with the fountain pen. After the last one is written in, she reaches into another drawer and pulls out a wooden rack that holds a bunch of colored beads mounted on slim iron rods. The first time I saw it, I thought it was some kind of weird rattle-toy, but Toad wasn't being completely goofy when he mentioned the abacus, because that's exactly what it is.

While the index finger of one hand moves slowly down through the numbers she just wrote in the ledger, the index finger of Banker Berniece's other hand dances over the abacus, flicking beads back and forth. I can hear soft little *click-clack* sounds as she works her way down the page. When she adds in the last number, she writes it in the ledger and circles it. Then she adds everything up again, puts a check beside the number in the ledger, and turns the heavy book so Toad can sign it. Then she writes the same number on a piece of paper, signs and dates it, and hands it to Toad along with an envelope. He initials the piece of paper, seals it in the envelope, and writes his name and today's date across the seal.

Now I hand her my slips. When she smooths out the piece of paper that shows how many BarterBucks I got for Porky Pig, I watch for her reaction, because for me, it's a pretty big number, but Banker Berniece's expression doesn't change. She just goes straight to flicking the abacus. Toad says that's part of why he trusts Banker Berniece. She treats everybody and every number just the same. You don't want somebody who's oohing and aahing over the details, Toad says, because that's the kind of person that will be just dying to tell someone else. Actually he said "deceasing to yammerize the populace," but sometimes it's easier just to say things my way.

After I sign and date my envelope, Banker Berniece turns to the safe and, standing so we can't see, spins the dials, flips the handles, and swings open the safe door. Following her inside, I take a key from a string around my neck and insert it in the lock on a safety deposit box. Banker Berniece puts a key in the other slot, and we both turn until the door springs open. I put my envelope inside with the envelopes from previous trips, close the door, then we both turn our keys again and the box is locked. At the end of the day Berniece will lock the ledger in the safe also, but the "envelope system," as we call it, is Berniece's way of making sure there's a backup record of how many BarterBucks each person has.

After Toad locks his envelope away, Banker Berniece places the ledger on a shelf inside the safe, then closes and locks the heavy door. On our way out of the bank, Toad turns and says, "Thank you, Berniece," just as plain as you please.

"Yes," says Banker Berniece.

Back on the street, Toby has fed and watered all the animals. While he goes in to settle up with Banker Berniece for the fish he sold, Toad reaches into a compartment on the *Scary Pruner*, pulls out a small canvas bag, and tosses it to me. It jingles when I catch it. "Arm the secret weapon!" says Toad, and I sigh. In addition to the chain mail he made for the dogs and oxen, Toad made Hatchet a pair of razor-sharp spurs, a set of tiny barbs that attach to the tip of each wing, and a stainless steel pick that clamps over the tip of his beak. We usually wait to put these things on Hatchet until the more dangerous ride home, and it's always a painful tussle.

Suddenly I realize I left Magical Mercantile without taking Dookie's red rubber ball. I toss the bag back to Toad.

"Gonna leave that to you and Toby," I say, over my shoulder, as I run across the street.

I find Mad Mike at the counter. He's packing Porky Pig into a crate. "Aren't you going to put him on the shelf?" I ask. Mad Mike looks down at the pig already half-ready to ship, then back at me. It's like he's taking a moment to form a careful answer. "Well, I . . ." Then he just sets the pig aside and says, "I have a customer who likes these sorts of things. He has a standing order for anything that fits his memory space."

"Memory space?"

"We all grew up in a certain time and place. And for most of us, as we get older our memories of that time get sweeter. Especially if everything else in our world has changed in ways that make it hard to keep up, or remember how things once were. So some people like to surround themselves with objects that remind them of those times. That's what I call a memory space. It's not so much a *place* as a *feeling*.

"I know it's hard to believe, when you look around at this world and what people *really* need," says Mad Mike, "but you can make a living scavenging memories."

"Well, if I ever have a memory space, about the only thing in there will be a knuckleheaded brother and a stick for digging in the dirt," I said.

Outside I hear an explosion of flapping and squawking.

"And a rooster," I say. "A *stuffed* rooster."

Outside, Toad has the *Scary Pruner* turned and pointed back up Main Street. Monocle is panting happily. Hatchet is on his perch clucking grumpily and looking dangerous. Toby is sitting silently at the rear. The only sign that he's been wrassling Hatchet is that his ears are a little redder than usual. I wish I had seen that.

Two hours have passed since we arrived in town. We need to get going. It would be nice to eat lunch at the diner, but the longer we stay the more active the GreyDevils will be, so we've each taken a sandwich to go. I climb up beside Toad and as easily as if he were ordering those sandwiches, he says, "Okay, boys, here we go," and Frank and Spank lean toward home.

The GreyDevils start trailing us pretty much as soon as we leave town.

19

THEY ARE GHOSTLY AT FIRST. JUST HINTS OF SOUND AND FLITS OF movement. A shadow on a tree trunk. A twig snap. A shift in the tall grass. The sun is still high, but suddenly the countryside *feels* darker. I grip my ToothClub tightly, and check the strap on my helmet. My eyes dart left and right, trying to spot something—anything. Then a GreyDevil steps into the open. It is draped in rags. Its face is sooty and smudged. It shuffles toward the wagon, staring hungrily at our cargo. "Back off, you tatterdemalion mummy-breathed flat-footer!" yells Toad. The GreyDevil stops, its yellow eyes staring as we pass. Its grubby face is cut with tear streaks and snot streaks. I guess I'd have a snotty nose too if I was breathing the smoke from all the things they burn on those bonfires.

Another GreyDevil approaches from an angle, and sidles

up near Frank and Spank. Hatchet fluffs his neck feathers and cackles like he's trying to hack up a fish bone. Wrapping the reins around the buckboard rail, Toad reaches for his bullwhip. I hear the *splap!* of leather on skin, and the GreyDevil yelps and grabs one arm. A trickle of sickly dark blood seeps from between its grubby fingers.

Frank and Spank just keep moving along, and another GreyDevil approaches from my side of the road. I pull out my SpitStick and hit it right between the eyeballs with a pepper-pea. It grabs its face and drops to the dust, moaning and rolling into the ditch.

"Well played!" hollers Toad.

"That'll run the ol' eyeliner," I say. I've seen makeup ads in Toad's old magazines, and some of those women look a lot like GreyDevils. Yet another GreyDevil puts a hand out toward Frank's flank. Once again Toad flicks his whip and—*pop!*—the Devil yanks back his hand and stands there sucking on the sore spot.

It's fun to talk tough about Toad pinging GreyDevils with his bullwhip, or about toasting their butts with rock salt, but this is not just an armchair adventure story. I would like to do nothing but sip tea and read poetry with Ma, but sometimes you have to dig in the dirt to survive. Sometimes you have to go out into danger in order to survive. And sometimes you have to strike out in order to protect yourself, and your things, and the people you love. Right now the *Scary Pruner* isn't just filled with things we *want*, it's filled with stuff we *need*. And if the GreyDevils take our stuff, it's not like the old days when you could just get more stuff. So we can't politely ask the GreyDevils to leave us alone.

For two or three miles the pepper-peas and whipcracks do the job. The GreyDevils come in close, more for a look than an attack, and only one or two at a time. Toby pops one on the forehead with the end of his fight-stick just as easy as if he were shooting snooker and that GreyDevil's head was a cue ball. The Devil drops to the ditch, and Toby hasn't even shifted in his seat.

It's even kinda fun for a while, like shooting silly targets at a carnival. But GreyDevils are beginning to line the roadside ahead, and when I look back, I can see a growing cluster of them gathering behind us. Just like stray dogs, GreyDevils can be troublesome on their own but are most dangerous when they start running in packs. Although GreyDevils aren't really healthy enough to run. *Shuffling* in packs, I guess. And they're not so bright, what with their brains all cheese-holed by chemical smoke and PartsWash, but they're hungry and they're desperate, and they know travelers are easy pickings. Especially if the travelers are in an overloaded wagon pulled by *dos oxii*.

Mainly we just want to keep them at bay as long as possible. We learned a long time ago that it's a long haul home, and you don't go straight for the Whomper-Zooka. We carry plenty of extra saltpowder packs but the supply isn't endless, and you don't want to use up your precious reserves on the early stragglers. The Whomper-Zooka is built for a crowd. So we stick to smaller weapons as long as we can. Some days we can get all the way back home without blasting anyone.

Today doesn't look like one of those days. Like bees in a swarm, the GreyDevils aren't capable of planning an attack, but once they get worked up and swirling in the same direction they become a terrifying force. And now they're starting to do just that. The sound of their feet never stops. It's like a thousand snake bellies slithering over dirt. I can hear their rattling coughs, and even the sound of their breathing is creepy, like someone blowing bubbles in warm cheese. They wear anything they have found—rugs with armholes, T-shirts advertising soda pop or music festivals, strips of old curtains and carpet they've ripped from abandoned homes. Some are wearing rough sandals made from discarded tires, although they've been known to tear those off and pitch them into the fire. During snow snaps they bundle up in furs and scavenged insulation, decrepit tarps—whatever they can find.

They are sickly and undernourished, and their sore-infested skin looks like a cranberry biscuit rolled in coal dust. You can't tell if they are male or female. You can smell the stench of them and their crusty, weepy wounds.

And now they're moaning. A sad, long, mournful sound like someone trying to howl with a hand clapped over their mouth. Once the moaning starts, you know trouble is not far to come. Now all the GreyDevils within earshot know there is treasure on the road.

Toad takes his helmet from its hook and puts it on his head.

"Snooky holer-tables!" he says.

And then he flips his visor down.

20

ONE OF THE GREYDEVILS STUMBLES IN AND REACHES OVER THE side of the buckboard. With all my strength, I bring my ToothClub down and the GreyDevil stumbles backward into the weeds, clutching one arm to its chest. Then a hand grabs me by the ankle, tugging at my boot. I whirl and face another GreyDevil, so close I can see its runny eyes and feel its humid breath, sour as pickled earthworms. I swing my ToothClub again. It connects with a solid *thunk*, and the fingers gripping my ankle release. I know what would have happened to me if the Devil had dragged me down, and I don't feel bad for a second. Don't have *time* to feel bad.

And then, in a single eerie moment, all the howling and moaning blends into a single sound, and the mob stops swirling and comes at us in a single dirty wave. If we were in one of Toad's cowboy books, this would be the part where Toad snaps the reins and hollers *"Heeyah!"* and the horses bolt, sending our stagecoach careening wildly out of danger. Unfortunately, Frank and Spank have only one gear, and it is low. You can *"Heeyah!"* all you want, but two miles an hour is still two miles an hour. Instead, Toad puts his helmet on, drops the visor, and hollers, "Scale the raven cradle!" Even in this dangerous moment, I grin behind my mask as I climb into the crow's nest. The idea that Toad can still play word games even while crunching GreyDevils makes me think he's nuts *and* the coolest guy ever.

With all the GreyDevils closing in, it seems like a good time to try out the flingshot. It's already loaded, so I spin the bike pedals as fast as I can. After about ten spins the trapdoor flies open and a shower of rocks flies out in all directions. Several GreyDevils fall back, holding their heads and moaning. But I also hear a loud *"SQUAAAACKK!"* and look over my shoulder to see Hatchet flapping angrily at the end of his dog leash, a stray rock having knocked him off his perch.

Oopsie, I think, smiling to myself.

I attempt to reload the flingshot and immediately run into trouble. First of all, I have to lift the bucket of rocks over my head. That's tough enough to do, let alone while standing in a crow's nest that's rocking side to side with every bump in the road. Then as I'm pouring them into the drum, we hit an extra-big bump and one of the rocks falls out of the bucket and bounces off my helmet.

I spin the pedals and send another load of rocks flying through the air. When I bend down to lift the third bucket, I get hit in the back with a rock, and then another. And then I realize: the GreyDevils are picking up the rocks and throwing them right back at us.

"Might notta thought the flingshot thing all the way through!" I holler to Toad, as another rock bounces off my stovepipe armor. Now in addition to rocks, they're throwing branches and heavy chunks of wood, and whatever other flingable things they can lay their clammy hands on.

The GreyDevils are really closing in now, but Toad hasn't called for the Whomper-Zooka yet, so I wait until several GreyDevils are trying to reach over the sides, then pull a handle attached to a cable. The side-whackers fly outward, and a group of four GreyDevils flops over backward. I crank the reset winch as fast as I can and trigger them again, and another cluster of GreyDevils goes down.

All around below me, I see chaos and swirling dust. Hatchet is cackle-clucking and flapping his barbed wings. Monocle is yipping and nipping, his tail spinning in a waggy blur. I can hear the *thwack!* and *smack!* of Toad snapping his whip and Toby cracking craniums with his fight-stick. But it's funny, even with all this happening, it seems quiet here on the wagon. It's like the eye of a hurricane. Frank and Spank with their ears flattened back but still plodding along. We're just working. Doing what we do. It's like we have a list of chores, and one of the things on that list is "*whack*

GreyDevils." And nobody is whacking more GreyDevils than Toby: on his feet now, standing wide-legged, his fight-stick whirling so fast it is invisible, but all around him GreyDevils falling away or grabbing their bloody, crushed noses, or tipping over backward knocked out cold, and all the while Toby's expression as still and solemn as if he is studying his reflection in a fish pool.

We're not keeping up though. The commotion has attracted even more Devils. When I look out around me from the crow's nest it seems we are at the center of a writhing pile of two-legged maggots.

And then I hear the command I've been waiting for.

"Ford Falcon!" hollers Toad. "Whomp at will!"

21

HEARING TOAD CALL ME FORD FALCON MAKES ME FEEL TEN FEET tall, that's for sure. But if I stand around with a swollen head, I'll end up with a swollen head.

I pull the Whomper-Zooka from its hook, drop a salt-powder packet down the barrel, and tamp in a wad of paper. Then I click it into the swivel straps, grab the two wooden handles, swing it around to point at the thickest clot of Grey-Devils, and yank the striker string.

For a split second, nothing happens. Then I hear a faint sizzle, and . . . *WHOMP*!

The stovepipe belches rock salt and a wad of flame the size of a pig, followed by a gigantic burp of black smoke. The smoke rolls out over the GreyDevils, and from within the cloud I hear ragged moans as the stinging salt goes to work. The smoke drifts clear and I can see GreyDevils all over the ground, flipping and flopping like their skin is on fire.

There is no time to enjoy the view. I drop in another bag of saltpowder, rewrap the striker string, swivel the Whomper-Zooka to the other side of the wagon, and touch it off again.

WHOMP!

More yowling and howling, and more fish-flopping Grey-Devils.

At the rear of the wagon Toby's fight-stick is a blur. A GreyDevil heaves a stone his way and while it is still in mid-air, Toby shifts both hands to the far end of the stick and bats the rock right back into the chest of the GreyDevil, knocking it flat. Keeping his hands in the same position, he bats another GreyDevil smack on the butt, knocking it face-first into the dirt. Toby is amazing to watch, and I pay the price for goggling at him when a big chunk of tree root comes end over end through the air and slams into my helmet, ringing it like a bell. I go cross-eyed and wind up knocked half over the railing. I am angry with myself for getting distracted. *Maggie!* I think. *Pay attention! You need Ford Falcon focus!*

Toby's rapidly becoming outnumbered back there. He needs some Whomper-Zooka assistance. "Clearing the rear!" I holler. "In three . . . two . . ."

We've practiced this move over and over. When I holler "One!" Toby flops flat and I let fly with another blast right through where he was standing a second ago. Another ragged moan goes up, and for a moment a gap opens in the slobbery ranks, but then the GreyDevils close in again.

It takes four more Whomper-Zooka blasts before we get the mob thinned out and we can go back to picking them off one by one. When things calm down even more, Toby puts aside his fight-stick and practices with his whip-bow. Instead of sharp arrows he's shooting dumdum pepperheads, which are basically pepper-peas on sticks. He's amazingly accurate. Fifty yards away a GreyDevil takes a step toward us. Toby flicks his wrist, the dumdum shaft flashes through the air, and a red pepper puff blooms at the end of the GreyDevil's nose. As it claps its hands over its eyes and stumbles backward, Toad and I both turn toward Toby and applaud.

Our applause is interrupted by an explosion of scratchy screeching. We swivel our heads back around. A GreyDevil is approaching Frank and Spank, head-on. Toad raises his whip, but before he can crack it, Hatchet flaps into the GreyDevil's face, flailing his spurs and epaulet blades like a frazzle-feathered fighter jet. The GreyDevil falls to the ground, and Hatchet dives after it, his beak spear flashing back and forth like a sewing machine needle. He's cackle-screeching like someone took a buzz saw to the chicken coop. The GreyDevil struggles to its feet and stumbles into the ditch. It turns to look back and its face looks like someone dragged it headfirst through the briar patch.

Hatchet tries to get back up to his perch, but he's tuckered and his weapons are heavy. After a few fruitless flaps and cackles, Toad punches the "retrieve" button and the dog leash zips Hatchet back to roost. He clucks grumpily and sticks his chest out.

There are no more GreyDevils in sight. As the dust and feathers settle, we take inventory. Toby has a cut to his forearm. I have a bump over my right eye. "A-OK, not DOA!" hollers Toad, hanging his helmet back on its hook and grinning like he just got off a neat ride at the Bubble City amusement park. Frank and Spank are plodding along at the same pace they've maintained all day. Monocle is flopped on the buckboard floor, panting happily. Hatchet is tut-tutting, fluffing and resettling his feathers just the way he does on any given day in the barnyard. Most important, all of our supplies are intact. I bandage Toby's arm with gauze and dressings from the first aid pack. Toby doesn't look at me. Instead, he keeps his eyes moving, scanning the road and ditches for troublesome stragglers.

And up on his perch between Frank and Spank, Hatchet fluffs his feathers and tips his needle beak to the sky.

"Cock-a-doodle . . . *aaack-kack-kack-kack*!"

Yeah. We're fine.

22

TILAPIA TOM IS WAITING FOR US AT THE CURVE ALONG BEAVERSLAP Creek. Toad and I help him and Toby unload their supplies, then we say good night and head down the road. At the gate, Monocle barks until Arlinda lets us in, and Toad drives the *Scary Pruner* into the barn. While I still have all my armor on, I wrestle Hatchet off his perch and out of his gear, then carry him to the coop in a headlock. I throw him inside and slam the door before he can get at me. As I walk away I can hear him clucking importantly. He'll probably keep the hens up half the night with his bragging.

Arlinda has put a bowl of water out on the porch, and Monocle is lapping it up. Tripod is purring and rubbing up against Monocle's legs, letting him rest so they can get back to chasing each other.

I help Toad unhitch Frank and Spank. We give them water and feed and brush them while they eat. Then I help Toad unload the *Scary Pruner*. Finally, I go over each piece of my armor, checking for broken straps or missing pieces—anything that could leave me in danger. You repair your armor before you need it, because you never know when you'll need it. When I've made sure everything is in good shape, I give it a polish and oil the leather, then hang it up in my locker so it's all ready to go.

Arlinda invites me in for supper, and it smells wonderful, but the sun is already dropping, and I want to get back to my family and my Ford Falcon bed. "I figured," says Arlinda, handing me a package of food wrapped in cloth. It's heavy and warm. I tuck it in my backpack next to Ma's tea and the other supplies and begin my climb out of Hoot Holler and up to Skullduggery Ridge.

By the time I get home, dusk is gathering. I can see a glow through the plastic shack window, so I stick my head inside. Dookie is asleep, and Ma is at the table, reading by candlelight.

"How did it go, dear?" asks Ma.

"Oh, fine, nothing too much," I say. I figure it's not a lie if you don't get too specific. Plus, Ma has enough to worry about.

"I got you something to go with your poems." I place the brown paper package beside her book.

"Oh, Maggie," says Ma as she picks it up and begins unwrapping it. "You shouldn't . . ."

"Turns out that pig was worth quite a bit," I say.

"Oh, Maggie!" she says. "Earl Grey!" She cracks the lid, closes her eyes, and takes a long sniff. When she opens her eyes they glisten in the candlelight.

"Go ahead and make some, Ma."

She's hugging me now. "No, just that one sniff took me to another world, dear Maggie. It's enough. Oh, thank you."

I look around the shack. "Where's Dad?"

She lets me out of the hug and turns away.

"I . . . I don't know, Maggie. He went out a little while ago. For a walk, he said."

"At sundown?"

"Maggie, you know he needs his time alone. It isn't easy for him. There are things . . . he . . ."

She pauses, and I feel awful that I've taken her from being happy about the tea to feeling bad about Dad.

"It's all right, Ma. I know. I'm used to it. I shouldn't have asked."

She looks at me, trying to smile.

"G'night, Ma."

"Good night, Maggie."

"Ma?"

"Yes, Maggie?"

"Tomorrow it's Emily and a visit with the Earl."

Before heading down to the Falcon, I check the root cellar door. It's locked. No light leaking out. I stand there for a moment, remembering my vow to dig up those carrots, and wondering where Dad might be. Where he goes on these walks of his. Up atop Skullduggery Ridge I can see the empty flagpole silhouetted against the last of the fading light.

And next to it, another silhouette: Dad.

I walk up the trail. This time I don't try to be quiet, but Dad doesn't seem to hear me coming anyway. He's standing still as a statue, staring at the countryside below. I walk to within a few feet of him and look in the same direction. I can see the faint yellow square of Toad and Arlinda's kitchen window, and dotted all round them the orange pinpoints of GreyDevil bonfires winking to life. I step up beside Dad. He has his arms wrapped tightly around himself, as if he is cold. He is so still I can't even see him breathing, but even in the last of the fading daylight his eyes are bright. Not weird glow-in-the-dark bright, but feverishly bright. Like he's trying to see so hard his eyes are watering.

"Dad."

His head snaps around immediately, but it seems like he stares at me for a second or two before he actually sees me. Then he blinks and his arms drop, and he says, "Oh—*ah*— hi, Mag—*Ford.*"

"You all right, Dad?"

"Oh. Sure." He doesn't sound sure. "Sunset," he says. "I like to watch the sunset. Reminds me of back when things were . . ." He trails off.

We stand there for a moment. Then he squares up his shoulders, all businesslike. "Well! Better hit the hay!"

We walk quietly back down the trail.

At the door of the shack, he hugs me. "G'night, Maggie."

"G'night, Dad."

I watch him enter the hut and close the door. I listen until the bar drops, and wait until the candlelight goes out. Quietly unlocking the root cellar door, I enter, and close it behind me. After feeling my way down the stairs in the dark, I kneel down and fish the jacklight from my pack. I scratch a match and touch it to the wick, shielding the glow by leaning over it as I dig through the sand pile. The carrots look weird and wiggly in the shaky yellow pool of light. I dig and dig, sweeping the sand to the side and stacking the vegetables, being careful not to scrape or bruise them. All the while I am wondering what I will find.

Finally all the sand and carrots are swept and stacked to the side, and there in the jacklight glow I see . . . nothing. Just that bare slate floor. I sift the whole pile of sand through my fingers to be sure I haven't missed something.

Still nothing.

I even hold a handful of sand up close to the jacklight and pour it from one palm to another, just to see if I can spot anything. It's just sand.

Whatever Dad had hidden with the carrots, it's not here now. I cover them back up, then snuff the jacklight and quietly sneak out of the cellar. I stare at the shack, a darker square in the dark. *Maybe*, I think, *he just wanted a carrot.*

But that wasn't what his eyes told me.

Down at the Ford Falcon, I stand on the hood and look at the stars. I do this nearly every clear-sky evening. Just take a moment to stand there wide-footed with my head tipped back and my hands on my hips, and gaze at the whole twinkling-sky universe.

The stargazing helps me somehow. Makes me feel lonely sometimes, sure, but mostly it just makes me realize that no matter how big the troubles here seem, even the type of troubles that can drive the people of a great nation under bubbles, well, these troubles don't amount to a fly speck on the moon compared to all of space and time. Somehow knowing that just takes the pressure off.

"*The stars about my head I felt,*" I whisper. Emily Dickinson wrote that. Alone in her room. I wonder if she ever waited until dark and snuck out to look at the stars.

I crawl back inside the Falcon and roll into my bedding. It feels good to stretch out beneath my own blankets. The trip to town, trading Porky Pig, the GreyDevil battle, it all seems like another day, another world. But over and over, as I try to drift off, I keep thinking about Dad. About his mysterious walks. About the root cellar. About how strange it is to know someone so well they hug you good night, but to be in the middle of that hug and suddenly realize he too is part of some other world.

23

WHATEVER SORT OF WORLD YOU LIVE IN, IT WILL GET BORING IF you live there long enough. In the week since my last trip to town with Toad, nothing exciting has happened. I may be surrounded by solar bears and GreyDevils and corn that grows like it's trying to tickle the sun, but that doesn't mean every day is an adventure. There are the hoop house gardens that need to be watered and weeded, the chicken coop that needs to be cleaned, whirligigs to make, vegetables to pick and preserve, pigs to feed, weapons to make and repair, clothes to make and wash, and every day more "gold" to be dug out of Goldmine Gully.

Even if you're doing them on the moon, chores are still chores.

I'd be a lot more bored if I didn't have my family. Although

I'm still happiest when I'm hiding out in the Falcon all alone, I look forward to the times Ma and I read poetry and have tea, or the times we just *talk*. There are things only a mother can tell you. Or only a mother can hear. Dad, on his good days, still makes me smile—although lately he's been disappearing more than ever, sometimes even during the day. The last time he straggled home he was all scraped up. He said he slipped and fell into a gully. "Maybe you need to eat more garlic," I said, but I wish I hadn't, because I could see it hurt his feelings.

In his own weird way, even Dookie helps: just when I'm becoming bored enough to chew off my own toenails he jumps out of nowhere two inches from my face and hollers "*SHAZZ-WHIFFY!*" or "*FUZARKUS!*" or some other nonsense. I've also grown used to that dang red rubber ball coming out of nowhere to bounce off my head. I never should have gone back to get it from Magic Mike. Still, even as I'm giving him the third noogie of the day, I have to admit— at least for as long as it takes to rub a red patch into his noggin—I don't stay bored long.

I'd really go nuts, though, if I didn't get to go down to Hoot Holler and work with Toad. Today he and I will be sorting scrap, so as soon as Hatchet's first evil crow-hack wakes me, I crawl out of the Ford Falcon in the dark, hoist my pack, and hike to the flagpole. It's too dark for flags, but lately Toad and I have been experimenting with a semaphore. It looks a lot like a jacklight, only the box is bigger, and instead of a tin reflector, there is a curved mirror that we got by very carefully taking apart a headlight from one of Toad's junkyard cars. The glass on the side where the light shines out is covered by tiny little shutters that can be rapidly opened and closed with a small handle. Toad learned Morse code when he was a boy, and he quizzes me on it when we work in the junk piles. I see a light in Toad's house far below, so I whistle three long and three short. Then I strike a match and touch it to the candle in the box.

Pointing the semaphore toward Toad's house, I flash out a few words.

"Ford Falcon descending."

I wait, then a light in Toad's yard winks back at me:

"O-K."

I smile, partly because our system is working—old Daniel Beard would have loved this giant version of his jacklight—and partly because I realize the most powerful thing about Toad's semaphore lamp is how it forces him to speak in plain and simple words. Then I smile even bigger when I wonder how long it will take before he figures out how to do semaphore spoonerisms.

Because I'm not gathering ferns or chasing down Dookie, I make good time getting down the ridge. Halfway along I see a patch of wintergreen, and stop to pick some. Wintergreen leaves are like nature's chewing gum. It's hard to believe a shiny green leaf can taste so much like candy. Like with most things, it's that first taste that's the best, so I pop in a leaf and chew it, stopping just for a moment to enjoy fresh, sweet flavor.

It's getting lighter. Through a gap in the trees I can see the countryside below. Things look a lot different down there right now, because it's almost harvest time. Instead of brilliant green, the Sustainability Reserves are flat tan. It changed about five days ago, just like someone threw a switch, which Toad says is basically what happens, because that is how the corn cells are programmed. It takes the corn about one month to cure. Then the big harvesting machines will arrive, the cornvoy trucks will be running night and day, and the Grey-Devils will be all stirred up and crazier than usual.

I've chewed all the flavor out of the wintergreen leaf. I ball it up on my tongue and—*ptooey*—spit the cud into the bushes. Bending to pluck another one, I hear a twig snap behind me and freeze in a crouch. Listening intently for any other sound, I realize I'm in the same area where we ran into the solar bear. *Coulda used a "shibby-shibby,"* I think while slowly dropping one hand to my ToothClub and fishing in my pack for a pepper-bomb with the other. Still in a crouch, I look for any motion, listen for any sound. Nothing. Just my own heart, thudding in my ears.

But I *know* I heard something. And I could tell by the *snap!* that the twig was too thick to be crunched by a squirrel or a rabbit. Something's behind me, and it's big.

In one smooth motion, I draw my ToothClub and whirl.

The eyes are staring at me through the leaves from about

twenty feet away. The pupils are dark, almost black, and the whites are not white but yellow—as a matter of fact, these eyes are *really* yellow—and even before I make out the rest of the figure in the brush, I think, *GreyDevil!* And sure enough, when the eyes blink and the figure turns to run crashing through the brush, I see the pale, sooty skin, the knotty, matted hair, and the trailing tattered rags of clothes.

I don't chase. Toad has always taught me: if trouble is running away, you let it run. Instead I stand there, listening and looking for other GreyDevils, but soon the silence settles and the normal forest sounds resume, and it's clear it was the only one.

It's odd to see a GreyDevil this far up the ridge, and it's odd to see one out and about this early in the day. They don't tend to stray too far from their fires or the roadways. Maybe they're getting hungrier.

And it *ran*. I've never seen a GreyDevil *run*.

24

TOAD AND I SPEND THE MORNING TEARING APART OLD CARS AND
farm equipment. It's hard, tough, loud work. Lots of banging
and ripping and hacking. Certain things have special value:
big hunks of sheet metal, heavy shafts (like the axles we took
to Freda on our last trip), and copper wire. Toad says in the
old days he would have just cut everything apart with a blow-
torch, but these days we work with tin snips and bolt cutters
and a pry bar with a blade that looks like a giant can opener.

We're having one of those spitty cold days that seem to
come out of nowhere these days. A cold wind is blowing,
swirling together a mix of light rain and sleet. My hands
are numb and I'm shivering. But I love working with Toad.
Whether we're cleaning fish or pulling copper wire from a
pile of old vacuum cleaners, Toad just keeps talking. Stories,

jokes, silly words, history, it all just rolls out of him. If you didn't know Toad, you might think he was just an odd old man who talks funny, but even with all the nutty talk, he has a way of teaching me things without making me feel like I'm getting a lesson—which of course is the best way of learning. And even though his favorite book is written by Daniel Beard—the man who thought girls should stick to "pretty store bows"—the main thing I like about Toad is that he doesn't talk to me like I'm a girl. He just talks to me.

The weather keeps worsening. Arlinda sticks her head out the door.

"Even a chicken knows enough to come in out of the rain, you knuckleheads!"

Toad and I stow our tools in the shed and head inside. The kitchen is warm and filled with the smell of fresh biscuits. Arlinda puts one on my plate. It looks like a fluffy white cloud that has been browned around the edges. I split it, and a puff of steam rises to the tip of my cold nose. I drizzle a spoonful of honey on both halves and let the honey melt in before I take a bite. Arlinda puts out three mugs of fresh-brewed chamomile-and-clover tea, and as the sleet hits *tickety-tick* against the windowpanes, I can't imagine a cozier place to be.

Up on the ridge, I know Ma and Dookie are cozy too. Ma will have a fire going in the shack stove, and Dookie will be playing with his whirligigs. If Dookie gets too stir-crazy, Ma will hold him and hum the songs she hummed when he was a baby. Sometimes that's the only thing that can settle Dookie down.

And Dad . . . I hope he's in there with them and not on one of his mysterious walkabouts. Surely he wouldn't go out in this weather.

While the honey soaks into my biscuit and the tea cools, I pull an old newspaper from a stack by the door. "GOV'T UNVEILS BUBBLE CITIES, ALL INVITED," reads the headline. Beneath that, a smaller headline reads, "Declaration Day Set." The "invited" part was true. I knew that from talking to Toad and Arlinda. No one was forced to go Under-Bubble. But basically the invitation boiled down to this: UnderBubble or OutBubble, you choose by Declaration Day. And if you choose OutBubble, yer on yer own. For good. No do-overs.

The article was illustrated with a picture of a beautiful shining city under a clear bubble. The bubble was filled with happy people doing happy things—there was volleyball, just like in the brochure, but also people having picnics and having sack races and playing catch. Everybody looked happy and healthy. *Really* healthy.

"Toad?" I ask. "Did you have any doubts on Declaration Day? Did you ever think of going UnderBubble?"

Toad snorts like a grumpy hog. "Ot-nay or-fay a sit-splecond!"

"We saw it coming for a long time," says Arlinda. "And knew we wanted no part of it."

"The tolipicians!" says Toad. "After they got done yam-slammering, I wouldn't have gone in their blankety-blank bubble if they'd have sent me an enraged invitation and a magic flying welcome mat to float in on."

"And when they cut a deal with CornVivia, well, that sealed it for us," said Arlinda.

There is a photo of two politicians smiling with their arms around a fat man in a business suit. The caption says the politicians had "set aside their differences for the good of the country" and were thanking companies like CornVivia for joining together with the government "in a Patriotic Part-nering that will allow every citizen of this great nation an opportunity to live life free of hunger, want, or danger."

"Yah," says Toad, pointing at the photo, "when politicians agree to set aside their differences, you know you're in for it."

Toad and Arlinda have told me before how it turned out. Most people had already gone from feisty to fearful and were happy to head for the nearest Bubbling Centers. You could say all the trouble brought people together. That sounds like a good thing, I suppose. But most of those people were giving up everything they owned—and most of what they said they believed in—in return for safety. Arlinda and Toad say the roads were jammed in the months leading up to Declaration Day. People in little vans and big trucks and everything in between—when it came down to it they wanted a guarantee that everything would be all right.

We sit at the kitchen table for a long while. Outside, the

141

wind just keeps blowing harder and the air gets colder. The sleet snaps against the windowpanes. Toad keeps stoking the stove, and Arlinda keeps cooking, so it's hard to imagine leaving. Even after the biscuits, my stomach is growling like a grumpy solar bear. I look at the pans bubbling on the stove, then I peek out the window toward the ridge. The sleet has stopped, but the wind is still blowing a thin rain.

"It's nasty out there," says Arlinda. "You might as well stay the night."

I start to say no, then a spatter of sleet hits the window and I catch a whiff of biscuits. "Okay," I say, "but first I have to call my parents."

I step out to the back porch and whistle three long and three short. Then I light Toad's semaphore lantern and wait. Soon a flickering light appears beside the flagpole.

Staying here tonight, I flash. After Toad taught me, I wrote out the Morse code alphabet for Ma. She learned it in half the time it took me.

O-K, winks the light from Skullduggery Ridge. Then a gap and a final set of flashes: *Love, Mom*.

I smile. Then I smile again, and flash one word: *Smile*.

Later, when I am curling into my blankets in the barn, I think of how sometimes I feel trapped between being a GreyDevil-fighting scavenger and just a girl who wants to cuddle in her mother's arms. I wonder what my life would have been like if I had been born before all this Bubble silliness. Before solar bears and giant corn I can't eat, when you could just drive to town without a Whomper-Zooka. I think of my few hazy memories of those other times . . . of flickering televisions, of my own room, and dolls, and Dad and the red balloon floating away. . . . When I finally drift off to sleep, I dream of a GreyDevil battle that swirls on and on and on. Toby and I fight and never fall, but they just keep coming, and I wonder why Dad isn't there to help. Somewhere in the midst of it all, I dream I hear a whistle: three long, three short.

25

I WAKE TO A GRAY DAWN. THE WIND HAS STOPPED, BUT A COLD rain still drizzles down. The hike up the holler will be miserable, but I know when I get to the shack Ma will have tea water on the boil. We'll sit beside the window to read poems and listen to the rain trickling down the plastic. There won't be quite enough light, so we'll light a candle and lean together with our hands wrapped around the tea mugs to catch the warmth in our palms. Ma says sometimes there's nothing better than reading a good book in bad weather.

The thought of this cozy scene keeps me going through the long, soggy climb. At the crest of Skullduggery Ridge, I pause for a moment to look down through the rain at the coop, the shack, the garden patch, the root cellar, the Ford Falcon down below. . . .

Something isn't right.

I look again. The shack door is gaping open, hung from a single broken hinge. The chicken coop is knocked sideways. The garden is trampled, the hoop houses smashed and tattered. The cellar door is kicked in.

I drop my pack and run to the shack.

Just outside the door I stop and call out. Softly, so if there are still attackers nearby—GreyDevils or whomever they might be—they won't hear me.

"Ma?"

Nothing.

"Dad? Dookie?"

Now it seems even quieter than before I spoke.

Lurching forward, I kick aside the kindling that used to be the door.

"MA!"

I'm hollering now, completely forgetting that I may be in danger. There is no answer, and in the half-light I see no one. I sweep the lumped-up blanket off the bed, flip the upended table. No one.

I run to the coop. Nothing. A few feathers in the straw, some broken eggs, and silence.

I run around crazily, hollering and checking behind and beneath every object and surface. Everything in sight is tipped, bent, or broken. Someone has stomped across the roof of the Falcon, and muddy water has pooled in the dents. A giant spiderweb of cracks crisscrosses the front windshield.

I peer though a side window, afraid of what I'll find, but see nothing.

I run the perimeter of our little homestead. I claw through the salvage piles, kick over the compost bins, even dig my hands into the chicken manure pile in a desperate attempt to find anyone or anything. I find nothing but a single chicken, huddled wetly beneath a tree.

Finally I come to a stop, so ragged and out of breath I have lost the ability to be frantic. I stand with my chest heaving and empty hands dangling. Foolishly, I have left my weapons on the ground in my pack, but there is no one to strike. This is not a problem that can be solved with a ToothClub or a SpitStick.

The root cellar! I think. *I haven't checked the root cellar!* And now I'm running again, up to where I dropped my pack. I scrabble around inside and bring out my jacklight. Pulling aside what remains of the door, I raise the jacklight. Everything is a mess. The shelves have been ripped from the walls. I can smell tomatoes and sauerkraut and applesauce. The ham that was hanging from the rafter is on the floor and torn to shreds. There are rutabagas and carrots and sand everywhere.

But no sign of any person—or thing.

I go back up the stairs. As I walk back around to the front of the shack I hear a crunch beneath my feet and look down. There on the ground is the old window Dad had promised to put up in Ma's reading room. All the little wooden dividers are smashed. Dad was so excited the day he found that window. I don't know if he ever would have gotten around to building the reading room, but when I saw how happy he was to show Ma the frame, or how carefully he wrapped each new pane in deerskin to protect it, I knew he meant it with all his heart. Ten paces from the ruined window I find a flat piece of tin. The day Dad pulled that from Goldmine Gully he said he would nail it on the roof above Ma's reading window so she could listen to the raindrops drumming while she read on days like today. Now the tin is bent and stomped and twisted, and something red is snagged on one of the sharp corners. I lift the tin, and there is Dookie's red rubber ball, torn and flat.

It doesn't even feel like me walking as I trudge to the Shelter Tree, place my back against it, and slide to the ground.

I am so wet, so cold, so tired. So lonely for my family. So lonely for my days as Maggie, when I had no responsibility for those around me. I lay my head against the root, and I cry.

I cry quietly, but I cry hard.

26

IT IS A LONG TIME BEFORE I CAN GET MY BREATHING RIGHT, BEFORE I can take a breath that isn't a gulping hiccup. I steady myself, and, cradled in the exposed roots of the giant tree, I try to gather my thoughts.

Tha-thump. Tha-thump. Tha-thump.

The root. I can feel a faint thumping in the root against my back.

Tha-thump.

Faint.

Tha-thump.

Steady.

Tha-thump.

Like a heartbeat.

A heartbeat? In the wooden root of a tree? For a moment

I am too frightened to move. Is it a GreyDevil? A solar bear that crawled in to get out of the rain? Is it one of the attackers who ripped apart my home and stole my family?

I stay frozen, listening as hard as I can. Now I hear a softer sound. A rise and fall, like breathing. I move slowly to my hands and knees and peer carefully into the tangle of roots.

And there, nearly invisible in the cavelike darkness, sticking out of the mud, is a miniature boomerang. "Dookie!" I gasp, and reach for it. Moving too quickly, I slip and fall forward, scraping my cheek on a gritty, mud-covered root. I stretch an arm out to catch myself, but the heel of my hand slides right past the boomerang and bumps into something at once soft and solid. At first I want to yank my hand out, but then I pat the object and . . . it's a foot!

A small foot. Just the size of . . .

"Dookie!" I holler.

"Dookie!" I holler again. I squeeze his foot. There is no reaction. The foot is cold, and I panic now, desperate to have him out of there. I tug and yank at his ankle, pulling backward with all my strength. I am breathing hard, and hollering "Dookie!" over and over, loud now, not caring who might hear. By the time I pull him out I am wild-eyed and weeping again, my hair a sodden tangle. I gather him up tight: Dookie, my snot-nosed, whiny-shorts, cranky-pants, angry-making brother, all loose in my arms like a flat balloon. I stop crying. Somewhere within me comes strength I didn't know I had. I hold Dookie tight and pull my shoulders back square, and I strike out for Hoot Holler.

A long time later when I get to the security gate I'm too out of breath to whistle. Instead I call Toad's name, over and over, and then Toad pulls the gate open, and for once in his life he doesn't say a word, just takes Dookie from my arms, carries him into the house, and places him ever so gently on a blanket beside the woodstove, which is roaring with a fire.

Arlinda goes straight to work cleaning Dookie's wounds, applying patches and poultices, putting cool cloths to his brow. The worst bruise is above his right eye. There is an egg there the size of a bar of soap. Dookie moans and moves a little now and then, but he will not open his eyes. When Toad pulls Dookie's eyelids up and shines the jacklight in his face, Dookie's pupils squeeze smaller.

"It's a good sign," says Toad, but his voice is very solemn.

We move him into Toad's taxidermy room, which is filled with animals Toad stuffed using directions from Daniel Beard's book. All afternoon I sit among the cockeyed, crooked creatures and wait for Dookie to awaken. I hold his hand, and sing the songs Ma used to sing to him when he got upset. I watch him for the slightest flicker of recognition, but there is nothing.

At nightfall I go to the barn and bring my blankets into the house so I can sleep right beside Dookie. Tripod follows me in from the barn, and I'm glad, because I've never needed the comfort of her purring as much as I do now. When I get settled, I reach over and give Dookie's hand a squeeze. He doesn't squeeze back. I keep his hand in mine while I try to sleep, which seems impossible. How can I sleep not knowing where Ma and Dad are? Or if they're even alive? Every time I close my eyes I see smashed doors and shattered glass. Every time I put my head down I hear my heart in my ears and flash back immediately to the sound of Dookie's heart vibrating the roots of the Shelter Tree. Squeezing my eyes shut, I put everything I have into listening to Dookie's breathing; in and out, in and out, quiet and steady, a sound like the surf of a faraway ocean I've never seen, and slowly, wave by wave, I drift out on a peaceful sea of sleep.

Sometime in the night I wake. I don't take a breath until I am sure I can still hear Dookie breathing. There is faint lamplight from the kitchen and when I rise up on one elbow I can see Arlinda has moved her rocking chair in beside the stove and has been sleeping sitting up, her head tipped to her chest, a candle guttering on the stove. She must have heard me move, because she opens her eyes and raises her head. Quietly, I rise from my blankets and go to her. She puts out her arms and I sit on her lap like I am a three-year-old and lean my head into her chest, and she holds me while I cry. When I finally look up I can see her cheeks are wet and shiny too.

"Oh, Arlinda," I say, when I have my breath again. "It's so awful . . ."

"It is, child," says Arlinda, and I feel confused. Why is she agreeing? Why isn't she trying to comfort me?

"I won't give you false comfort," she says, in the gentlest voice, as if she has read my mind and my question. "Something awful *has* happened. That is where we begin. Moment by moment, hour by hour, day by day."

"But my ma . . ." I'm crying again.

"We don't know, child. We don't know." It feels so good to have her arms around me. She holds me for a long time, and then, ever so softly, she says, "We know that we have your brother. And that he needs us now. That is where we begin."

I stand up, thumbing tears from my face.

"That is where we begin," says Arlinda again. I feel the quietness of her voice spread inside me. I turn to go back to Dookie and see Toad, standing in the bedroom door. He steps backward into the darkness, but not before the candlelight glistens on the tear tracks down his own cheeks.

Back in my blankets, I take Dookie's hand again. Arlinda snuffs the candle, and this time when I close my eyes, rather than broken boards and shattered glass I see a tiny light winking, as if from a great distance: *Love, Mom . . .*

27

BY THE FIRST MORNING, DOOKIE IS RESTLESS. BY THE SECOND morning, he is opening his eyes. By the third morning, he rolls over, looks at a cross-eyed stuffed muskrat, and whispers, *"Fshazzle,"* which in most folks' case would be a sign that his brain was addled, but in Dookie's case is just the sort of thing he always says anyway, so it's hard to tell.

Then his eyes flash to mine. *"Sh-shibby?"*

"No, Dookie," I say, gently. "No danger. You're safe now."

Then I turn away, so he won't see the tears in my eyes.

I leave Dookie with Toad and Arlinda and return to Skull-duggery Ridge to look for any sign of my parents. I search every inch of the ransacked shack, looking for scuff marks on the floor, for bits of cloth, any hint of what might have happened or who might have taken them. Under a broken chair in a dark corner I find Ma's Emily Dickinson book. I snatch it up and clutch it to my chest.

Outside, I lift every bit of junk, peek under every stone. I crawl through the chicken coop on my hands and knees. Returning to the front door of the shack, I walk in ever-widening circles, marking my progress with peeled and sharpened aspen sticks, moving them out six feet every time I make another round. Every morning I walk new trails. In the evenings I armor up and skulk from bonfire to bonfire, spying from the darkness, hoping to catch a glimpse of Ma and Dad.

I see nothing but GreyDevils.

One day, before I leave to search for Dad and Ma, I take Dookie outside. He walks slowly, blinking in the light. We stroll over to the fish tanks, but when I hand him his under-water water-telescope he shows no interest. I hand him a boomerang, and he studies it like he's never seen one before, then lets it drop to the ground. "How 'bout berries, Dookie? Let's pick some berries." Dookie always liked picking berries out in the brambles behind Toad's barn. But now he is standing stock-still and staring straight up into the sky.

"Dookie?"

"*Sh-shibb . . . Shib . . .*" He can't get the word out. I look around quickly. What possible danger could there be? We're only a few feet from the house and inside the safety fence.

"*Sh-sh . . .*" Dookie's hands begin to flutter. Then his arms stiffen. And then he drops to the ground, his whole body jerking and twitching.

"Toad! Arlinda!" I holler, and they both come running out the door, but there is little we can do except kneel beside Dookie and make sure he doesn't hit his head on something hard or cut himself on something sharp while he's flailing.

Dookie has never had a seizure before. It has to be the hit on the head. He is foaming and chewing and clenching his fists and paddling his feet. Eventually the clenching stops and the paddling slows, and then he is still again. I check that he is breathing, and he is. I feel his pulse and it is thumping along. As I let go of his wrist, his eyes blink open.

"Fshazzle."

"You okay, Dookie?"

Slowly he rolls over to his hands and knees. Then—still slowly, like he's moving in molasses—he stands.

"Dookie—you okay?"

He bends to pick up the boomerang at his feet, holds it up before his face, then spins and sends it whirling into the air. It flies out beyond the barn, curves up and out of sight behind the tall silo, then comes winging back into view headed straight at me. I hit the dirt, flailing like I'm having a seizure of my own, and the boomerang clangs off the hood of a junk car.

Dookie dances around me, pointing and giggling. Then he grabs the water-telescope and runs off to spy on the tilapia.

I'm so happy to see him up and around I don't even give him a noogie.

28

EVERY DAY I SEARCH FOR MY PARENTS, OFTEN WITH TOAD AT MY side. But on the one-month anniversary of their disappearance, I tuck my ToothClub into my belt and prepare to leave the farmhouse on yet another search only to find Toad standing before me, blocking the door.

"No more."

I look to Arlinda. Her eyes are filmed with tears, but her voice is firm.

"No more."

I narrow my eyes and stick my jaw out, but inside I know they're right. In another time, I might have been able to run around in search of my parents until I died trying. But here in the AfterBubble world, every day that I spend wandering and searching is a day I am doing nothing to feed myself or

Dookie. It's a day I'm not pitching in with Toad and Arlinda.

I don't like what I am being told, but I know it is how it has to be.

"You—*we*—will never stop searching for your parents," says Arlinda, who has been watching Dookie for me all this time, "but you can't keep walking the same circles."

I know what she means, even though it's hard to hear it.

I decide it's time to move back up to Skullduggery Ridge. Toad and Arlinda have told me that Dookie and I are welcome to live with them now, and I couldn't imagine life without the Hoppers—especially now that Ma and Dad are gone—but I feel like Dookie and I need to reclaim our territory. To hold it for all it's worth. I admit my pride is probably getting the better of me, that there is some selfish part of me that wants to prove myself by taking Dookie back up the ridge, but I'm in no mood to fight it.

Toad and I pack tools and lumber up the ridge and spend several days repairing doors and getting things cleaned up and squared away. We rebuild the shack and cellar doors and reinforce them with steel strapping. We set the chicken coop right and Arlinda sends two more laying hens up to join the one that had been left under the tree. Last thing, Toad fits an old sheet of clear vinyl in the shattered windshield of the Falcon. "Dome-say we'll rix it fight," he says. It was good to hear him talking silly again, although his voice was solid and serious.

When we have the place put back together, I hike down

to fetch Dookie. Together we climb back up the ridge, and together we begin our new life as orphans.

Hatchet and the parrots still squawk every morning, the GreyDevils and solar bears are still dangerous, and even with Dad and Ma gone, we have to keep living and working. When Toad and Arlinda hatched out a batch of chicks, they gave three to Dookie, and every day he tends them so gently I'm not even sure it's him. He holds them tucked beneath his chin and hums quietly. I keep scavenging for scrap and building whirligigs from Daniel Beard's book. On the days I go down to help Toad sort scrap, Dookie comes along and spends the day staring at fish and flicking miniature boomerangs. On the days I go to town with Toad, Dookie stays in the house with Arlinda, helping her bake but mostly sitting in the taxidermy room having mystery conversations with the cross-eyed muskrat.

On every trip to town with the *Scary Pruner* I watch for any sign of Dad and Ma. In particular, I keep an eye out for GreyDevils wearing any of their clothes. That'd be about the worst thing I could see, but at least it would be a clue. It's the hardest thing, not knowing: Dead? Or alive? Either way, at least I'd know what to do with my heart.

I miss them so much. I have Dookie, sure, but I feel like a boat with no keel, moving forward but sliding sideways now and then. I keep up the tough talk and steady face for Dookie's sake, and even for my own sake—sometimes you have to fool yourself into being strong—but I feel hollow where my heart should be.

Every day while I am working I puzzle over what happened to Dad and Ma. Something about the attack doesn't make sense. It could have been GreyDevils that came up the ridge to plunder Goldmine Gully, but they rarely travel that far—although there was the GreyDevil I saw on my way down the ridge that day. But even if a stray GreyDevil wandered up this way, it'd be even rarer for them to be organized enough to manage an attack like this.

The other thing that was weird was Ma and Dad being gone. It was possible that something had gone wrong and Ma and Dad were overwhelmed in the attack. But what didn't make sense was them being utterly, completely, without a trace, absent. GreyDevils don't take prisoners. They might kill or maim in order to get what they want, but they'd leave your body behind. And as far as taking someone hostage, they haven't got the attention span to come up with a plan, and if you've ever watched them howl and swirl at the sight of a kernel of URCorn, or pitch over on their faces after drinking PartsWash all night, you know they'd never put it together to hold someone prisoner and arrange a ransom.

As horrible as it was to consider, I had been ready, in my searching, to find their bodies. But to find nothing?

It didn't make sense.

29

ONE THING I DIDN'T THINK ABOUT WHEN I DECIDED TO MOVE BACK to Skullduggery Ridge with Dookie was how much work it would be just keeping track of him. I don't know how Ma did it. He's forever wandering off. And now I'm always worried about him having a seizure and hurting himself. I can't leave him alone, so I've had to move out of the Falcon and into the shack with him.

Yesterday when Toad and I finished scrapping and I came to get Dookie from the house, Arlinda met me at the door with my supper wrapped in a cloth. "Leave the boy down here tonight," she said. I could see Dookie in the kitchen, playing spoons.

"No, I . . ."

"Leave him here. Toad and I are jerking fish tomorrow.

Dookie can run the net." Dookie dropped his spoons and stood up, grinning. He loves to dip the tilapia from the tank before Toad guts them and Arlinda preps the fillets for drying and smoking.

"But I should . . ."

"You need the time alone," said Arlinda. "We'll see you day after tomorrow, when you come to help Toad load the *Pruner*."

I started to step back off the porch, then stopped.

"Go," said Arlinda.

I sleep so hard in the Falcon that the parrots and Hatchet's crowing don't wake me until the sun has climbed high into the sky. I get up, let out the chickens, and then crawl right back into Falcon and sleep until noon. I eat some fish jerky, drink some water, and sleep some more. Now I'm awake again and the sun has crossed the ridge into late afternoon. I can hear the rumble of cornvoy trucks in the distance. Harvest is in full swing now.

I make some tea, pull *The Complete Poems of Emily Dickinson* from the glove box, where I've been keeping it since the shack was ransacked, and sit on the hood of the Falcon. For a long time I just hold the book in my lap and stare out across the distance. Sometimes the grand view makes my heart soar; other times it makes me feel hopelessly small. Today as I stare out over the world I am feeling the weight of Emily's words on my lap, and how she scratched them out, one by one, all alone at her desk. I used to think it was weird how Emily never wanted to leave her room. How she got to where she would only peek out from behind her door. I understand that now. This old station wagon is my Emily room.

In one of her poems Emily wrote *"To fight aloud is very brave, / But gallanter, I know, / Who charge within the bosom, / The cavalry of woe."* I guess the Whomper-Zooka would be "fighting aloud." But what I am facing now—losing my parents and facing my own *cavalry of woe*—that's much harder. Toad can teach me how to fight GreyDevils, but when it comes to fighting the sadness in my bosom—my *heart*—I need Emily. I think Emily is telling me we are more than one part, and we have to balance all those parts. And there is a part of my soul or heart, or whatever it is that makes us *us*, that Emily wrote down for me all those years ago. It was like she was writing notes to me.

I remember Ma saying that sometimes she felt the only person who ever would have understood her heart was Emily. I remember asking her if she wasn't worried that Emily was too gloomy. If Emily's sad poems might drag Ma down and actually make things worse. "No," said Ma. "No, sometimes you just want to know someone knows. Knows the trouble you feel. Knows the thing the people closest round you can't seem to understand."

She paused for a moment and looked out over the countryside.

"Someone," she said, "who knows your lonely. Not someone who knows *you are* lonely. Someone who knows *your* lonely."

Now I whisper that to myself. *"Someone who knows your lonely."* Sometimes I feel like Emily knows my lonely so well that I don't even have to read her poems. Just holding the book is enough. The words speak softly to me from between the covers.

I open the book to a poem called "The Mystery of Pain." Emily writes about how when we are in pain we cannot even remember what it was like before we had the pain. I think about how lost I have felt since Dad and Ma disappeared, and how it's hard to even remember the happy times.

Now I start reading Emily's poems one after the other. As fast as my eyes can scan. Page after page. "Weak tea, Maggie," I hear Ma saying, and I know she wouldn't approve, but the poems sweep everything away. I'm not even reading them, I'm swimming through them and not stopping to come up for air.

And then I close the book and sleep again. I sleep all night long, even forgetting to put in the chickens. When I finally wake they are clucking beside the Falcon. I open one eye, shake my head, and peek out. The sun tells me it is nearly noon.

I feel like I slept for one hundred years.

And then I hear the whistle.

Three long, three short.

It's coming from Hoot Holler. Toad.

Again: Three long, three short. Quicker this time. More urgent.

I run for the flagpole.

30

THROUGH THE BINOCULARS I SEE CHAOS. A CORNVOY TRUCK HAS run off the road between Toad's barn and the Sustainability Reserve and lies on its side beside the Leaning Tower of Pisa, which—amazingly enough—is still standing. The front of the truck has knocked a section of Toad's security fence flat and the silver trailer has split open, spilling URCorn across the road in a beautiful yellow fan. As I watch, the trucker crawls out of the cab and runs for the safety of another truck. And closing in from all directions, looking like scarecrows on the march, I see hordes of GreyDevils.

I take off at a dead run. I'll still never get there before the GreyDevils do. I can only hope Toad can hold them at bay until I arrive.

But all that URCorn! They'll be in a frenzy. *And Dookie's*

down there! I think, and run even faster. Already my lungs are aching and my mouth tastes like metal. I keep pounding downhill, my pack jouncing on my back, my ToothClub in my hand. Whenever the trail passes through a place where Hoot Holler is visible, I see the snaky lines of GreyDevils have become thicker. Now I hear a *pop-pop-pop*. That means the first of the GreyDevils have arrived and the Sustainability Security crews are firing at them. Sure enough, at the next clearing I can see the Sustainability Security crews standing in a semicircle around the crashed truck and firing their weapons, and there are dead GreyDevils on the road and other injured ones crawling here and there. So the crews are using real bullets. But the GreyDevils are showing up in clots now, and just like when they attack the *Scary Pruner* there will be a point when there get to be so many that the Sustainability Security crews will be hopelessly outnumbered. Sure enough, soon the *pop-pop-pop* sounds stop, and at the next clearing I can see the Security crew has jumped into its vehicle and is retreating behind the giant BarbaZap gate, which immediately begins to roll closed behind them.

Now I'm encountering GreyDevils myself. We're all moving in the same direction, but they're so focused on getting to the URCorn they don't even notice me. They just shuffle-run, their lungs making horrible cheesy-wheezy sounds. Actually, right now my lungs don't feel much better.

HA-WHOMP!

Toad! The Whomper-Zooka! Just as I break into Hoot

Holler, the Security crews are closing the electric gates of the Sustainability Reserve, using the last rounds from their weapons to knock down the GreyDevils who think it's their chance to get into those fields of giant corn. Mostly they're all swarming the capsized truck, but as the gate slides the last two feet, it traps a pair of GreyDevils. First it fries them, then it crunches them. The Security crew just watches as they sizzle.

The first GreyDevils to reach the spill have thrown themselves headfirst into the kernels, shoveling handfuls into their faces or biting mouthfuls like hungry hounds swimming through a pool full of dog food.

"TOAD!" I holler, banging at the gate just down from where the truck has crashed through the fence.

"FULLY OCCUPIED, FORD FALCON!" Toad hollers back. I hear another *HA-WHOMP!* and immediately realize: Toad is too busy fighting to get the gate, and Arlinda is probably in the house guarding Dookie.

The only way in is through the breach in the fence.

Which is currently clogged with slobbering GreyDevils.

31

THIS ISN'T ONE OF THOSE TIMES WHEN YOU THINK THINGS OVER. I draw my ToothClub, raise it high, and rush forward. At first the going is pretty easy because I'm going with the Grey-Devil flow, but as I get closer to the gap in the fence and the mountain of spilled URCorn, the jostling and bumping begins. "Outta my way, snot suckers!" I holler, and start smacking heads. An elbow whacks me in the ribs, making me go *whoooofffh!* A heel smashes down on my steel-toed boot, making me happy I am wearing steel-toed boots.

Now things are really getting clogged up. I high kick the GreyDevil ahead of me. He pitches headfirst to the dirt and I dive into the opening where he used to be, but immediately I am jammed shoulder to shoulder with more creepy crawlers. The stench of their unwashed rags and bodies makes me retch, but I think of Toad and Arlinda and Dookie, lower my head, and barge forward another three feet. I holster my ToothClub because I don't even have room to swing it now, and even when I punch and kick the bodies around me there is no response. They're so obsessed with getting to the URCorn that it's like I'm not even there. I'm just being carried forward by a greasy, grimy tide of GreyDevils.

And then everything stops.

I can't move, and I'm being squeezed tight, so tight I have to work to make my breath go in and out. My arms are pinned to my sides, and now I admit I'm freaking out a little. I struggle, but it's no use. And I can hear a sound . . . a wet, smacky, grindy, *odd* sound. Now I realize—it's the sound of GreyDevils chewing and gnawing and slobbering and smacking as they gobble the kernels of URCorn. The GreyDevils beside me must hear it too, because suddenly I feel something wet and warm run down the back of my neck. GreyDevil drool!

"This is NOT HAPPENING!" I holler, although it's hard to holler when you're trying not to hurl. I kick, elbow, and claw with every ounce of energy I can summon. The tiniest gap opens before me and I shoot both arms up, grab a GreyDevil by its greasy shoulders, and by scrabbling up its back with my knees, basically do a pull-up until I am high enough up its back to get a knee over its shoulder. I grab its horrible head in both my hands, lever myself up so I'm standing on its shoulders, and launch myself into a forward dive. As I take flight, I can see I'm headed for a pile of GreyDevils who are

169

burrowing into the URCorn. I belly flop onto the pile with a thump, then climb and claw and crawl like mad, doing whatever it takes to keep moving over the giant squirming glob of GreyDevils gorging themselves on crazy corn.

When I get near the peak of the pile I reach out to the torn steel where the trailer has split open. Grabbing the lip with both hands, I do a chin-up myself, then kick one leg over and hoist myself atop the trailer, only to see Toad about to pull the striker on the Whomper-Zooka.

"FOLD YOUR HIRE!" I holler.

Toad's eyes widen, then his face breaks into a big grin.

"FORD FALCON!"

Even in all the craziness, Toad's smile warms my heart in a way it hasn't felt in months, and for just a split second I imagine how heroic I must look standing astride the tanker, rising above all odds to come to the rescue of my friends and family. After months of frustration and futility and worry I have something to *do*. As awful as this situation is, at least I can *fight it*.

Flap-flap-WHACK!

Oh, for the love of cock-eyed nuts.

Hatchet.

I rip him from my hair and throw him into the pile of GreyDevils, where he belongs. As I jump from the tanker into the compound, he's already pecking furiously at a GreyDevil's earlobe. I dive behind Toad and he lets loose another Whomper-Zooka blast.

"We gotta keep 'em out!" says Toad. "That corn's holdin' 'em for now! Once it's gobbled, they'll be roarin' all over the place, hauling everything off to the Juice Cruisers!"

"Dookie!" I holler. "Where's Dookie?"

"In the house," Toad says. I look over my shoulder and there's Arlinda on the porch, cradling a Mini-Zooka Toad made especially for her.

I can stop worrying about Dookie, then.

32

FOR HALF A SECOND I CONSIDER MAKING A DASH FOR MY ARMOR, but then a stray GreyDevil lurches my way and I realize there is no time for that. I clobber the GreyDevil a good one with the ToothClub and it staggers back toward the tipped-over truck. While Toad reloads the Whomper-Zooka I stand guard before him, whacking at GreyDevils and thinking we're in for a long night.

And then rising from behind Skullduggery Ridge, I hear a distant moaning sound. I swivel my head around, half expecting to see an army of ravenous GreyDevils come over the ridge, but instead I see a gigantic helicopter rising over the horizon and coming straight for Toad's place. As it draws closer, I can see the national flag and the CornVivia logo on its side.

When it gets directly above the crashed cornvoy truck, the helicopter hovers high in the sky. I'm expecting a thunderous roar, but the two big propellers at either end just make that low moaning sound. A small hatch opens in the belly and a long, long tube snakes downward toward the ground. The tube is about as big around as my waist, and the end is covered with a spiky steel grate. Someone in the helicopter must be controlling it, because now it's twisting and, like an elephant's trunk, nosing its way into the pile of GreyDevils. Suddenly the air is filled with a sizzling *Zap-snap-zap!* Sparks fly from the nozzle spikes and the GreyDevils howl and scatter. URCorn begins whooshing up the tube.

"Toad!" I holler. "It's a giant vacuum cleaner!"

One of the GreyDevils gets too close and in an instant is sucked up tight against the grate that keeps it from being inhaled by the tube. The hose retracts, raising the GreyDevil about ten feet in the air. Then someone in the helicopter flips a switch, the whooshing stops, and the GreyDevil drops to earth. Immediately, the nozzle roars to life and starts sucking corn again.

The helicopter keeps vacuuming corn and zapping Grey-Devils, and it is really something to see, but it also means that the GreyDevils are being scattered and some of them are winding up on our side of the fence.

"Whomp at will, Ford Falcon!" hollers Toad, reminding me that I needed to stop being a spectator. Over the next twenty minutes, while the helicopter crew sucks up corn out of every nook and cranny of that wrecked truck, I do my best to keep the GreyDevils at bay, shooting the Whomper-Zooka now and then, but mostly using my ToothClub and pepper-bombs. Monocle is helping too, chomping and gnawing and growling, his tail spinning happily—for him this is not a fight, it is like recess—while Hatchet flaps and pecks and scratches. I hear a *whock!* as yet another GreyDevil gets sucked against the end of the tube. The tube raises him kicking and flailing into the air and then just like a cat playing with a mouse, the hidden operator flicks the nozzle, flinging the GreyDevil right at us.

The trouble is, the hose also flicks a scatter of URCorn our way, and as the nozzle sparks and zaps its way back into the truck, a mob of GreyDevils turns and comes charging, crazy to get the URCorn that just sprinkled down on us like yellow hailstones.

I blast them with the Whomper-Zooka and it's no better than blowing kisses. They just keep swarming. I lay into them with my ToothClub, and I hear Monocle yapping, and Hatchet cackling, and for the first time that I can remember, I'm truly scared. There are just so many of them, and they are so crazed. It's terrifying to realize they aren't after me personally. It's simply that they are in a frenzy to get to something and they'll go through me to get it. It's like standing between a pen full of fat pigs and a pack of starving solar bears.

Stepping backward, I catch my heel on a rock. I stumble, then fall on my butt. I struggle to rise, but the wave of charging bodies knocks me flat. GreyDevils close in all around me. I can't see any one particular face, just shapes and ragged silhouettes blocking the sky. I'm trying to curl into what Toad calls "armadillo position"—knees and chin to chest, fingers clasped behind my neck—when suddenly something jerks at my collar and I feel myself being dragged backward.

"Rise and retreat, Ford Falcon!" It's Toad, pulling me to my feet. We run for the house, where Arlinda is holding the door open.

Just as we reach the porch, I look back over my shoulder.

And stop dead in my tracks.

"Ford!" hollers Arlinda. "In the house! Now!"

But I am already running back toward the GreyDevils. Or rather, toward one GreyDevil in particular. It is kneeling with its back to me, gobbling corn. It is wearing a tattered T-shirt. The shirt is stained and grimy, but I can see it was once blue.

And across the shoulders I can see the image . . . of an old-fashioned door lock.

That's my *father's* shirt.

33

THE GREYDEVIL IN THE BLUE T-SHIRT IS SNUFFLING IN THE SPILLED corn like a rabid pig. Stopping just behind it, I raise my Tooth-Club high. I am filled with rage. Seeing my father's shirt on that *creature*, imagining how the shirt got there, what was done to my father in order to steal it, I want to smash and maim and make someone else suffer just a fraction of what my father must have suffered. Of what our *family* has suffered.

"You can stop stuffing your piehole, skunk-monkey," I say, cranking the ToothClub back like Toad taught me to do with Hatchet, "because I'm about to *fetch* you silly!"

The GreyDevil freezes, then turns its head.

I stop my swing halfway, and then I freeze too, staring at the face before me. It's a typical GreyDevil face, all sooty-sweaty and pocked with sores and streaked with snot tracks. The lips are dripping with spit and little chunks of half-chewed URCorn. The cheeks are hollow and the eyes are sunken . . . but something about them is different. They are watery and sickly, but not as yellow as most GreyDevils'. And most GreyDevil eyes look as dead as a fish's after three days on the beach, but deep inside this GreyDevil's eyes I can see a tiny spark of light—of *life*.

I look at the shirt again. The front. A key, and two words: "Bon Hiver."

Now the eyes again.

My voice is so quiet it is nearly a whisper.

"Dad?"

If I am expecting the faint spark in those eyes to melt into love, I am dead wrong. Our eyes lock for a split second, then the GreyDev—*Dad*—makes a mournful half howl, staggers to his feet, and lurches toward the gap in the fence.

I run after him and throw myself on his back. He totters and falls, and I cling to him as he struggles to rise and run again. He feels so bony and frail in my arms.

"TOAD!" I scream, and Toad is on us in an instant. When he sees the face of the creature I am wrestling, his eyes widen, and in a ragged voice he says, "Snooky holer-tables!" Dad struggles terribly, but we hold him down until finally he goes still as a rag doll. We pull my father to his feet, Toad and I each gripping one of his arms.

"Shig ped," says Toad, and he says it so firmly I don't

think he's spoonerizing, he's just having trouble talking. I have never seen him so shaken.

I'm shaken too, and don't move. Now Toad's eyes snap, and suddenly he is all strap iron and steel again, and above the swarm of GreyDevils and the hum of the helicopter his voice is like a whipcrack.

"Now!"

Dad starts struggling again, fighting us, kicking with his heels, trying to get away. When we get to the shed and push him through the door, Toad has to peel Dad's fingers from the doorjamb so I can swing it shut without crushing them. The pigs squeal and scoot as we shove Dad through another door into the small feed storage room in the back. I slam the feed room door and Toad drops the bolt in place. The thick walls muffle the howling and moaning, but I can hear clawing and thuds against the door, and I feel sick.

But there is no time to dally. Toad cracks the pig shed door and I can see GreyDevils milling around the yard, some of them holding pieces of iron stolen from our scrap pile. We burst out of the door and make a run for the house. As we hit the porch, Arlinda steps out between us and touches off her Mini-Zooka. When I turn, I see the helicopter is drawing its giant vacuum cleaner back into its belly now, and the Grey-Devils are rushing back in to claw through the last kernels of URCorn remaining in the corners of the ruined truck. As the helicopter rises, flying up and away over the ridge, the Grey-Devils in the yard are thinning out. Now that the URCorn has been vacuumed up, they're all trying to figure out how to get through the BarbaZap and into the Sustainability Reserves, and there are only a handful rummaging around in Toad's junk piles. Between Toad's Whomper-Zooka, my ToothClub and pepper-peas, Monocle's joyful biting, and Hatchet's bad attitude, it takes us about two hours to round up the last one and run it off. By then the cornvoy truck has been towed away. By the time we get done stringing barb-wire back and forth across the hole in the fence, evening is coming on.

I want so badly to look in on Dad, but when I reach for the pig shed door, Toad puts his hand against it.

"But, Toad, I . . ."

He shakes his head, and we walk to the house. In the kitchen Arlinda hugs me, then pours a mug of tea. When I pick it up my hand is shaky. I've never been so tired, but my eyes are wide, and I'm trembly inside, like I've seen a ghost.

"There is a way to get your father back," says Toad. "But it will take time. And what lies ahead is far worse than anything you saw tonight. You cannot help him right now. There is nothing for you to do right now but rest and gather your strength."

I can't imagine what awful things have happened to make Dad this way, and I can't imagine how we will ever get him back from the animal I left in the pig shed. But I also have new questions about Toad: if he knows how to get Dad back, he must know what has made him this way.

"Toad . . . Dad . . . what . . . ?"

"Tomorrow," says Toad. "Now you must sleep."

"And Ma? Is she out there somewhere? In the same shape? Or worse?"

"We don't know," says Toad.

And then a small hand slips into mine. Dookie. And so I drink the tea, and then Dookie leads me into the room with Toad's strange stuffed animals and he pats the blankets on the floor and like a tuckered child I lie down and I sleep.

The next morning I wake to the smell of fresh-baked apple pies and the rumble of cornvoy trucks coming and going. I look out the window at the pig shed, then look back at Arlinda, packing pies into crates.

"Those hungry truckers only show up twice a year," she says, pointing out to where the cornvoy trucks are lined up waiting for their loads of corn. "Gotta make hay while the sun shines!"

34

TOAD SAID IT WOULD BE HORRIBLE, AND IT WAS. DAD WAS LIKE AN animal. He *was* an animal. Whenever we stepped inside the pig shed I could hear him in the feed room, moaning hoarsely and pounding the walls. Scratching at the door so hard his fingernails ripped. There were times in the beginning when we had to tie him down. We had to give him water in a wooden bowl because when we gave him a glass he bit right through it and cut his lip.

Every time Toad or I went down, we carried slop buckets and gave the pigs some feed. Toad wouldn't tell me why. He just said it was important to make it look like we were just going down there to feed pigs.

"Do you think someone is watching us?" I asked, and he nodded. Remembering how he snapped at me when I hesitated about dragging Dad into the shed, I realize now he knew we had to act fast when we were still surrounded by the swarm of GreyDevils and the distraction provided by the giant helicopter vacuum in the sky.

Every morning Arlinda ground up a small potion of herbs and grains, then boiled them into a porridge that we slipped beneath the door. Once I made the mistake of peeking through to see if Dad was eating the porridge, and when I saw the way he tore into it with his bare hands, nearly chomping his fingers as he stuffed the mash in his face, I couldn't believe this was the same Dad who was joking with me about Hatchet the day I discovered Porky Pig in Goldmine Gully.

Finding Dad really messed me up about Ma. Of course I had been missing her terribly, but I had settled into the idea of not knowing. Now I had to wonder if she was out there somewhere, crazy on PartsWash and trading with Juice Cruisers to survive. What if she was in that crowd I climbed over at the URCorn spill? What if she was one of the Grey-Devils shot by the Sustainability Security crews? I couldn't believe I was thinking this, but it was almost easier to think of her being dead than being one of *them*.

Dookie had no idea Dad was in the pig shed, and we didn't tell him. We were worried if Dookie saw Dad in this condition it would freak Dookie out forever. I told Arlinda it seemed wrong to keep a son from his father, but she said, "That is not the boy's father . . . and won't be for some time." The next time I delivered his porridge and he backed into the corner and snarled like a wild dog, I realized she was right.

Then came the day I saw an ember of softer light in his eyes. That day Toad gave him a plastic cup of berry juice, and Dad drank it slowly, not like before when he frothed and chomped. Finally we could open the door and hand him his food and he wouldn't run to the far corner and hiss like a mad cat, or try to claw his way past us to freedom.

But the healthier he got, the quieter he got. He went from looking me straight in the eyes like a crazy man to quietly turning his back and refusing to look at me at all.

"Time, Ford Falcon, time," said Toad when I told him.

By the end of the first week Dad's skin was less gray. The sores and the runny nose were clearing up. When we left him a washcloth and water he sometimes used it. We left clean clothes and after three more days he put them on.

Then one morning I take Dad his porridge, and after eating it quietly, he speaks.

"You shouldn't have saved me, Maggie." His voice is scratchy, weak, and croaky.

"Dad, you're back . . . it will be okay now."

"No," he says. "No."

"But, Dad . . ."

"You don't understand, Maggie. I don't *deserve* to be alive."

I just look at him.

"Your mother," he says.

"What about her?" I am afraid of what he will say next.

"It's because of me . . ."

"What's because of you?"

"It's because of me . . . that . . . that she's gone."

I just sit there. Waiting.

"They . . . they were looking for me."

"They? Who's 'they'?"

"The Bubble Authorities."

I look at him, so confused I have no idea what to say.

"I carry secrets, Maggie. Terrible, terrible secrets."

35

WE EACH SIT ON AN OVERTURNED SLOP BUCKET AND FACE EACH other, knee to knee.

Dad takes a deep breath and lets it out.

"You know I met your mother when we were both in college," he says. "Your mother was a word nerd, but I was a science geek. After we got married, your mother gave up school and went to work while I did research and piled up science degrees. I don't think I wanted an education as much as I just wanted to live in the laboratory. It was my favorite place."

I'm looking at him now, this man I've known only as my mostly bumbling dad with the lopsided smile—and most recently as a raving GreyDevil—and trying to imagine him as an eager young man looking through a microscope.

"One day some people from CornVivia visited the college. My instructors showed them my grades and my work, and they offered me a job."

"You worked for CornVivia?" I wrinkle my nose like I just found a worm in the porridge.

"They promised to pay off all my tuition if I agreed to work in their laboratories for two years," says Dad. His voice is scratchy and weak, and there is sweat on his brow, but he is looking me right in the eyes. "Your mother was working so hard. We had no money, and we owed so much on tuition I thought we'd never pay it off, and now here was someone offering to wipe it away. Besides, I *loved* working for Corn-Vivia. I was given my own laboratory. I had all the latest tools and technology. At the end of my second year the company gave us a nice car, and offered us enough money to buy our first house if I would stay on."

I'm still trying to picture Dad in a lab coat.

"It was a good life," he says. "I loved your mother, I loved my work, and I especially loved seeing my research put quickly to work in the real world."

Now he looks down at the ground, and his voice gets quieter.

"For a long time, things just kept getting better. Corn-Vivia paid me more and more. Your mother went back to school and was able to finish her studies, and we lived in a beautiful house. I hired a man to build your mother beautiful bookshelves, and she filled them with beautiful books. I even had the man engrave a quote above the shelves: '*she ate and drank the precious words*' . . ."

"Emily Dickinson," I say, recognizing the line. "It's from a poem about how books give us wings. Ma and I memorized that one! It was our favorite. It actually says 'he,' not 'she,' but you must have changed that for Ma."

For just a fleeting second I see the shadow of a smile cross Dad's face, but then he grows serious again. "The more Corn-Vivia paid me, the more they pushed me. They wanted more and more ideas, more and more ways to grow more and more food faster and faster."

"Dad! Did you work on URCorn?"

He doesn't answer the question. "Then came the Secrecy Signings," he says. "I had to sign papers promising never to reveal what I was working on or discuss any of my inventions with anyone outside the laboratory."

He stops now, his elbows on his knees and rocking forward with his shoulders hunched, like he's working his courage up. When he speaks, his voice is so quiet I have to lean in to hear him. "One day several men in suits visited my lab. They sat me down in a little side room. One of the men explained that because the knowledge I carried in my . . . in my brain . . . was patented and owned by CornVivia it was considered 'intellectual property.' And because of the Patriotic Partnering Act, it was also classified as a state secret. He said it was Corn-Vivia's right and duty to make sure the information didn't fall into the wrong hands, so a small tracking chip would be implanted beneath the skin of my right cheek in case I was kidnapped by someone trying to steal their secrets."

"You let them *do* that?" I say, angrily.

"They quadrupled my pay," he says, catching my eyes and then looking away. "Our life was so good. We had everything we needed and all we could want." Then he looks up. "You were a toddler and Ma was pregnant with Dook . . . Henry. We lived in a nice house with a nice yard, we had the best medical care, and when CornVivia and the government announced their Bubbling program, we were guaranteed a special place in the capital Bubble City, with everything the same as we had it, right down to your mother's bookshelves."

I feel like I'm falling through the air. My hands are balled into fists, like I'm trying to grab hold of something to slow me down. Dad just keeps talking, his voice quiet and his face expressionless.

"Right after Henry was born, they put me in charge of a big new project," he says. "Top secret. Related to the Bubbling. When I figured out how it was being used, I wanted no part of it. But it was too late—I *was* part of it. And Declaration Day was coming. I knew too much and was terrified about what would happen if I tried to leave. So before they could do anything, Ma and I packed up you and Henry and took off."

"But the chip? How did you avoid being tracked?"

"On my way home from work that Friday, I bought a red balloon."

I jump to my feet. "I remember that! You gave it to me in

the backyard, and it flew away before I could grab it."

For the first time, I see tears in Dad's eyes. "It wasn't an accident."

"You did that on *purpose*?" I sit back down.

"Yes, Maggie." He is hanging his head down again. "It was a terrible thing to do. But there was always the chance someone was watching. I had to make it look like an accident. Like I was trying to give my little girl a balloon and it just got away."

I'm upset, but mostly I'm just confused. Dad can see I don't understand.

"The chip," says Dad. "In the bathroom, in the house, before we came outside with the balloon, I numbed my face with ice, then cut it out."

My mouth falls open. The bandage on his cheek that day! His goofy lopsided smile!

"When I let go of that balloon, the chip was taped to the string. As we watched that balloon disappear, it took our old life with it."

He pauses. "I have never forgiven myself for not thinking to bring a second balloon."

"But there was a second balloon, I remember it."

"Yes, I dug it out of a drawer. It was left over from a birthday party. It didn't float. You didn't like it."

"Yah," I say. "I remember stomping it."

We sit for a moment. I can hear the pigs grunting softly outside the feed room. Dad continues. "We did the best we could to disguise our escape, driving away like we were going on a camping trip. We had two backpacks filled with everything we could carry that would help us survive without returning to civilization for a long, long time. Nothing extra. No frills. Except for the Emily Dickinson book and *Little House on the Prairie*. I understood what that meant to your mother.

"The day before, I bought a brand-new car for cash from some guy I didn't know. I didn't tell him who I was, and he didn't ask. You could get cars anywhere then—everyone who was planning to go UnderBubble was getting rid of them."

"The new-car smell!" I exclaim, the memory of it coming back.

"Our plan was to drive as far as we could, all weekend long, knowing that when Monday came and I wasn't at work, the questions would begin, but hoping by then we'd be hundreds of miles away and that balloon would have carried the tracker far, far away in the opposite direction."

"But we started 'camping' that same day," I say, furrowing my brow.

"Yes. All day your mother and I listened to the car radio— we had left our phones behind so they couldn't be traced. We'd only been driving for half a day when we heard that the balloon had been found. I don't know what happened. Maybe it got caught in a downdraft. Maybe it set off an alert because it was traveling too far in a straight line. It didn't matter. We knew now that the authorities would be hunting us. So we drove the car deep into a logging road, abandoned it, and just started hiking."

I stare at the man in front of me. Here he is, nearly healthy again and looking like the Dad I knew, but with every sentence out of his mouth it's like I am hearing from someone I've never met before.

"I've always known they were coming for me. That's why we lived on the run for so long. That's why even after we did settle I never went to town with Toad. It was because I knew the Bubble Authorities might have someone out there looking for me. I know I said it was because I was staying back to protect Dookie and Ma . . . but . . ." He stops, and his eyes fill with tears.

"Was that who attacked the shack?" All this talking, and now I realize I haven't asked him what happened to Ma.

Now the tears are running down his cheeks.

"I don't know. Probably."

I reach out and grab his shoulders. "You don't know? You can't even guess? You were there! You were supposed to be protecting them! What did you see?"

Before he speaks, he tips his face into his hands. When his voice comes out, it is choked and muffled.

"I wasn't there."

"You weren't there? But . . ."

"I was already with the GreyDevils."

"The GreyDevils! Why?"

Now he looks at me again. The light in his eyes is gone.

36

I STAND UP SO QUICKLY I KNOCK OVER THE SLOP BUCKET. EVER since Dad began talking I have gone from sad to terrified to happy to freaked out to confused, and now I feel myself taking a sharp turn toward angry. Having just learned that he abandoned Ma in the worst moment possible, and after the story about the red balloon, I am in no mood for tenderness.

He reaches out his hand, but I turn away. He sighs, and speaks again.

"Do you know what makes URCorn work? Why it cures disease, why it will heal your wounds overnight, why it will keep you alive for a hundred years . . . unless you get hit by a cornvoy truck?"

I shake my head, still not looking at him.

"What happens if *you* eat URCorn?"

"It makes me sick."

"Why aren't all the people in the Bubble—who eat URCorn every day—getting sick?"

"I dunno. You're the science genius." I shouldn't have said that, but I'm really not in the mood for Twenty Questions.

"It's because they've all been treated with Activax."

"Activax?"

"Think of Activax as the key that turns on all the good things in URCorn. If you don't have Activax, URCorn is just a quick way to puke. If you do have Activax, URCorn is a miracle—but there's a catch."

"Yah, the last twenty minutes have been just *full* of catches." I'm really not in a very good mood. I sit back down on my slop bucket with my arms crossed.

"Once you have the Activax, you have to have URCorn. If you don't get it, you develop a terrible hunger. A hunger that claws and digs at your insides. A hunger that takes over your brain. A hunger that becomes the only thing you can think about. A hunger that will drive you to do anything you can to get URCorn. A hunger that will drive you to do anything it takes to make the hunger go away, even if it's only for a little while."

Now I'm paying attention, because I'm starting to understand something. I straighten up.

"The GreyDevils!"

"Yes," says Dad. "The GreyDevils. Based on everything I've seen, I'm certain every one of them has been injected with Activax. And every one of them will do whatever it takes to make the hunger go away."

"That's why they throw themselves at the BarbaZap!" I say. "That's why they swarmed the cornvoy truck."

Dad nods. "And that's why they guzzle PartsWash. It's awful, but it makes the craving stop."

Then it hits me. Dad snuffling at the URCorn. Dad howling in the pig shed. Dad all haggard and slimy. Dad the *GreyDevil*.

"Dad . . . you had the Activax!"

"Yes, Maggie. Before I left CornVivia. I was one of the first."

"But . . . how did the GreyDevils—those *people*—get the Activax?" It was odd to suddenly think of the GreyDevils as people. Like my dad. "And where do the new ones come from?"

"I don't know," says Dad. "I have my suspicions, but I don't know. . . . I'm not sure we *want* to know."

"What about Ma? Did Ma have the Activax?"

"No . . . at first—when I took it—I really believed in all the good it could do. By the time it was ready for mass production, once I suspected how they intended to use it, I had too many doubts. Too many suspicions. I wouldn't let her— or you children—get it."

"But all this time . . . where have you been getting your URCorn?"

"When I knew we were leaving, I began sneaking it home.

We had bins of it at the lab. The day I tied that chip to the balloon and we took off, both your Ma's pack and mine were half full of URCorn."

"But that couldn't have lasted you this long . . ."

"You're right. I ground up and ate as little of it as possible and planted the rest. To prevent anyone from planting their own URCorn, it will not sprout unless it is treated with a CornVivia sprouting agent. The URCorn I brought in my backpack had been treated, but once it ran out, I wouldn't be able to grow any more. I could only plant a few stalks here and there. I planted them far apart so if something happened they wouldn't all be lost. And I had to plant them where the GreyDevils weren't likely to go. That's why I chose Skullduggery Ridge. Goldmine Gully was part of it, but mainly I did it to avoid the GreyDevils.

"But I hardly ever had enough. Each year the plants had a tougher and tougher time surviving. In the Sustainability Reserves they have the advantage of all the sprays and chemical boosters. And now and then some stray GreyDevil would stumble on my little patch and devour it in a minute.

"This past year, I finally realized I couldn't keep up. When you caught me in the root cellar, I had just counted my last few kernels, figuring out just how many more days I could go."

"But I looked! There was nothing down there but carrots."

"Maybe you stopped looking too soon," says Dad. I start to ask what he means, but he continues his story. "I kept cutting down, trying to wean myself off it, but already I could feel the gnawing in my gut and the aching in my head. I started sneaking out at night with a jacklight, checking for spillage outside the Sustainability Reserve gate. I walked the cornvoy routes to try and find stray kernels before the Grey-Devils got to them in the light of day. But they were so few and far between, and the gnawing and the aching just got worse and worse.

"Then one night when I had been walking all night and hadn't found any URCorn, and the gnawing was the worst it had ever been, in the gray light of dawn I came to a Grey-Devil bonfire. They were all lying about unconscious and I dipped a little Partswash off the bottom of the cauldron. It was awful. But the gnawing feeling faded. I snuck out again a few nights later. And a few nights after that . . . and soon, as my URCorn dwindled down to nothing, all I could think of was how I was going to get my next dose."

It is all beginning to make sense. Why Dad went from being the healthiest person in the family to being sickly or overtired so often in the morning. And why he was scraped up—not from a tumble off the trail but from making his way through the brush at night. Now I'm remembering the night I caught Dad up by the flagpole, staring off into the distance to the GreyDevil fires. He wasn't just staring, he was preparing to go.

"But now you're fine!" I say. "How . . ."

"Do you remember the day you ate the URCorn and got sick?"

"Kinda hard to forget," I say. "I thought I was gonna yak up my liver."

"Do you remember that I went back out to see if I could find more?"

"I remember," I said. "You wanted to make sure Dookie didn't eat any."

"Well, that's true . . . but I was also hoping I'd find more *for me*. And I did. Just a couple of dusty kernels. I was stuffing them in my pocket, and when I looked up I saw Toad watching me through the gate.

"He didn't say anything, but he knew."

"But . . . you're getting better now, so you must be eating URCorn!"

"I am," says Dad. "Arlinda's been putting it in the mash."

"But where did she get it from?" For a moment I was thinking Toad might have scooped up some of the corn from the crashed cornvoy truck, but that didn't make sense, because he would have had no reason to do that unless he knew we were going to find Dad, and by the time we did find Dad all the URCorn had been vacuumed by the helicopter or gobbled by the GreyDevils.

"What was Arlinda doing the morning after you put me in here?"

"Baking pies."

"For?"

"For the cornvoy truckers."

"And do you know what she charged for each of those pies?"

"Uh . . ."

"Let's just say those cornvoy truckers are loaded with it."

"So Arlinda knew too?"

"Yes," says Dad. "And your mother, of course. She knew I was getting worse. She knew the URCorn had run out and that I was sneaking away for PartsWash. There was nothing she could do but wait at home and hope I came back safe."

For a moment we sit quietly on our buckets. Then Dad speaks.

"And then came the attack."

37

"IT WAS COLD AND SLEETY AND WET AND RAINY ALL THAT DAY and most of the night. You remember—you were down here working with Toad."

"Yeah," I say, "and it was because of the weather I stayed down here that night."

"I knew it would be miserable, and I didn't want to go out into it," says Dad. "But the gnawing . . . I just couldn't take it anymore.

"When I got to the first bonfire just beyond Toad's farm, I hung back beyond the light of the flames. I always did that, always waited until the Devils were mostly knocked out from the PartsWash. Just for my own safety. But this night something odd was happening. While most of the Grey-Devils were lying around on the ground and the fire was dying down, there was a group of about ten that were still up and around. And there was something about the way they moved—it just wasn't right. And the faces—they were gray and sooty and streaky, but the cheeks weren't hollow enough. And the eyes . . . they were yellow, but almost *too* yellow.

"The group was milling around, and as I watched I realized they weren't drinking PartsWash. Then, almost as if there had been some silent command, they all left the bonfire, headed toward the trail leading to Skullduggery Ridge.

"And then my blood went cold, because I realized: these weren't GreyDevils, they were people who wanted to be *seen* as GreyDevils! And that could mean only one thing: they were with the Bubble Authorities."

I sit up straight, and my eyes widen. "Dad! That day! That day on my way down to help Toad, I met a GreyDevil on the trail! I remember thinking it was strange to meet one that far up, especially traveling alone. And *its* eyes were bright yellow!"

"Colored contact lenses, probably," says Dad. "Part of the disguise."

"Must have been scouting our place," I say. "Looking for you."

"Yes," says Dad, "if you want to skulk around, why not dress up like a skulker?" Then he takes a deep breath, and when he speaks next, his voice is soft. "When they all set out, and I realized they were heading up Skullduggery Ridge— toward our shack, where Henry and your mother were sleeping—I knew I had to follow. Try to get ahead of them and warn your mother, then turn myself over to the Bubble Authorities—it had to be me they were after. But there was still some PartsWash in the cauldron, and I had to have some. For courage, I told myself.

"I took one drink. And then another . . .

"When I woke, it was well into the next day. I stumbled up to the Ridge. I was in such bad shape. It took me a long time. I lost the trail. I stumbled off course. When I finally came to the shack . . ."

He stops. His voice cracks and tears rise in his eyes.

"No one was around. I saw what you saw. I found Henry's little boomerang by the Shelter Tree. I found the drag marks where you pulled him out. I saw your tracks, your boot heels deeper from carrying his weight. I stumbled up to the flagpole and looked down with the old binoculars just in time to see Toad let you through the gate. And I saw Ma wasn't with you . . ."

I was remembering that day now. How frightened I was, how Dookie felt in my arms, how Toad took us in. I grab Dad's shoulders, make him look at me. "You *knew*? And you never . . ."

Now the tears are streaming down Dad's face.

"I was so ashamed. I had failed my family. But I knew you and Henry were safely with Toad and Arlinda. And the gnawing . . ."

"COWARD!" I jump to my feet and scream the word, my

arms iron-straight at my sides, my hands clenched in fists.

Dad just sits there, tears falling off his jaw.

"You did *nothing*!"

"I became a GreyDevil."

Have you ever felt like someone took all your breath and your insides and every part of you and left you emptier than empty and like nothing you ever knew was true?

I sit back down. My knees are too weak to hold me up. Dad is crying. I can't say anything.

I don't know how much time goes by before he speaks.

"Maggie."

I can't look at him, let alone talk to him.

"Maggie," he says again, his voice just a croak. "Your mother is alive. I believe it with all my heart."

I am staring at my boots.

"If it was the Bubble Authorities—and it has to be—they took her UnderBubble. To the capital, where the government and CornVivia have their headquarters. And there is only one way to get her back."

Still I say nothing. I have no feeling left in me.

"I have to turn myself in. They have your mother, but it's me they want. Me, and my biggest secret. I have to go UnderBubble."

Now I yell at him again. "Your *biggest* secret? If those other secrets were tiny . . ." I let my words trail off, then very quietly I ask, "What is the biggest secret?"

"I can't tell you." Dad's voice is barely a whisper.

"What?"

"I can't tell you. I haven't even told your mother."

And now I'm really yelling. Everything comes out. All my anger. All my fear. I yell at him about all the times he was gone at night. I yell at him for getting us into this trouble in the first place. I yell at him for abandoning Ma. I yell at him for being an awful father. I yell and yell until I just have no energy left. I stand up, and look down at him sitting there. I stare at him for a long, silent time. Then I step backward through the feed room door and gently close it. I refasten the lock and double-check it.

Toad is standing on the porch. The feed room walls are thick, and I can't tell if he heard me yelling, but he can tell by the look on my face that I know things now that I didn't know an hour ago.

"Keep him in there," I say.

And then I walk away.

38

LEAVING DOOKIE WITH TOAD AND ARLINDA, I HIKE UP TO THE FORD
Falcon and spend the rest of the day alone. I just can't face
my father. Can't face anyone. Not even Dookie.

When I stepped out of that pig house I felt like I'd been up
and down Skullduggery Ridge fifty-seven times with rocks
in my pockets. Now my anger is gone and replaced with
numbness. I have no idea what to do.

So I sit beneath the Shelter Tree with Emily.

At first I just page through the book, not sure where to
begin. I find a poem called "Childish Griefs." It is only two
tiny verses. I read it twice. It seems like Emily is writing about
how the things that make us sad when we are little children
become almost sweet after we experience real trouble. Some
people would say I am still a child—and there are certainly
times when I can be childish—but I am living through

troubles now that most grown-ups never face. I think about the red balloon, and how sad I was when it floated away, and yet now I realize that grief was nothing compared to the grief I am feeling now.

I close the book and let it rest in my lap. I miss Ma so much.

I walk down to the Falcon. I stow Emily's poems in the glove compartment, then climb up on the hood to watch the day drain away. The sun is going down behind me, and the horizon to the east is already darkening. I can see just the faintest hint of the Bubble City glow.

Ma, I think. And because it has been so long, I say it out loud: "Ma."

Gone three months now. Vanished, like that final semaphore flash from Skullduggery Ridge.

Three months since I've seen my mother's face. Three months since I felt my mother's arms around me.

She is out there, I think, as I stare into what is now nearly complete darkness.

Or UnderBubble, I think, turning my eyes back to the growing glow. I don't know for sure, but it's the only thing that makes sense. As if any of this makes sense.

Dad says he still has one more secret. But he's already told me what I need to know: whoever took Ma had actually come to take him.

And then I decide.

It is time.

In the morning, I am going.

I am going to trade my father for my mother.

39

BACK DOWN IN HOOT HOLLER THE NEXT MORNING, I CARRY THE usual bucket of fake slop to the pig shed. Dad is in the feed room waiting. As if he had a choice.

"I'm going after Ma," I say. "I'm going UnderBubble. To the capital."

He shakes his head. "No, Ford. No. She is my wife. I am the father. I am the *man*. This is my responsibility."

When he says he is the *man*, a nasty answer jumps to my throat. It makes me think of Ma telling me how *men* changed Emily Dickinson's poems before they published them. It makes me think of Daniel Beard and his dumb "pretty store bows." I manage to swallow the nasty answer and instead I say, "How do I know you'll make it, Dad? How do I know a group of fake GreyDevils isn't out there just waiting to grab you? How do I know they won't just haul you off? Or what if they just snuff you on the spot? Either way, I'll never see you or Ma again. And how do I know you won't use up the URCorn Arlinda got with her pies and get the craving again? How do I know in three weeks you won't be right back at the GreyDevil fires, guzzling PartsWash?"

Dad looks away. I know I'm hurting him, but I have to speak the truth.

Now I speak more gently. "Besides, you are our only leverage. If your secret is as powerful as you say, it's the only thing we have. Without the promise of getting you, they have no reason to give up Ma. If you go alone, they'll just grab you—and then I won't have any cards in this game."

"So now I'm a card in your game?"

I wait a moment, carefully arranging my words.

"I did a lot of thinking up on Skullduggery Ridge yesterday. I came to understand some things. I know now you were under terrible pressure. Pressure I probably can't begin to understand. I'm still angry and sad about parts of it, but I don't blame you. I think you've done the best that you could, in the best way you knew how.

"But, yes: right now you are a card in my game."

It is quiet in the pig shed. Inside, I'm thinking I don't really have a game. I don't even know for sure if Ma is being held UnderBubble. Or how to get to her if she is. That's the part of this game that is a gamble.

Dad speaks. "But what is your plan?"

"I'm just going to walk up and knock on their door. If they want you as badly as we think, they'll let me in."

"One card," says Dad, shaking his head. "You've only got one card."

"Yes. It's a gamble. The biggest gamble of my life. But, Dad? The stakes in this game? The stakes are our family."

Now there are tears in both of our eyes.

"Our family—together again."

This time before I leave with my empty slop bucket, I hug him.

"You cannot go alone."

I have just explained my plan to go to the capital. Arlinda is standing in front of me with both hands on her hips, her feet wide apart.

I frown and stick out my chin.

"Affirmer-ized," says Toad. Him, I ignore.

"There is no courage," says Arlinda, "in simple-minded stubbornness."

I cross my arms and push my chin out another quarter inch.

"Maggie, bravery ends where blockheadedness begins."

"But . . . ," I say.

"Do you remember when you stumbled and fell during the GreyDevil battle?" asks Arlinda. "One silly little accident, and there you were, at their mercy. If you had been fighting that battle alone, if Toad hadn't been there to grab your collar and drag you toward the house, you would have been stomped, maimed, or dead—not brave or courageous. Toad and I—as much as we love you, as much as we depend on you—can get along without you. But Dookie? Dookie needs you. And he needs your mother even more. Even with help there is no guarantee you will make this journey safely. But going solo would be silly and selfish."

During this entire conversation, Arlinda hasn't raised her voice. She is speaking firmly and quietly and that tone doesn't change as she passes her final judgment, but she lays each word down as solidly as if it were a brick.

"You take Toby."

Toad is no longer looking at me. He is staring at Arlinda and silently nodding.

I stalk out of the farmhouse without saying a word, but I know Arlinda is right.

So. Me and Toby then.

40

FOR THE NEXT FEW DAYS, I PLAN AND PREPARE. TOAD SAYS THAT, depending on weather and trouble, we can walk to the capital Bubble City in a week. We will take only what we can carry on our backs. Actually, that's not true: if Toby really did bring what he could carry on his back, we would be packing two Whomper-Zookas and half the *Scary Pruner*.

That boy is massive.

But we'll be traveling light. We can't cover that much country on foot while wearing all the gear we use on our trading trips to Nobbern. We'll take our weapons, of course (Toby has attached a bayonet to the end of his fight-stick), and I'll wear my breastplate and gauntlets but that's it. We pack fish jerky and dried vegetables and salt, basic cooking utensils, and water flasks. We have knives and rope, a first aid kit, and a sewing kit. In addition to our jacklights, we pack several pitch-sticks, which we make by wrapping string around the forked end of a stick and then soaking the string end in pitch. We got the idea from Daniel Beard's book. He called his version Wicktorches. They're quicker to light and burn much brighter than a jacklight.

It would be simplest to follow the old interstate that loops up around to the north, but it would be much too risky. Too many other travelers, too much chance of running into Bubble Authorities, or GreyDevils attracted by the cornvoys. And even more than any of those things, too much chance of attracting attention. Instead, Toad draws maps of old hunting trails and deer trails that will lead us away from Skullduggery Ridge with the least chance of being observed. Then he gives us a tattered road map with what is now the capital Bubble City marked by a red X. Once we reach what is left of the roads and highways, we'll use that map for the rest of the trip.

The day before I leave, Dad says, "I would like you to bring me the Emily Dickinson poems."

"Dad, you're not the word nerd of the family," I say. "You've never read a poem in your life."

"The poems in that book are as close as I can be to your mother now."

I hadn't planned to hike up to Skullduggery Ridge today because Toby and I will be leaving that way tomorrow morning, but when I look at my father, so alone there, the decision is easy. When I leave the next morning he has Emily by his side.

We leave before dawn and climb Skullduggery Ridge using our jacklights. I grab a few things from the shack, and then Toby and I pause to rest our packs on the hood of the Falcon and stare off to where we'll be heading. It is the deepest, darkest part of a starless morning. The last of the GreyDevil fires have gone out, and the glow from the nearest Bubble City is pushing up against the horizon like a dirty gray cotton ball. We stare at it silently for a moment, then set out on the trail, dropping slowly from the heights of Skullduggery Ridge to the valley below, the shadows cast by our jacklights shuddering and sweeping weirdly across the trail ahead.

The bird chatter and parrot calls grow louder as the sky lightens. We extinguish our jacklights and hike into dawn. I lead the way, making Toby follow. I am being prideful, I know. But this trip is my responsibility. It's my mother we're after. It's my family I'm trying to save. This isn't Toby's problem; it's my problem. In fact, I'm not sure why Toby even agreed to come along. Or why his father allowed it. Arlinda made the arrangements. Maybe they were just afraid to say no to her.

We stop frequently to check Toad's maps. For now it looks like it doesn't really matter if we take the fork to the left or the right, as long as we're heading in the correct general direction, because eventually all trails lead to roads that lead to the capital.

The sun climbs, and soon it's hot and humid. We're walking through the rumpled foothills I can see from the hood of the Falcon. The trail rises and falls, winding through a forest that is jungly and green. Vines twine and dangle from the branches, and we pass through glades thick with fern. Some of the low spots open into marshes. The ground here is squishy, and the air smells salty-sweet. It is also filled with bugs—mostly nasty little gnats, mosquitoes that seem the size of horseflies, and—of course—horseflies. We rub our necks and forearms with a mix of vinegar and herbs Arlinda prepared, and that helps some, but they still buzz around our ears and zip in for a nip now and then.

We drink from our water flasks, forage a few snacks here and there, and once I find a patch of wild strawberries. But mostly we just walk. And walk.

When we finally stop, I squint up at the sun. It is near noon.

"Lunch?" says Toby. It's the first thing he's said all day.

"Yah," I say.

We sit and eat jerked fish in silence. I think about Dad back in that pigpen and wonder what he's doing now. I wonder if Arlinda is out trading her pies for URCorn, and if she will be able to get enough to keep Dad going until this is over. She can only make so many pies, and the truckers can only slip her a few kernels at a time. And when harvest ends, so will the cornvoys.

After eating, we walk another two hours, then choose a campsite hidden in the trees. Our plan is to have one person sleep from midafternoon to midnight and then take watch while the other sleeps until dawn. Toby unrolls a sleeping mat woven from dried canary grass. "You take first watch," he says. I'm just about to tell him I don't take orders from a boy when I realize he's giving me the easiest watch. The one where you don't have to wake up in the middle of the night and stay awake until the parrots squawk. So I just say thanks.

I arrange a simple campsite, set a cooking fire, and make a stew with dried vegetables and smoked pork. Toby awakens, eats some stew, and goes straight back to sleep. I put out the fire so it won't attract attention in the dark. Then, after a brief circuit of the camp, I place my back against a tree with my weapons at hand, and wait for night to come. Well, here we are, I think. On our way. With pretty much no plan, just this idea that I can somehow walk to the biggest Bubble City and make things happen.

Day turns to dusk, and dusk turns to dark. The moon is a sliver, but the sky is clear. Every now and then I catch a nose-stinging whiff from a GreyDevil bonfire. Some of the solar bear howling is closer than I would like. By the light of the fingernail moon I can see the lump that is Toby sleeping ten feet away, his fight-stick at his side, and I admit that makes me feel better.

I stay on watch until the stars have spun well past midnight. When I nudge Toby's shoulder with my foot, he awakens without a startle. "Got it," he says, and as he stands I roll into my blanket.

41

THE NEXT THING I KNOW THE PARROTS ARE SCREECHING AND IT IS day again. For a moment I am disoriented. Then I want to cuss the parrots. But I smile when I realize at least I don't have to listen to Hatchet.

Then it's another day of silent hiking. More trails, more bugs, more signs that other travelers have passed here—but not a single GreyDevil. Today is a tough slog. Yesterday we still had the fresh sense of adventure. But today, we just walk and walk and walk. When we finally stop to camp, Toby doesn't say a word, just unrolls his mat and goes straight to sleep while I set a fire and make another stew. Later, when he wakes to eat, I wait until he's seated, hand him his stew, then say, simply, "Thanks for walking with me."

"Yep," he says, stirring the stew.

"I don't know why you're doing it."

"Arlinda told me to. . . ."

"But I still don't know—"

He cuts in before I can finish. "Your ma. She was good to me."

I realize he is looking me in the eyes for the first time in two days. Maybe for the first time since I've known him.

"I never met my ma, you know."

It's getting dark. The firelight flickers on his face as he turns back to the stew. I don't say anything.

"I asked Pa about it once. I was tiny. He picked me up and held me tighter than he'd ever held me before. 'Your mother was better than all of us,' he said. I could feel his tears soaking through my hair."

He's staring into the fire now.

Then he takes a breath and continues. "That's all he'll ever say about her. Not another word. He just goes back to feeding his fish."

The fire is dying down. We both gaze into the flickery licks of orange, lost in our own thoughts. Then I shake my head and look away—it's dangerous to stare into a fire. If something—or someone—comes at you from the dark, they'll be on you before your eyes adjust. It's like being temporarily blind. I scoot forward and, using the heel of one boot, start kicking dirt over the coals.

The howl of the solar bear freezes us for just an instant, and then it is coming at me through the air, a dark blob against the starry, moon-slivered sky, its claw-studded paws and shiny-toothed jaws spread wide.

42

THE SOLAR BEAR KNOCKS ME FLAT BACKWARD, WHICH IS A GOOD thing because if it had attacked from behind I would have been crushed face-first into the fire.

I don't *stay* flat backward. Even as I realize what's happening I flip to my stomach and curl up armadillo tight, just like when the GreyDevils swarmed me in Toad's yard. I hear the solar bear's jaws snap and take a terrible clunk to the head as a fore-tooth rakes my skull. Immediately, I feel the warm blood flow. The bear's breath is awful, like spoiled meat and rotten berries. A claw scrapes my back as the beast tries to turn me. I desperately want to unfold and run for it, but I know I'm vulnerable enough without exposing my belly and throat. Back when we were living on the run, I saw how solar bears could gut a wild hog, and I don't feel even a little bit like being bacon.

The teeth are at my skull again and I'm bracing for the crunch when the bear gives a loud grunt and tumbles into the brush. I crack one eye open to see the dark lump of Toby and the animal rolling on the ground at the far edge of the fading firelight. Jumping to my feet and drawing my knife, I turn it blade up like Toad taught me, and start circling, but I can't see well enough to safely make a stab. I kick a dead branch into the fire. The flames flare, and now I can see Toby clinging to the solar bear's back, riding it like a rodeo bull. Toby's split-second decision to plow into the bear probably saved my life, but it left him no time to draw his knife, so for the moment, it's a wrestling match, with Toby using every trick his cage-fighting father ever taught him in a desperate attempt to stay just beyond the reach of tooth and claw.

Holding my knife with the cutting edge up, I stab at the air and holler as loud as I can.

"HEY, BEAR!"

The solar bear rears into the air, and Toby uses this momentum to grab it by both ears and pull it over backward. It works, and they hit the ground with a flop, the bear's paws paddling the air. In an instant, Toby locks his ankles around the bear's upper chest and snaps his arms into a choke hold around the bear's neck. The animal writhes and roars, and rakes at Toby's ankles with its hind legs. Toby's leather boots can stand the clawing for a while, but not forever. And if the claws catch him higher up the leg they'll strip the flesh from his bones.

I keep circling the two tumbling figures, desperate for an opening. Lunging for the bear's belly, I get caught square in the chest with a back paw and flung backward. I scramble to my feet and swipe my blade across the bear's rump. Hardly the best way to kill a bear, jabbing it in the butt. But that's the target I was offered. Blood swells through the caramel-striped fur and the bear does stop tearing at Toby's legs long enough to drop to all fours, whirl around, and face me. "Fight-stick!" hollers Toby, his voice muffled against the bear's hide.

I don't want to take my eyes off the bear, so I back toward Toby's sleeping mat in a crouch, feeling behind me with my one free hand. My fingers touch the rough canvas of Toby's pack, then the softer fabric of his bedroll. The pack has been kicked over, and everything is spilled. I feel a wooden shaft, but the instant my fingers close around it I realize it's too small. It's a pitch-stick. I drop it and pat the earth again, and now I find the fight-stick. I sheathe my knife (Toad has trained me well), grab the fight-stick in both hands, and raise it high above my head. With the bayonet attached it feels heavy and unbalanced. Toby and the bear are back to rassling. Realizing he'll never choke the bear, Toby has given up his neck lock for a lower position. I think he's just trying to keep the bear occupied—and himself alive—until I can stab it with the bayonet, but his ankles have come unlocked and he is slipping dangerously sideways. Suddenly the bear spins, and Toby is flung crashing into the brush. The bear is on him in an instant, and just as quickly I am on the bear, driving the bayonet deeply into its back. The bear howls and spins, swiping at me with one paw, and this time I am the one flung into the brush.

Snapping and flopping like a giant beached shark with fur, the bear turns itself into knots trying to reach the fight-stick. The branch I kicked in the fire is still burning and in the half-lit crazy shadows thrown by the flailing bear, I edge my way back to Toby's pack and pick up the pitch-stick. Plunging it into the coals, I raise it flaring to the sky just in time to see the bear bite the fight-stick, pluck it from its flank, and flick it through the air. Then the animal turns and launches itself at me with a roar, its mouth a cavern of drool-covered stalactites and stalagmites. There is no time for my knife and no time to dodge. Instead I rush straight at the beast, thrusting the pitch-stick before me. Another gust of death breath hits my face, and then, even as its bloody forepaws close around me, I drive the flaming pitch-stick deep into the bear's maw and down its throat. The bear rears up and its arms loosen. I drop to the ground and scuttle backward like a freaked-out crab stuck in reverse. The solar bear is pawing at the pitch-stick lodged in its throat when suddenly it throws its head back and gives out a strangled howl. Toby has leaped from the shadows and is driving the bayonetted fight-stick into the bear's body again and again and again, until finally Toby is just standing there heaving for air and the bear is lying stone-still, a piece of the pitch-stick dangling from its mouth like a busted toothpick, a wisp of smoke curling from between its lips.

For a while there is only the sound of two people trying to catch their breath.

Then I hear a soft chuckle.

It's Toby. In the firelight I can see his sweaty, dirty, bloody face scrunched up in a grin.

"Hey, BEAR?"

I roll my eyes, and then we're both laughing. Even with the blood caking on my brow and the tattered, bloody strips of cloth hanging from Toby's legs, we're laughing and laughing, the relief spilling out of us and echoing in the dark forest all around.

43

WHILE I DIG THE FIRST AID KIT FROM MY PACK, TOBY STOKES THE fire. We need the safety of darkness, but we need to boil water to clean our wounds. Besides, we just had a howling solar bear fight to the death and the air is filled with the scent of fresh blood, so it's kind of hard to worry about attracting attention. We do shield the flames as best we can with our packs, and dress the cuts and gouges by jacklight, using rag strips and Arlinda's healing paste. We got off easy: the backs of Toby's legs are gashed in a couple of places, but nothing deep enough to catch muscle or tendon. His tall boots took most of the abuse and will need stitching and patching. When Toby parts my hair and looks at my scalp wound, he says it's about three inches long but he can't see bone. It's driving me nuts to think of the bear spit in there, so I clamp my teeth and tell him to scrub it good before he packs it with paste. He does, and it hurts so bad I pound my fist into my thigh. Then he threads a needle and drops it into the boiling water to sterilize it.

"Here," he says, handing me a stick. "You might wanna chew on this."

Then he starts sewing.

Even when the pain is making me squeeze my eyes shut so tight I feel like they'll pop, I notice how gently his giant palm is cradling my head, and how tenderly his fingertips work around the wound. You'd never guess it from such a big lug. I wonder if maybe he's that way because he didn't have a ma, and he had to learn tenderness from his giant pa.

"Okay," he says, as he knots the last stitch and ties a rag strip around my head. "That oughta do it."

"Good enough," I say, standing and squaring my shoulders. "Let's eat some bear steaks!"

If we were back home, we'd spend the next day turning that bear into food and a rug and tallow candles and the best ToothClub ever, but out here we simply don't have the tools or time. We weren't hunting—we were fighting for our lives. Still, as a scavenger, I hate to let anything go to waste. So even though we just had stew, and even though we should put the fire out, we skin one of the bear's haunches and Toby cuts two big steaks. We spear them with sticks and broil them over the flames. When we tear into the meat it is still a little bloody inside, but we are so famished from the fight and the butchering we just can't wait. It's strange, eating that steak, knowing that an hour ago it wasn't clear who would be eating whom.

After Toby turns in, I snuff the jacklight and sit the rest of my watch. The solar bear fight has taken everything out of me, and it's all I can do to stay awake. By the time I wake Toby and roll into my bag, I'm so tired it feels like the insides of my eyelids are vibrating. My head is pounding from the solar bear bite, but I fall straight to sleep, my mind spinning into a dream of fighting the bear. In the dream the bear comes at me again and again, but just as it closes me in its arms I see its eyes, and they are yellow, GreyDevil yellow, and then the bear becomes a big, laughing fat man, and even in my dream as I dive away I wonder why. But now I am an armadillo, curled up tight and rolling, rolling, rolling. . . .

44

THE PARROTS WAKE ME EARLY. TOBY IS USING THE FIRST LIGHT OF day to stitch and repair his torn boots. For breakfast I eat two leftover strips of bear steak. Toby is still working, so I walk over to the body of the solar bear and skin out as big a chunk of hide as I can without rolling him over. Using the flat side of my knife blade, I scrape the underside of the hide clean, then, using my thumbs, work cooking salt into the skin. Before I roll the hide up and stow it in my pack, I cut off two little strips and use my sewing kit to stitch one strip to the front of my shirt, and the other to Toby's shirt. Operating on Toad's *Scary Pruner* theory, I'm wanting people to see that solar bear fur over our hearts and wonder how we came to have it. It might be the sort of thing that spares us a fight.

Finally I pull out my whetstone and spit on it. *"Knull dife, lort shife*," I say, smiling as I run the blade back and forth.

We get a late start. Right away my head wound is pounding. When the trail takes us past a swamp, I stop to cut some willow whips and chew on them while I walk. Arlinda told Ma and me once that bull moose chew willow when their antlers hurt. They don't taste like much, and maybe it's my imagination, but it does help some.

For five more days, we hike, make camp, break camp, and hike again. There are no more solar bears. We just trudge, day after day. By the third day the trails become wider and more well-worn, and there are more and more open spaces between the trees. Here and there we see little tents and shacks and chicken coops and people looking up from hoop house gardens, and I realize how easy it is to think I'm the only one living the way I do. Sometimes the people wave, but mostly they just stand and watch us pass, like they're worried we might turn into trouble. I notice I'm more on edge, too, studying the face of everyone we meet on the trail, moving to the side ahead of time, letting my hand rest on my Tooth-Club until they've passed. I'm used to being on guard against solar bears and GreyDevils, but I'm finding that strangers make me more nervous by far.

And we're headed to a place where everyone is a stranger.

On the fifth day the trails become old roads. Now and then we meet someone with an oxcart, and once a team of spirited, trotting horses pulling a scrap wagon. Nobody is driving anything even remotely as amazing as the *Scary Pruner*. Usually the sight of Toby is enough to keep them moving with their eyes cast elsewhere. We see the ruins of buildings and what used to be small villages. Unlike Nobbern, these villages have almost no life to them. Nobbern may be ragged in a lot of places, but at least it's got actual businesses and residents, and Magical Mercantile. There is nothing like that here. We see ragged, dirty people lurking in the buildings, but they just peek out at us. I keep looking for GreyDevils, but we haven't seen one for two days now. I've puzzled on this some, but I suppose the answer is pretty simple: there aren't any Sustainability Reserves in this part of the country, and they don't want to travel far from that crazy corn.

I stop puzzling on GreyDevils and start puzzling on what I'm going to do when I get to the capital. Last night I spotted the faint glow of it against the distant sky. My heart jumped, and I felt a cold ball of fear in my stomach. I still don't have a plan beyond walking right up and knocking on the door. And even if I did have a plan, it's one thing to imagine it while sitting all alone in an old car on a faraway ridge. It's a completely different thing to actually put that plan up against reality. What if they just grab me and no one hears from me again? What if they just ignore me? What if they don't even have Ma? And for that matter, who exactly is "they"?

All I know is they want Dad, and I want Ma. I guess my plan amounts to putting one foot in front of the other.

I don't have a better one.

On the sixth day we're walking on the shoulder of a wider road, and instead of little villages we're seeing acres of empty, tattered houses. They seem to go on forever, joined by cracked, weedy roads that wind all around and eventually come together. The sound of cornvoy trucks is louder, and sometimes if the land rises we can see them moving back and forth in the distance. And there is something odd: the more closely packed the abandoned buildings become, the fewer people we see.

We stop to eat lunch. For just a moment I lean back against my pack, close my eyes, and cross my arms over my chest to rest. My wrist brushes the patch of solar bear fur, and for an instant I don't recognize what it is. It's weird how just a few days and a few miles can make something seem like it never really happened. Or that it happened to someone else. I could almost believe I dreamed it, except that my head still feels like someone used it for a volleyball. I chew some more willow bark.

We study the map, then set out again. Last night there was a glow against the sky all night long. Today or tomorrow we will reach the capital. Now we're seeing a few taller buildings, or what's left of them. Many of the windows are broken out, and some of the bricks have begun to crumble. There are weeds growing on windowsills. Turkey vultures skulk on the rooflines and flop their wings to catch some sun. Just when I am wondering what they would find to eat around here, a grubby figure emerges from an alley ten feet away. It's a small man wearing a shapeless poncho that appears to be made of close-cropped gray fur. The poncho is belted at the waist, and several wire snares hang from one belt loop. Two plastic buckets dangle from either end of a wooden bar he's carrying across his shoulders. He looks surprised to see us, and for a minute it seems as though he might run. Then he smiles a gap-toothed smile.

"Want some rat?"

As he says it, he dips a shoulder so I can see into one of the buckets. *Ugh*. Yep. Rats. *Dead* rats. *Big* dead rats. Solar bears I can handle. Rats freak me out.

When he sees the look on my face he grins.

"Fresh caught!"

I look at Toby. He's just standing there like Toby, although I see he's quietly moved his fight-stick to the ready.

"I'll even skin it for you," says the little man, "but you'll have to cook it yourself."

"Yeeeah . . . ," I say, backing up a step.

"And I get to keep the skin!" he interrupts, patting his hairy poncho. "I sew 'em together. Make these ponchos and sell 'em! Handcrafted! One of a kind! Shed the rain! Tough! Cozy!"

"I believe every word but *cozy*," I say. Probably shouldn't have, but I did. If it hurt his feelings, he didn't show it.

"Nobody wants to eat a rat, nobody wants to wear a rat," he says. "Until they're starving and freezing." His grin grows bigger, and he looks at me expectantly.

"Not starving," I say. "Not cold."

"Don't see many people in this part of town," the little man says. "Usually it's just me and the rats."

"Are you the city rat-catcher?"

"Me? I work for no one! 'Specially not the guvvermint. I'm a self-employed rat-repre*neur*!"

He fishes something out of the pocket of his poncho and holds it up. It looks like a shoestring with gangrene. "Try some rat jerky?"

I nearly barf on his boots.

Suddenly I see his face change. He backs up a step and points at my shirt.

"S-solar bear?"

"Yah," I say, real breezy like. "*Fresh* solar bear."

"W-wow . . . you . . . *you*?"

"Yah," I say again. "Me."

"And him?" The rat man points at Toby.

"He did assist, yes."

"Does he talk?"

"Not really."

"Who are you?"

"Ford," I say. "Ford Falcon." I say it real firm, so he'll get the idea.

"Um, do they still *make* those?"

This is not the effect I had hoped for. I decide it is time to move on and start to step around him. He turns to watch us go.

"Um, no offense—I know you're *Ford Falcon* and all—but do you know where you're going?"

I just keep walking.

"You—you and your large, nontalking bodyguard—may be able to handle a solar bear, but I'm not sure you can handle what's up there." He points up the crumbled street to a long rise and a hill, where on the distant ruined horizon the old buildings stand tallest of all.

"Just beyond the rise," he says. "The Clear Zone."

Toby and I just look at him.

"Nobody crosses the Clear Zone."

45

WE LEAVE THE RAT CATCHER AND WALK ON. IT IS TAKING US MUCH longer than we expected to reach the buildings on the horizon, and daylight is fading. And yet, above the ridge, even as darkness falls, a great white glow is rising.

Bubble City. *The* Bubble City. The capital.

The buildings to either side of us are even taller now, but still cracked and empty and—because of the darkness behind us and the light ahead—filled with long, strange shadows. We are bone tired from the day, and my head is throbbing again. But now that the capital Bubble City is within reach we find ourselves determined to get there. To finally see this place we've only heard about. To see if anybody is playing volleyball and eating ice cream cones, like it showed in the brochure and the newspaper photos.

The higher we hike up the hill, the brighter the light grows, until finally it is just a blinding whiteness pouring between the tall buildings and down the street toward us.

And then there are no more buildings. Just space. White, white space. Away to the left, away to the right, and far ahead of us, only whiteness. What has only appeared as a dirty smudge against the night sky is now so pure I swear I feel it thrumming with electricity.

Toby comes to stand beside me. We shield our eyes, and now I can make out a few things—it isn't one giant light but rather banks and banks of them, mounted on high poles and pointed outward, stretching either way for what seems to be miles. It's hard to tell how far away the lights are, because the space between is acres and acres of flatness.

I can hear cornvoy trucks rumbling again.

"Um," I say, "it might not be so wise to be standing right out here in the world's biggest spotlight." I duck into the doorway of the last building. Toby joins me.

"Rest. Wait till morning," he says, using up four whole words.

I agree. Partly I am itching to go, and partly I realize I have no idea what is next and that I better sleep. I can't imagine how I'll get to sleep, but it would be dumb not to.

"I'll take first watch," says Toby. It's not the way we've been doing it, but I'm too tired to argue. I undo my bedroll in a corner of what must have once been a lobby, curl up, and try not to think about rats.

In what seems to be ten minutes Toby is shaking my shoulder and it is morning.

I scold Toby for staying up all night. He just ignores me. He looks as tired as I've ever seen him. When he reaches for his pack, I say, "No way."

He looks at me.

"You stayed up all night for me. You're in no shape for anything. We don't leave until you sleep."

"I . . ."

"Sleep," I say.

He unrolls his bag and is out in half a minute. When his breathing becomes deep and settled, I study his sleeping face for a moment. I think about his father, and what the two of them have been through together. I think about how Tilapia Tom will get along if Toby doesn't return. What it would be like to lose your wife and your only child.

I've been thinking about this for the last three days. Toby's job was to get me here. Arlinda was right to send him—if I had been alone when that solar bear attacked, right about now I'd be reincarnated solar bear poop. But from here on in, this is my battle. I have no right to drag Toby into it. I look at him one more time sound asleep on the floor, his fight-stick by his side. I have no idea what sort of trouble awaits me, but I don't think it will be the kind that can be solved with a fight-stick. I take my finger and write a note on the dusty tiles: "Stay. If I'm not back in two days, go home. You did your job."

Now I step outside and into the Clear Zone.

In the bleak morning light all the mystery is gone. Rather than a wondrous bubble, I see an endless wall, stretching high into the sky. It was painted white once, but now it is streaked and dusty, and ringed with BarbaZap. What looked like white space before us last night is just plain old gravel, a wasteland with not a weed or plant to be seen. The banks of lights are still burning, but up facing real sunlight they appear thin and weak. I can see a dome, but it sticks up like a tiny little bump. There's no way it covers the whole giant place. I remember Toad telling me not to believe everything I read.

I put one foot on the gravel. It crunches beneath my boot, and I stop. Nothing dramatic happens, so I take another step. The noise of the cornvoy trucks seems to be off to my left somewhere, so I angle that way, figuring they are going to a gate of some sort. Inside I admit my stomach feels like it's full of cold tadpoles, but what else is there to do but keep going? I straighten up and try to walk like I cross this patch every day, but with every step I expect the ground to explode beneath me.

Moving at a diagonal, I am nearly halfway across the Zone when I hear a soft buzzing noise. Seconds later a tiny object with four propellers hovers above me. I can see what looks like a glass eye. Now I hear engines and see a cloud of dust coming my way. I freeze. My heart is pounding. Toad told me once that anytime a cowboy-book cowboy rode a new trail, he'd stop to look back every now and then so he could recognize the landmarks if he had to return. I spin on my heel and look back to the building where Toby is sleeping and burn the image into my brain.

And now I turn to face what is coming.

They stop about a hundred yards away and holler for me to put my hands up. I think, *This really is like the cowboy books*, and raise my arms. About twenty people in uniforms spill out of the vehicles, fan out in a semicircle with weapons drawn, and slowly walk toward me. I stand stone-still.

"You are in the Clear Zone," says one of the security men. He has more stripes on his sleeve than the others. His face is obscured by a mirrored visor.

"Thank you, Captain Obvious," I say. When you don't feel brave, you gotta act brave.

If my smart-mouth comment makes him mad, I can't tell, because the only thing I see in his visor is a tiny version of me standing in a field of gravel. We stand there a moment, then I hear him speak. "Paddy wagon: advance!"

"Paddy wagon?" I can't help myself. "Paddy wagon? Like for taking someone to jail in an old detective book? That term's even older than *station* wagon. Surely you could come up with something more menacing."

Nobody so much as twitches. Apparently they aren't into comedy. A long vehicle with what looks like a square box on the back separates itself from the other vehicles and drives forward. When it pulls even with the security men, they begin walking beside it until they're ten feet away.

"Place your hands on your head and turn around," says Mr. More-Stripes. I do, and immediately someone grabs each of my wrists and lowers them behind my waist. I hear two *ziiipp!* sounds and my hands are tied behind my back. I wiggle my wrists. Tight. Then Mr. More-Stripes turns me back to face him—or, actually, to face myself in his visor.

"You have violated the Clear Zone and will be repatriated."

"Well, aren't you handy with the fancy words," I say. "Nope, you're going to take me inside the Bubble."

"Negatory," says Mr. More-Stripes.

I giggle. Maybe I shouldn't have done that. But really, *negatory*?

"You got a boss?" I ask.

Silence.

"Someone I can give a message?"

More silence.

"Well, since you're all wearing uniforms, I assume you have a boss. You tell your boss I have something you want."

Silence. Realizing I haven't been perfectly clear, I point at the Bubble.

"Something *they* want."

The man takes me by the arm and pushes me toward the van.

"You ever hear the story about the man who tied his

Security Chip to a red balloon?"

Everyone freezes. Then they all turn to look at me.

"That guy is my dad."

They stand there like mirror-faced statues.

"I know where he is."

Mr. Paddy-Wagon-Negatory walks away a short distance, then speaks quietly into his helmet radio. After a brief moment, he returns.

"Come with us," he says.

"Kinda seems like the only choice," I say, and climb into the van.

46

IT'S ANOTHER DREAM, AND THIS ONE IS SO MUCH BETTER BECAUSE instead of a stinky solar bear with yellow eyes and big teeth, I see Ma, and instead of assuming the armadillo position and rolling away, I'm running toward her with my arms open, but then the dream is turning because she keeps wavering in and out of sight like a human mirage, and then there's nothing around her but whiteness, and in the dream I worry that I'm just losing her again, so I holler out:

"MA!"

"I'm here, Maggie. Right here."

And she is. Ma, in the flesh, slowly coming back into focus. And now I know I'm not dreaming, because my head feels like someone shot it out of a Whomper-Zooka. I grab it in both hands and squeeze, trying to stop the throbbing, then quickly let go when I remember the stitches.

Except the stitches aren't there. I feel around again, carefully.

No stitches. Only a shaved spot on my scalp and a little scar-like ridge where the cut was.

I must have been out for a long . . .

"Maggie."

It really is Ma.

I stumble to my feet and stagger across the room to her arms. We fold each other into a powerful hug and just stay that way, as if somehow we can gather up everything we've lost and crush it back into our souls.

I remember being pulled from the paddy wagon. I remember walking down a long hallway into a room with people waiting. I remember bright lights and clean floors. I remember . . . that's the last I remember. Now here I am, with a raging headache, hugging Ma.

Ma feels stouter than I recall. Less like a bony bird. She's no Arlinda Hopper, but her arms are strong around me. She's been eating well, then. I stand back and hold her by the shoulders, like I am the grown-up here, and we stand face-to-face. Her cheeks are a good color. Her hair is shiny and full and swept up into a knot. Her face is clear and she looks well rested. But her eyes . . . her eyes are a swimming mix of love and sadness.

"Oh, Maggie," she says.

She reaches up and takes both my hands in hers and leads me to a corner of the room, where we sit facing each other on two hard white cubes. Everything in here is white: the floor, the ceiling, and three walls of the room. The entire fourth wall is a mirror.

"Oh, Maggie," says Ma again, taking my hands in hers.

"Ma . . . ," I start to say, but my voice cracks and fails me. It is so good to see her. So good to hear her voice. I don't want to sit there on my cube, I want to crawl right up into her lap and have her hold me in her arms, rock me like she did when I was tiny.

I am *so sick* of always being strong.

I look at us in the giant mirror. Here I am, nearly as tall as Ma, my face all dirt and streaks from woodsmoke and the days on the trail and my hair all ratted, my legs laced into tall leather boots, my arms deep brown from all the time in the sun, the strip of solar bear hide stitched to my shirt. . . . If I jump into her arms now it's gonna look like some nice lady being attacked by a GreyDevil reject.

Ma puts me back at arm's length, looks me up and down from head to toe, and speaks. "You look . . . you look . . ." I can see Ma trying to find the right way to put it. I can imagine what is in her head. How she is trying to look through the image of what it is before her now and see the girl she last saw three months ago. I am taller now, and stronger.

"You look like a woman, Maggie."

"Oh, Ma . . ." I shuffle my feet.

"A strong, powerful woman."

"Yah, who smells *strongly* and *powerfully* like she sleeps in the back corner of a solar bear cave and rinses her hair with possum guts."

"Maggie, that's not what I mean, and you know it." The sharpness in her voice makes me feel like a little girl again, and I guess I had it coming. I straighten up on my cube.

"Ma, I came to take you back."

47

THE SECOND I SAY I'M HERE TO TAKE HER BACK, MA'S EYES SHOOT
to the mirror-wall, and then back to me. "Oh, Maggie, no . . .
no . . . I'm afraid it isn't possible."

"What do you mean, Ma?"

"I . . . I . . ." She's looking at the mirror again.

"Ma! Have they hurt you?"

"Oh, no, Maggie. Quite the opposite. I have been treated
very well. I have a room of my own, Maggie. A room with
a window. Books on a shelf, and Earl Grey tea whenever I
wish, and I never was happy OutBubble, and I . . . and . . .
and . . ." She is speaking rapidly. Too rapidly, as if she's trying
to head me off, keep me from going down some dangerous
road. All the while she is still clutching at my hands, squeezing and unsqueezing them as if somehow this will keep her

distracted from the trouble surrounding us. "And now that you're here, you should stay. You're . . . you're all I have."

"But what about our family, Ma?"

"We have no more family, Maggie!" Ma says this so sharply and squeezes my hand so tightly that I cry out and jump back, but she clings to my hands even tighter, and her fingers are clutching at mine.

"Maggie, your father abandoned us! And Henry . . . Henry . . ." She is sobbing now, terrible sobs, sobs that shake her whole body. I have called Henry "Dookie" so long it takes me a second to realize she is referring to my little snot flicker of a brother.

"Dad didn't abandon us, Ma! There were things . . . things he couldn't . . ." I keep looking at that mirror. I don't know yet how much I should say.

"No, Maggie, no. Your father *abandoned* us. That night, before the attack, we had a terrible fight about him being gone all the time. He took his pack and said he was heading for the northern territories and I'd never see him again. For all I know he's . . . he's *dead*."

I know this can't be true. Ma and Dad got grumpy with each other, but I never once heard Dad raise his voice against Ma. And Ma *knew* what Dad was doing those nights when he was out wandering. Suddenly, I realize: someone *is* listening and Ma is trying to protect Dad by throwing them off his trail.

"Ma, he was . . ."

"Oh, Maggie, there is so much you don't know."

"But, Ma, I . . ."

"And after losing Henry . . . oh, Maggie, when I saw them beat Henry and drop him lifeless to the ground . . ."

"But, Ma, they didn't kill Doo . . . *Henry*. Henry's alive! I gave him a noogie just last week!"

Ma's eyes fly open, and her sobbing stops. "But I saw them . . . with their clubs . . . he fell . . . I knew . . ."

She tells me the story now, how she was up late worrying about Dad and trying to keep her mind occupied reading *Little House on the Prairie* by candlelight and worrying about Dad yet again when the attackers came screeching around the shack, how she knew immediately they weren't GreyDevils because their voices weren't right and at that hour any real GreyDevil would be at the bonfires drinking PartsWash. And then she knew for sure when they broke through the door because despite their rags and dirty faces, they moved like healthy men and their breath didn't smell like spoiled turpentine, their yellow eyes were *too* yellow, and then if there was any doubt remaining, they were all wearing headlamps and carrying weapons. She says the lights were blinding as two of the invaders grabbed and held her while the others smashed the chicken coop and tore up the house and stomped the Falcon and went into the root cellar looking for Dad. The men kept threatening Ma and demanding to know where Dad was, and she kept telling them she didn't know, which was true. Dookie kept running in circles, hollering

"*Shibby-shibby-shibby* . . ." Then he grabbed Ma and tried to pull her away from the men. One of them raised a club and hit Dookie in the head and he crumpled to the ground. She tried to go to Dookie, but the men grabbed her tightly and hustled her away. The last thing she saw, she says, was Dookie's little body lying on the ground, lit by the flash of a headlamp. Then she was dragged off into the night.

"Ma . . . Dookie . . . *Henry* . . . he survived! I found him in the roots of the Shelter Tree. Where he used to hide out and wait to scare me. He must have come to long enough to crawl in there."

"He's alive?" says Ma, as if she didn't hear me the first time.

"Alive, Ma. And he needs you." I leave it at that. I don't tell her about the seizure.

She is quiet now, squeezing her eyes against tears that sneak out anyway.

"They will never let me go."

I shoot a glance at the mirror. Wondering who's back there.

"They want your father."

"I know, Ma. That's why I'm here."

The light in the room changes, and as if someone has thrown a switch—as someone has—the mirrored wall becomes a window.

And behind the window are two men.

48

THE TWO MEN ARE SEPARATED BY A WALL, ALTHOUGH THERE IS A window in the wall that allows them to see each other. The first man is a skinny fellow with skin so pale and limp it reminds me of wilted lettuce. He is standing in a clean white room the same as ours.

The second man is big. Big as Tilapia Tom, plus a fat hog's worth of blubber. His face is creased and oily, like a greased prune with eyeballs. His hair is thick and black. He's wearing a suit and a tie. They're tight around his neck and belly. He's sitting behind a massive wooden desk that looks as if it was built just so he could pound his fist on it. Everything around him is a cluttered mess. There are shelves and cubbies on every wall, and every available surface is crammed with cast iron toys and tin soldiers and miniature steam engines and wooden-handled oddments and a hundred other things I don't recognize, every single one of them old. The walls are covered with rusty advertising signs and yellowed circus posters and framed postcards and a blinking neon sign that says "BEER."

And then, on the front corner of his desk, beside a stack of papers, I spot something that drops my jawbone to my toenails.

Porky Pig.

My Porky Pig. The one I dug up in Goldmine Gully. I recognize it by the rust spot right where its belly button should be.

The Fat Man—that's the name I decide to give him—must have seen my eyes bulge, because he chuckles evilly and picks up the statue.

"Nice, isn't it?" he says, waggling the little pig at me. His voice is coming through a speaker hidden in the ceiling.

I am trying to scowl at him and look tough, but he can pretty easily see that I am shocked and perplexed.

"I like old things," says the Fat Man, using a corner of his shirtsleeve to polish Porky's cap. "This little guy here, he reminds me of the old days, when I was a little boy, eating macaroni and cheese and watching cartoons on TV. Things were so simple then."

He looks at the statue and sighs. "I miss the old days . . . so I collect them. Well, I have *people* collect them for me.

"These things," he continues, waving his hand at all the objects surrounding him, "they tell me stories."

"Whatever," I said, trying to be cool again.

"They take me on adventures," he says.

I roll my eyes, even though I'm suddenly remembering how I felt when I held Porky that day under the Shelter Tree. Like I was being transported somewhere else also.

"And Porky here, Porky told me the best story of all."

"Sounds like you should get out more," I say. The Fat Man doesn't even blink. There is something about him that is familiar.

"This pig told me how to find your father."

It's all I can do to keep my mouth from dropping open again.

"I have been hunting for your father for a long, *long* time. Ever since he pulled the red balloon trick, as a matter of fact. He's a sneaky one."

Then he adds, "And a smart one."

For the first time since I don't remember when, I feel a little bit proud of my dad.

"Tough, too. Tearing that tracker out of his face. That took some guts." Then he looks at Ma. "Of course he had some help . . ."

Ma lowers her eyes.

"Yes, your father was quite a man," says the Fat Man. "And he was—*is*—quite a valuable man. The fact is, by running away, he *stole* from us."

"Couldn't have happened to nicer people," I say. I'm still trying to figure out why he looks familiar.

The Fat Man ignores me. "We had no choice but to pursue him. We knew he had to be out there. We had agents in the field, and eyes in the sky, but it's a gigantic country, and that balloon trick and new car had given him a head start. A week passed before we found the car. Half of that week it had rained, so there were no tracks or scent remaining.

"Pretty much it was a clean getaway."

The Fat Man cradles Porky in his hands, as gently as if he were holding a kitten. "Weeks became months, months became years. But we kept looking. We knew he needed URCorn. And we knew that sooner or later, that would lead us to him."

"And then one day one of my OutBubble collectors brought me this talking pig."

"That pig doesn't talk, you grease chomper," I say.

"Maggie!" says Ma, but I'm not gonna sit here all polite, no matter how much everything he is saying has knocked me sideways. I'm not gonna sit here like I'm one of Daniel Beard's pretty-store-bought-bow girls. I need to be Ford Falcon.

"It's just a dumb piggy bank. Look at the slot."

"Oh, I know about the slot," says the Fat Man, ignoring my attitude. He places Porky in the center of his desk now and sits straighter in his chair, like a professor about to deliver a lecture. Waving his hand at the objects surrounding him, he says, "Before any one of these items can be brought UnderBubble, they have to be Steri-Scanned, to make sure we don't admit any unexpected contaminants. Some of us UnderBubble are germophobic weaklings." At this he rolls his eyes and points his thumb at the wall on the other side of which the man with skin like wilted lettuce is standing.

"HEY!" says Lettuce Face, with a flouncy little huff.

The Fat Man chuckles. "And when we put Porky here through the Steri-Scan, well, we got a surprise: the sensors discovered traces of an organic substance not usually found on the inside of piggy banks—human blood."

I recall the stab of pain when I reached for the pig and sliced my finger on the glass. I remember wiping my blood from the pig but not wanting to scrub it too hard. I remember my blood seeping into the cracks and the coin slot.

"Naturally, the Steri-Scan includes a DNA analysis and database cross-check. Imagine my surprise when it came back as a relative match to the man we'd been hunting for so long—your father."

Once again, I find myself trying to keep my chin off the ground.

"We knew the scientist we were hunting had children—and the blood on this pig came from one of them. We could then assume wherever the child was—alive or dead, it was blood after all—the father would be nearby. The collector who brought me the pig was quite happy to tell me where he obtained it. I then sent some of my people to visit the proprietor, and after a brief conversation he quite willingly told us about the young girl who brought in the pig."

Mad Mike! He sold me out!

"After that, it was just a matter of waiting until the next time you came to town in that ridiculous wagon with that ridiculous old man. Our undercover people then followed you back, cased your place, and identified your father."

I think of the GreyDevil I saw the night I was hiking down to Toad and Arlinda's. No wonder it was so far up the ridge. Those too-yellow eyes, and the way it ran instead of shuffled. Just as Dad and I suspected, it wasn't a real Grey-Devil. It was a spy.

"Pretty smart," I say, grudgingly. "But not too smart, because instead of capturing the escaped scientist, your goons beat up my little brother and kidnapped my mom."

"IDIOTS!" roars the Fat Man, slamming his fist against the desk so powerfully that Porky gives a little hop. "Under-trained governmental laze-abouts!" He pokes his thumb in the direction of Lettuce Face. "Dinglefritz over here was in such a rush to make the capture that he gave the go-ahead before we confirmed that your father was actually in the shack that night."

"But-but-but . . . !" Lettuce Face is dancing in frustration. "We couldn't wait! Euro-Cornsortium . . . Pharmo-Fos . . . the Anti-Gen Collective . . . if they ever get the secret . . . we *could not wait*!"

"SHUT IT!" explodes the Fat Man.

And in that instant I remember the photograph from the newspaper article about the Bubbling. The one with the two politicians shaking hands with the *fat man* in the business suit. That's him! Older and a hundred pounds heavier, but it's him. And Lettuce Face must be one of the politicians.

I'll say this for Lettuce Face: he may look creepy, but he looks like he has aged better than the Fat Man.

49

INSTEAD OF SHUTTING IT, LETTUCE FACE CHANGES THE SUBJECT.

"So . . . ," he says, shifting his gaze from me to Ma. "This is your *mommy*." He's as slimy as a snail's belly.

Just the way he says "mommy" makes me want to drive my fist through that glass and into his nose, his nose that looks as thin as a slice of cucumber. Two minutes I've known this creep and already I dream of how his proboscis will feel when it folds over beneath my knuckles.

When that mirror wall first flipped, Ma jumped like she'd been sitting on an electric wire. Even now she is darting her eyes back and forth from the skinny man to me, her face tight with fear. As for me, I just glare right back at him. Give him my best Ford Falcon stare, like my gaze could melt the glass.

"My ma, yeah," I say, standing up and squaring my shoulders. I'm trying to look tough, and in some ways I am, but it suddenly occurs to me that knowing how to spear a solar bear or run a Whomper-Zooka won't do me much good in this place.

"You *miss* your mommy?" Mr. Lettuce Face is wearing what looks like an exercise suit made of blue tissue paper. His skin is so pale I swear I can see watery pink blood pulsing beneath it. His eyes are transparently blue, and his hair looks like a patch of thin weeds. When he talks he hitches his hips to one side, cupping his elbow in one palm and using the fingers of his other hand to tap his chin between smart-aleck comments.

I take two steps toward the window. "I'm here to take her home."

Lettuce Face scrunches up his face and makes a high, vibrating sound.

"*E-e-e-e-e H-e-e-e-e* . . ." It sounds like he's having a sneezy little asthma attack or gagging on a warbler. Then I realize this is just his way of giggling.

"Get to it," growls the Fat Man from the other side of the divider. Lettuce Face is still giggling. "NOW!" says the Fat Man.

Lettuce Face stops giggling and addresses me again.

"We would loooooove to reunite you with your mother permanently."

He is actually rubbing his veiny hands together when he says this.

"But?" I know there's a catch and I'm not giving him the satisfaction of hope.

"But we need something first."

"Well, good luck with that. I can offer you exactly one stinking dead solar bear, but yer gonna have to fetch it yourself."

The way Lettuce Face pinches his lips together, you'd think some of that solar bear stink made its way into his carefully sealed cubicle.

"The price for your mother is . . . E-e-e-h-e-e . . . it's . . . e-e-e . . ."

"WE WANT YER OLD MAN!" bellows the Fat Man.

"You give me Ma first," I say. "Then we'll talk."

"You want yer ma back, you bring in yer old man!"

"You heard what Ma said. He's gone. I have no idea . . ."

"LIAR!" screams Lettuce Face. Then he giggles. He really is full-time creepy. "You are correct. After the attack, he did disappear again. But you were kind enough to capture him for us . . . *again*, thank you very much. And you kept him in the pig shed."

"I . . . you . . . how?" I hate myself for letting them know I'm flabbergasted, but this time I can't help it: my mouth has fallen into full flytrap mode.

Lettuce Face changes the subject. "You know, you had a *na-a-asty* cut on your head when you came in here." He acts like he cares, but there's a sneer in there.

"Yah, well you shoulda seen the solar bear," I say.

"Oh, I'm sure it was all very entertaining," says Lettuce

Face, "but when you grabbed your head earlier, what did you notice?"

I feel around up there with my fingers again, then, grudgingly, say, "Um, it's pretty much healed."

"Yes, yes," said Lettuce Face, like some simpering night nurse. "Yes, our surgeons are magnificent. They removed the amateur embroidery, cleaned up the wound properly, probably saved you from a nasty brain infection—assuming there's a brain in there—and then applied some CellGen, a terrific CornVivia product that generates new skin cells in under twenty-four hours."

I put my hand up to the shaved spot again. Nothing but that little ridge, and even that feels smoother than when I first checked it.

"Personally, I wish they would have shaved off all of that nasty hair, but then we were interested in keeping you alive, not clean." He studies me through the glass a moment and then scrunches his celery-stick nose again.

"TELL HER," bellows the Fat Man. I get the feeling that if it wasn't for the wall separating them, Mr. Lettuce Face would be Mr. Limp Neck.

"While we were fixing your head, we gave you a little something for the pain."

That explains why I don't remember anything between the paddy wagon and waking up to see Ma.

Lettuce Face chuckles again. It's like a lizard giggling. "It made you woozy. You talked a lot of useless gibberish."

"Sorry," I say. "That's kinda your department."

"Oh, you're a rude one," says Lettuce Face, but he's still lizard giggling. "But among all the nonsense you kept saying you hoped a Toad would feed the pigs. And then you'd wink at us."

Oops.

"Of course we now know of your neighbors Toad and Arlinda Hopper. And that they have a shed where they keep pigs . . . and—sometimes—your father."

"Well, if you're so sure you figured it out, why didn't you just go get him?"

"Ah. We tried. Sadly, he had pre-skedaddled. In the report, I was told our representatives visited with the Hoppers. We learned that your father had convinced Mr. Hopper to release him from the pig shed but gave no indication of where he was headed. Clearly your father anticipated that we might get the secret out of you. We do have operatives on the case, but they are currently at the disadvantage."

My heart sinks. The URCorn from Arlinda's pie sales won't last long. What if he winds up back drinking PartsWash and passed out beside some bonfire? Or worse, in the hands of an undercover GreyDevil who will drag him straight back to the Bubble? They know he needs URCorn. Surely they'll be staking out the local fires.

"If you're hunting him, why should I hunt him? You've got helicopters and eyes in the sky and who knows what else . . ."

"The more the merrier! *E-e-e-H-e-e!* Yes, my dear, we are searching. And we do have the upper hand. But once again he has a head start. And from the moment he removed his Security Chip and flew it on that balloon, your father has proven adept at the hiding game. You know him. His habits. His tendencies. Your odds are better than ours. Plus, *you want your mommy back.*"

If looks could melt glass, Lettuce Face would be dancing a hotfoot.

"And," says Lettuce Face, "we will release her to you in return for only one thing: your old man."

There is a moment of complete silence. Then Lettuce Face speaks again.

"Well, you decide. It's up to you. Of course, if we find him first . . ."

My heart sinks. If they find him first, I will never see him again. Worse, I'd lose any power I had to make them return Ma. I might never see *her* again.

"There is a bit of good news," says Lettuce Face.

I just scowl at him.

"Despite everything our patriotic partners have been able to accomplish in the world of *corn*, a reliable so-called truth serum has proven elusive." At this, the Fat Man shoots him a glare. Lettuce Face just shrugs. "The best we can do is help someone relax and ramble. But after comparing your answers to those your mother has given us, we are confident your father never shared his biggest secret—the one we *really* care about—with her."

My scowl stays in place, but inside I feel a pang in my

heart. Does this mean they put Ma through a babble session too? And what about Toad and Arlinda?

"So if you bring in Dad, we can quite happily return your mother."

"Yah? Well, what if I go out there and blab? Tell everybody about Dad and CornVivia and why he had to leave, and what you're doing to Ma, and what you did to my brother, and . . . and . . ."

"Oh dear," says Lettuce Face after I run out of air and ideas. "Aren't you petulant? Number one, you want your mother back . . . and alive. Number two, you wouldn't know who to blab to. Number three, you wouldn't know *what* to blab. After your little *relaxation* session, we know your father didn't tell you the big secret either."

My memory flashes back to the pig shed, and me yelling at Dad. Suddenly I'm wondering: By refusing to tell me the big secret, was Dad actually protecting me?

I look at Lettuce Face. "So. I bring you Dad, you give me Ma."

Lettuce Face nods. The Fat Man just sits there, holding Porky Pig.

"How do I know you'll keep your word?" I say, still scowling.

"What choice do you have?"

I scowl at him some more. He's right, and I hate it.

"Good luck, Little Miss Maggie," says Lettuce Face, and the glass fades back to mirror.

"FORD FALCON to you, salad skin!" I yell.

The mirror switches back to transparent glass. The Fat Man has vanished, but Lettuce Face is still there, grinning like a sneaky cat. "You have five minutes to say good-bye to your mother."

I lunge forward, smashing my fist into the glass. Lettuce Face jumps back, then giggles again. The glass is at least two inches thick, and I can feel the blood ooze from my knuckles.

Lettuce Face disappears into the mirror, still giggling.

I go to Ma. She's trembling, and there are tears in her eyes. There isn't much to say. For the first time I wonder where we are. I mean, I know we're in this stupid white room, but I wonder where in the Bubble City we are. I think about the brochure, and I think about the time I sat on the hood of the Falcon and stared across the distance, and I wonder if right this instant there are other girls my age nearby, laughing and playing volleyball and eating ice cream cones.

A door opens, and two mirror-faced guards enter.

"I'll be back, Ma."

"Oh, Maggie."

50

THE PADDY WAGON DROPS ME IN THE SAME SPOT WHERE I WAS picked up. I don't look back, because I can't bear to see that endless, giant white wall and imagine Ma in there. Instead, I look to the far edge of the Clear Zone, identify the building where I left Toby, and walk straight to it. He's there with his pack on his back, waiting for me as if I just stepped out for lunch. "Let's go," I say, and without another word we begin the hike home.

With every step I take I try to figure out how to find Dad and get him back to the Bubble. I am in a race: if the Bubble Authorities find Dad before I do, I have no way of forcing them to return Ma. But I am also in a conundrum: they will be tracking me, so the minute I make contact with Dad, they'll just swoop in and take him from me.

For a week I hike, and for a week I puzzle on this.

When we round the trail on Skullduggery Ridge and I see my good old station wagon waiting, I want nothing more than to bid Toby good-bye, crawl inside the original Ford Falcon, and sleep for a week. But I know I need to get back to Dookie. I'm also worried about Toad and Arlinda after their visit from the Bubble Authorities. I have good reason to be worried: the Falcon, the shack, the coop, the root cellar—they've all been ransacked again. The Bubble Authorities want Dad bad. If ever there was any doubt that they are doing everything they can to find him, the sight of our demolished belongings erases it.

Tired as Toby and I are, we quicken our pace and half trot down the trail to Hoot Holler.

Hatchet hits me the second Toad lets us through the security gate. What I wouldn't give to wring that bird's neck. Instead I settle for three swings and three misses and then just run for the porch, Hatchet crowing victoriously behind me. Toby just strolls along with a grin on his face. I guess that rooster knows better.

Dookie runs out to meet us. It's good to see him. Right away I see he has a scuff on his cheek and a bruise over his eye.

"Another seizure," says Arlinda. "A bad one." I give him a big hug and he hugs me back for maybe half a second, then runs three laps around the house, yodeling, "*Ya-la-loo, ya-la-loo, ya-la-loo!*"

"Good to see you too," I say.

Then I notice Toad's face looks just like Dookie's.

"Toad—what . . . ?"

"Bubblers," says Toad. "Least that's what I figure. They were perusing fer yer pater."

It makes me queasy to think of how they got me to tell them about the pig shed, and it made me angry to think of them beating up Toad when they found that my father was gone again.

"They were pummelating me gritty pood until Arlinda pepped out on the storch with her Zini-Mooka!"

One person was no match for all those Authorities—not even Arlinda with a Mini-Zooka—but none of those Authorities were interested in eating rock salt, so they stopped working Toad over.

"Se-bides," says Toad, "the prize they prized had vaporized." Now his face shades over, and he reaches a hand toward me. "Ford Falcon, your father . . ."

"He's gone again," I say. "I know."

"But how . . ." Toad and Arlinda look perplexed.

We sit on the porch and I tell them the whole story then, from the solar bear fight right up to the moment I tried to punch Mr. Lettuce Face through the glass.

"*That* was dumb," I say, flexing my knuckles, which are still stiff and sore.

"No sow . . . ," says Toad.

". . . So now," I say, "I am hunting my own father. Again."

"The night after you left," says Toad, getting serious and abandoning Reverend Spooner, "he convinced me he had to go. Told me the whole story. Said as soon as you reached the Bubble they'd be sending someone after him here. In the morning I backed the oxcart into the pig shed. Your father climbed in, wrapped himself in a tarp with a breathing tube, and then I buried him in straw and pig manure."

I make exactly the kind of face one makes when one thinks of being buried in pig manure.

"Yep, I knew nobody'd want to check that," says Toad. "Also, the heat of the manure would help disguise your father's outline in case the Bubblers were peeking down from the sky with anything fancy. I hooked Frank to the cart and drove it down to Tilapia Tom's. We made a big show of talking about him using the manure for his methane fizzer, the one he uses to heat his fish tanks during cold snaps. We backed the oxcart into the shed that houses the fizzer, closed the doors, and unloaded your dad.

"He said his plan was to wait for nightfall, then slip into the woods behind Tom's fish tanks. I bet he took to the river. Arlinda and I figure he had enough URCorn to last a month, maybe less.

"That's the last I've seen of him."

It's quiet now, nobody saying anything. Dookie runs past us and into the house, so at least we know he's not in the fish tank.

"Oh!" says Arlinda. "Before I forget!" She goes into the dining room and comes back with the Emily book. "Your father made us promise that we'd put this back in your hands the minute you returned. He said whatever happened, you'd want Emily's help to get through it."

"Yeah, well, I'm not sure even Emily's up to this one," I say.

"There is one other thing," says Arlinda, looking at Toad. "The night before he left, your father asked for a pen and some paper. He said . . ." Arlinda pauses for a moment and looks at Toad. He nods. "He . . . he said he wanted to copy down some poetry to take with him."

"Boy, he kinda picked a weird time to get into poetry," I say.

"He said a good poem can lift you above all trouble."

"Yeah, Ma used to say that. But that was before we were being harassed all over creation by fake GreyDevils and angry fat men who collect antique toy pigs."

"Let's eat," says Arlinda matter-of-factly, as if that solves everything, and for now it does, because suddenly my stomach is roaring like a solar bear.

The moment I step inside the house, a miniature boomerang hits me in the head, so I guess I can stop worrying about whether Dookie is his same old self. If it isn't a crazy flapping rooster, it's a crazy boomeranging brother.

Soon Arlinda has the stove rumbling hot, and the kitchen air is filled with the smell of good cooking. It's all Toby and I can do to keep from eating straight from the pots and pans.

When we do sit down to eat, we spend the first five minutes in almost complete silence as we work through piece after piece of fried chicken, piles of mashed potatoes, buttered carrots and green beans, and biscuits so fresh that a curl of steam comes wisping out each time I tear one open. Even Dookie eats well, finishing everything except a neat little pile of cooked carrots before running off to hang out with the stuffed animals.

"Dookie!" I say, and he comes lurking back to the table. "Eat your carrots." Then, because Dad can't be here to say it like he used to, I say, "They're good for your eyeballs!" Dookie pops three tiny pieces of carrot in his mouth and scurries back to the taxidermy room. I figure I'll take what I can get and let him off the hook.

After the last bite, I suddenly feel bone tired. I wash my plate, then lie on the floor beside Dookie in the room with all the strange creatures looking at us with their cockeyed gazes. I hear Toby leave for home. For the first time in six days, I relax.

Soon Hatchet is crow-hacking and the sun is up.

We eat a huge breakfast: fluffy mounds of scrambled eggs, sausage and bacon, pancakes right off the griddle and drowned in maple syrup. When I finish, I tell Toad and Arlinda I need some time alone up on Skullduggery Ridge.

"Two-times-one two-times-two-burro-not-early a retrieval aircraft-minus-a-vowel one-less-than-five per yater?" asks Toad.

He must have been up all night working that one out.

"Yes, Toad," I sigh, after realizing by "burro" he meant mule, "to formulate a retrieval plan for my father."

Then I give Dookie a hug, gather my gear, and step outside. I'm just at the gate when Arlinda comes out the screen door, waving something in her hand.

"Your Emily book!" says Arlinda.

I tuck the book in my pack and climb up to the place where I think best.

51

UP ON THE RIDGE I LIGHT A FIRE AND HANG THE KETTLE. THEN I dig through the mess of the shack until I find the tin that held Ma's tea. It's scuffed and dented, but the cover is still on tight. When I pry it off I find just a few loose leaves. They've lost most of their flavor, but as the steam rises from the mug there is just enough of the bergamot to kick loose memories of sitting with Ma against the Shelter Tree. Tears fill my eyes. As the first one spills over I swipe at it and slop hot tea over my hand. As much as the scald of it hurts, it helps me get myself together. I set the tea on a rock to cool and pull Emily from my pack. *A good poem can lift you above all trouble.* We'll see, I guess. Returning to the tree, I settle in again and begin to read.

The sun is bright today, but rather than blazing down,

it's filtering through the leaves of the Shelter Tree, falling across my arms and shoulders and the pages of the book in shifting, shimmering splotches. Once again I can hear Ma telling me not to devour Emily's poems, but once again I just want to fill my head with these words, read the lines one after the other, not even stop to try to understand them. I just want to get lost in the *feel* of them. The *rhythm* of them. The *taste* of them. I want to read Emily's words until I feel like she is right here with me, or we are sitting side by side in her little room, and we are friends, and we have made a pact never to venture into the rough, dirty, messed-up, lousy world again.

I read and read and read, until my eyes go fuzzy. The tea is long gone, the last drop dried in a brown oval at the bottom of the mug. When I finally raise my gaze and stare off over the Falcon and across the landscape toward the Bubble City, my heart lurches when I think of Ma, somewhere out there in that white-dome, white-cube world. My heart jumps again when I realize that the voice I hear when I read Emily's poems is Ma's. I wonder for a moment if this is the worst thing I could have done—wasting time reading these poems that make me feel so lonely. But in a weird way, even the lonely feeling is comforting. To sit in the spot where I used to sit with Ma, to read the poems we'd read together, and to realize that whatever comes to be in the future I have the memory of those moments inside me for all time.

One last poem, then it's time to get back to real life. I leaf through the pages of paper to the poem Ma and I have always chosen for our favorite—the one about the joy of reading books. Ma and I shared it so many times that the Emily book falls easily open to it.

At first I don't think much of the folded scrap of paper, figuring it is a bookmark Ma had placed. Then I see the words "Ford Falcon" written on it.

Ma *never* called me Ford Falcon!

It had to be someone else.

I unfold the paper. It is grubby and wrinkled, and the handwriting is shaky:

> Dear Ford Falcon (Maggie, for your mother):
>
> Good girl. Your favorite poem. I knew you'd find it here.
>
> Fo gish.
> Do it like Dookie.
> Taller than Toby.
>
> Love,
> Dad

My hands are trembling. I raise my head and look all around.

Nothing.

I read the note again. The three nonsense lines in the middle. Clues—they have to be clues.

Fo gish.

Okay. That's a spoonerism for *Go fish*.
Seriously? *Go fish?*
I move to the next line.

Do it like Dookie.

I frown.

Taller than Toby.

I sit and stare at the little piece of paper until I notice my butt has fallen asleep. I need to move. Walk. Work. Sometimes my brain works best when my body is busy. I fold the paper back up along its lines, tuck it inside my shirt pocket, and start cleaning up the mess left in the shack by those government-approved vandals. While I pick up broken dishes and tipped-over chairs and arrange the few things that aren't broken back on the few shelves that aren't broken, I chase the phrases around and around in my head, try to link them up, try to get them to make sense.

Go fish.

There's the card game, of course, which Ma sometimes

played with me when I was younger, using an old dog-eared deck Toad dug out from a drawer somewhere. Was Dad trying to tell me to look in that old pack of cards? The drawer they were stored in has been pulled from the dresser and thrown against the wall in a corner, with all the contents spilled. I dig around until I find the pack on the floor beneath one corner of a ripped blanket. I go through the entire deck, card by card, front and back, jokers and all, but can find nothing unusual.

Go fish.

I suppose if Dad had been the kind of Dad who took me fishing this might be a clue to head for our favorite spot on BeaverSlap Creek and look for clues there, but the closest Dad ever came to taking me fishing was when we helped Toad harvest the fish tanks.

I drop the dish I'm holding and don't even feel bad when it shatters.

Go fish.

There's a big grin on my face as I think, *Got it, Dad.*

52

"TOAD!" I HOLLER, BANGING ON THE SECURITY GATE. I SHOULD HAVE let him know I was coming but I have to assume I'm being watched, so I didn't whistle three long and three short, or raise the flag.

When Toad opens the gate it's all I can do not to sprint straight to the fish tank. Circling it slowly, I look for any sign of a message, or digging, or a freshly replaced board. A hiding place of any sort.

Toad follows and watches me.

"Puzzlement, Ford Falcon?"

"Let's feed the pigs, Toad." He looks even more puzzled now, but if we're going to read that note we need to be out of sight. In the pig shed I pull out the note, unfold it, and show it to Toad. Naturally his eyes light up, because what we have here is a word puzzle.

"*Fo gish!*" he blurts. The man can't help himself.

"Yes, Toad," I say patiently, "already got that. Didn't really take me anywhere. No, I think the message was much more straightforward. Is there space beneath the tank, Toad? Space enough for a man to hide? Or leave a message?"

"Yes!" he says. "Down there amongst the plumbing and whatnot!"

"Isn't it time we give the fish tank a very careful inspection?" I ask, and give him a wink.

We walk to the base of the tank, and Toad pulls open a small hatch. We peer inside. Nothing. I crawl in and shine a jacklight over every surface. Still nothing.

In the shelter of the crawl space, I look at the paper again. *Do it like Dookie.*

"Last thing I wanna do, really," I say, "is do anything like Dookie."

Right on cue, Dookie comes whooping past, grabs the water-telescope from its hook, and climbs the ladder.

"Toad! That's it!" I speak urgently but quietly. "The water-telescope! Dad left some sort of message under the water!"

I clamber up beside Dookie. He's already hanging over, swirling the water-telescope through the water, jabbering and pointing at fish I can't see. It takes awhile, but finally I convince him to let me have a look. I scan every inch of that tank, sides and bottom. I see nothing but tilapia.

Back down at the foot of the ladder, Toad and I rack our brains.

Finally, Toad speaks.

"Y'know, there are a lot of fish in the barrel, and a lot of barrels full of fish."

"Yyyesss . . . ?" I say.

"*Taller than Toby*," says Toad.

I just look at him.

"Friend or foe, Daddy-O!" says Toad.

I look at him again. He raises his eyebrows and nods his head to the north. And suddenly I think of all those times we drove over to pick up Toby, and when we'd see his big bulk waiting alongside the road Toad would say, "Friend or foe?" and then Toby's dad would emerge to stand beside his son, and tall as Toby was, Tilapia Tom was taller.

"Daddy-O!" I exclaim, finally getting Toad's hint. With the water-telescope still in my hand I spin on my heel and speed walk toward the gate, trying hard not to run.

"Ford!" Toad stops me in my tracks with a harsh whisper. "Do you think anyone who might this very instant be watching us would be curious about why you were hiking down the road to Tilapia Tom's with a water-telescope in your hand?"

I hang my head. Toad is right.

"I believe it's time we helped Tilapia Tom inspect his fish for signs of scale mange," says Toad, and off we go to hook Frank to the oxcart.

There is no such thing as scale mange, of course, but it's doubtful any Bubble Authorities goon would know that. We meet Toby and Tilapia Tom in their fish-cleaning shack and lay out our plan.

"We think Dad left a message in your fish tanks."

Tilapia Tom nods. He talks about as much as Toby.

"Have you seen him?"

Tilapia Tom shakes his head.

Armed with a fishnet and a bucket, we head for the tanks and go through them one by one. As I peek through the water-telescope Toad talks loudly about the grave dangers of scale mange. Now and then Tilapia Tom nets a fish and he and Toby make a show of studying it. Now and then they toss one in the bucket.

Tank after tank, we find nothing but fish.

And then, on the bottom of the last tank, the one closest to the woods where Dad likely made his escape, I spy it: a rock, wrapped in plastic and twine.

Looking through the water-telescope, I guide Tilapia Tom as he nets the rock, which he swiftly dumps into the fish bucket. Trying not to run or hurry, we make our way to the fish-cleaning shack. Once inside, I tear at the plastic, and within is another note.

Dear Ford Falcon (if you're reading this you've truly earned the name):

I knew you could do it.

Visit the Earl for dos upside sunrises. Then upgrade your oculators. When you hit bottom, consider cooking cauldron-style.

When it is time, I will be ready. Just invite me to an upside-down dinner for lunch.

Love,
Dad

I am flooded with relief. Relief because Dad seems to be following through on a well-thought-out plan, which means he really is trying to reunite us. He isn't planning to run off and freak out with the GreyDevils.

But my relief doesn't last long. Now I have another riddle to figure out. What if I can't solve it? What if it takes me so long his URCorn runs out? I know what happened last time. And what if the GreyDevils catch the scent of his URCorn and come after him like they came after that cornvoy spill? Or what if the Bubble Authorities find Dad before I do? Lettuce Face said they weren't really going to try, but I don't believe that for a minute.

Another thing: surely the Bubble Authorities are watching me. What if they grab me and grab the note? But Dad seems to be thinking of that, too. They can't possibly know what it means. There are too many personal clues. And none of these clues seem to give away anything about where

Dad might be hiding. Even I can't figure that out. It's not a perfect trick, but it's a pretty good one: they're forced to follow along and figure it out on the fly, just like me.

Still, the first thing I do is sit right down and memorize that note.

53

I FIGURED OUT PRETTY QUICKLY THAT "*VISIT THE EARL FOR DOS upside sunrises*" was Dad's way of saying I should relax and do some reading on Skullduggery Ridge (the *upside*) for two days. Of course it was crazy to think I could relax, but also of course I knew he wanted me to do this for a reason. He didn't want me to go straight from reading that note to *upgrading my oculators*, whatever in the world that meant. He wanted me to move slowly, so as not to lead the bad guys straight to whatever he had planted for me.

But boy, oh boy, it is tough. I spend a lot of time under the Shelter Tree and on the hood of the Falcon with Emily on my lap, but the only way I keep from going nuts is to keep busy doing other things. I do some cleaning up. I make a few repairs. I unroll that solar bear hide and scrape it again and resalt it so it won't rot before I have a chance to tan it.

If I ever have a chance to tan it.

All the while I'm working, I'm trying to figure out the riddle: "*Then upgrade your oculators. When you hit bottom, consider cooking cauldron-style.*"

Oculators. That one sounds Toad-ish. Then I remember: The goggles he built for Frank and Spank. He called them "oculator protectorators." Which I assume means "eye protectors" to the rest of us. So how am I supposed to upgrade my eyes? Am *I* supposed to get goggles?

I let it go for a while.

The two days crawl by. As I struggle with the riddles, I begin to have doubts. That day in the pig shed when I told Dad he was just a card in my game, I was sure this was the right thing to do. Now I can't escape the idea that not only am I hunting my own father, I am hunting him *with his help* so I can turn him over to the enemy. Even though I want my mother back, even though I am still angry when I think of Dad drinking PartsWash while the fake GreyDevils tore up our home, beat Dookie, and took Ma, even though *Dad himself* has said I have to turn him in, the fact is I'll be sacrificing one parent for the other and I'm not sure I can do that.

It's not a decision anyone should have to make. But then, as Toad often tells me, "Fife is lot nair!" That's a three-letter forward flip—for experts only.

When the sun rises on the third day I have made no more progress on Dad's riddle. I spend half the day puzzling on it, then at noon I walk up to the flagpole and sit down where I can see out over Hoot Holler. I want to sit. Sit and think. I lean my back against the hutch where we store the old binoculars.

Bin*oculars*! What upgrades your eyes more than a pair of binoculars? Hands trembling, I open the hutch and pull out the binoculars. I turn them over, looking for any sign of a note or some sort of message. Maybe I'm supposed to spot something with them! Maybe Dad will send me a sign! I put them to my eyes and scan the valley below. I don't see anything out of the ordinary. I zoom in on Hoot Holler. There is smoke coming from the chimney. Toad and Arlinda are probably just now sitting down to lunch with Dookie. I'd be lost if they weren't able to take care of him. I hope he's behaving. I hope he's eating well and not causing any trouble.

"Eat your carrots, Dookie," I murmur, remembering what Dad always told him. "They're good for your eyeballs."

And blammo, it hits me. Dad's clue isn't about binoculars. It's about improving my eyesight by eating carrots! And where are the carrots? In the root cellar! And "*When you hit bottom . . .*" That must mean he wants me to dig down through the carrot sand. Oh, how badly I want to jump up and run right down there, but I think about who may be watching and instead walk very slowly back down to the Falcon, where I fetch my jacklight. ". . . *consider cooking cauldron-style.*" Of course. If I'm going to go into the root cellar under the watchful eye of some spook, I need a reason to be down there, and what better reason than making soup? I light a cooking fire in the flat-rock stove and remove the slate top so the flames can heat the cauldron. I pour in some water, and then, just as nonchalantly as you please, I walk to the root cellar and let myself in. Closing the door behind me, I follow my jacklight all the way down to the sand pit, where I caught Dad digging that night.

I kneel and dig with my bare hands. At first I find only one spindly, droopy carrot. Then another. With all that has happened, we never got our garden planted up here, so these are the last of the carrots I harvested with Ma.

I brush one off and take a bite. Although it's droopy, it's not rotten and tastes just fine. Unlike my brother, I like carrots. Plus it's nice to think of this carrot as something Ma planted and tended.

I dig deeper in the sand, using my fingers like rakes. Nothing, not even another carrot. I sweep all the sand away. Still nothing.

When you hit bottom, consider cooking cauldron-style.

Well, I've certainly hit bottom. And I'm already cooking cauldron-style. What am I missing?

This is not the first time I came down here looking for something other than a carrot and came up empty. Dad was stashing URCorn down here, and yet I couldn't find it. What did he say when we talked about it in the pig shed?

Maybe you stopped looking too soon.

I lift the jacklight and bend down closer to the cellar floor, sweeping away a few more grains of sand. The slate is smooth against my palm. No wonder it makes such a good stove top.

Yes, Ford Falcon, I think to myself, as my face lights up, a stove top you can remove when you want to *cook cauldron-style*!

I put my cheek nearly to the ground, and sure enough, there it is . . . a crack in the slate. I almost break a fingernail clawing at it, then I pull out my knife and—Toad would chew me out if he knew I was doing this—use the blade to pry one side of the flat rock up.

I lift it away and set it aside, and there, in a hollowed-out space, are four small objects. They are long and narrow, like pencil boxes. I pick one of them up. I undo the small clasp on the side, press a button, and the case springs open to reveal a slender glass tube corked with a rubber stopper. The tube is cradled in soft padding, and inside the tube I can see coils of what looks like . . . *hair*.

I snap the small case shut. There is a glass jar in the hole, with a folded piece of paper inside it. Unscrewing the lid, I remove the paper and unfold it. It's Dad's writing again.

Dear Ford Falcon:

I knew this day might come, and planted these items some time ago. If you're here, then I guess there has been trouble. But if you are here, that also means that against all odds, this plan is working.

285

I can't take any chances with this one, so it's mostly riddle free. It's terribly important that it not fall into the wrong hands. Memorize it as soon as you can, then destroy it.

Leave the tubes in their cases. The cases are waterproof and very strong.

Leave one case right here.

Regarding the rest, here is the plan:

I read the directions. They're written in plain English, but they're still pretty complicated. At the end, Dad wrote:

When everything is in place, invite the Authorities to visit. The Fat One and the Skinny One. Settle for no one else.

Love,
Dad

Possibly my life could get weirder.
But I'm not sure how.

I remove three of the cases and hide them—one in my shirt, one in my sock, and one in my ratty hair. The fourth I leave in the hole. I can't stay down here long enough to memorize the note without raising suspicion, so I fold the paper and sheath it with my knife. I replace the slate and heap sand on it. Then I take the last of the carrots and grab a limp parsnip. If someone is watching, I need them to believe I went down here to get vegetables for the soup.

Good thing, too. Because as I step out of the root cellar, I catch a glimpse of two very yellow eyes watching from the brush beside the trail. I take a big crunch from the carrot and hold the other one out in front of me.

"Hey, you fake!" I say, talking with my mouth full. "Want a carrot?"

Silence.

"Might help those sick yellow eyes of yours."

They blink, and disappear.

Just in case someone is still watching, I finish making the soup. It's pretty awful.

And then I prepare for the busiest week of my life.

And after the year so far, that's saying something.

54

IT TAKES ME A WEEK TO DO IT ALL. FIRST I MEMORIZE THE NOTE and burn it. Then I have to convince Toad to load up the *Scary Pruner* and go to Nobbern.

"Now?" he says. "But yer pater . . ."

"This is about *pater*," I say quietly.

Next I have to convince him to let me take his cross-eyed muskrat to town with us.

"But . . ."

"*Pater*," I say. Then, in the most respectful tone I can, I say, "Toad, in order for the plan to work, many of the details can be known only by me."

He never asks another question.

Two days later we make the trip. Among the scrap iron we deliver to the blacksmith shop is a short length of pipe. It is crimped at both ends, and hidden within—unbeknownst to anyone on earth but me—is one of the test tube cases. "Oh-ho-ho, I'm afraid that little hunka pipe's not worth the ink it would take to write up the BarterBucks slip," says Al. I just smile at him and follow Freda into the shop. With Al out of earshot I speak quietly. "Freda, this is an odd thing, but you are always honest in your dealings with us, so I am putting my trust in you." I hold out the pipe. "Put this high in the rafters in the darkest corner of your blacksmith shop. Someplace Al will never go. If a man arrives one day and says he is looking for a corn cob pipe, give it to him. Tell no one. *Especially* Al." Freda smiles and nods, like this sort of thing happens all the time in the blacksmithing business.

At Magical Mercantile I ask Toad to wait outside with Toby while I go in with the cross-eyed muskrat. Magic Mike takes one look at it and through gales of laughter says, "I can sell a lot of things, but I'll *never* be able to sell that."

I reach out and grab him by his polka-dotted bow tie. The laughter stops and his eyes go wide.

"Listen to me very carefully, Magic Mike." My face is about half an inch from his, and I can hear him gulp.

"I recently visited a Bubble City. I guess you could say it was a business trip, because it certainly wasn't pleasure. While I was there I got reunited with a pig. *Porky* Pig."

Magic Mike's face is now the color of his green eyeshade.

"Y'know, if word got out that a fellow like you, in a business like this—where you deal with some powerful and mysterious clients—couldn't be *trusted*, couldn't be relied upon to protect the sources of his most unusual merchandise, boy, now that could be real hard on business."

"I . . ."

"You're right about one thing, Magic Mike. You're not gonna sell this muskrat. You're gonna *stock* it, but even if someone is crazy enough to buy it, you're not gonna sell it. Unless—and this is very important, so stop swallowing your tongue and listen carefully—unless that person says he or she is looking for a cross-eyed corny gift.

"Those *exact* words, Magic Mike. Cross-eyed corny gift. Now put it on the shelf."

Just before I step out the door, I look back, and Magic Mike is already climbing down the rolling ladder. The muskrat is on a topmost shelf. And within his cotton-stuffed belly is a small case containing a test tube.

When we finally stop to see Banker Berniece, I again ask Toad to wait outside. When I explain my situation, her face remains as expressionless as the bun at the back of her head. It takes us awhile to sort everything out, and it is a highly unusual transaction, but from beginning to end her voice never changes from its usual flat tone, even when I thank her and she bids me good-bye.

We fight a few GreyDevils on the way home, but my heart really isn't in it. We still have to defend ourselves, and I will,

290

but ever since I found out about Dad, I've wondered just who might be behind those tortured yellow eyes.

After we drop off Toby, it's a quiet ride and I have time to think. Dad had left me two more clues I had yet to use. They weren't that difficult, and I had figured them both out easily.

> When everything is in place, invite the Authorities to visit.

When I was memorizing that line, it hit me: I've had this whole thing backward. I've been twisting my brain into knots figuring how to sneak Dad into the Bubble without the Authorities snatching him, when what I really need to do is make the Bubble come to me. They still have all the power, but at least my boots will be on home turf.

And so the day after all of the pencil cases are in place, I sit with Toad and Arlinda and lay out the rest of the plan. Then I hike up to Skullduggery Ridge, stand on the hood of the Falcon, and knowing full well there is a GreyDevil with fake eyes out there somewhere, holler, "I'm ready to give up my dad."

Nothing happens, but I know someone is listening.

"Knock on Toad Hopper's gate one week from now. And leave your yellow eyes at home."

How do you prepare to deal with someone who has all the power? We know if they want to they could crush us. Evaporate us. The only thing we have on our side is their uncertainty. And Dad's secret, I guess. Maybe the best we can hope to do is go down swinging, or at least telling them the truth to their faces. Like a frog swallowed by a stork, we can't escape, but we can maybe scratch their throats on the way down.

One week later I am helping Toad clean the chicken coop after lunch when a helicopter clears Skullduggery Ridge, passes above us twice, then settles in a cloud of dust just outside the gate. We walk to the gate to wait for the knock. When it comes, five men, four of them armed and uniformed, one in a suit, are waiting. Mr. Suit says, "I'm here to arrange the details."

"The exchange happens here," I say. Mr. Suit starts to argue.

"They want him, they come and get him. And they bring Ma."

He starts to speak one more time, and I cut him off again.

"And we only deal with the Fat Man and Lettuce Face."

"Who . . . ?" says the man, genuinely confused.

"Figure it out," I say. "We can't stop them bringing guards and soldiers and whatever else, but if those two aren't here, no Dad."

The man looks around nervously. GreyDevils have begun appearing. It's their time of day, and hearing the helicopter they think there might be corn about. The guards quietly thumb the buttons on their weapons, and the gunsights glow hot red.

"And if you're concerned about your safety, we can do the exchange inside the BarbaZap gate," I say. "But no one inside other than two pilots for that whirlybird, the Fat Man and Lettuce Face, and my ma."

More and more GreyDevils are appearing. They're getting worked up way more quickly than when they come after us on the *Scary Pruner*. The guards raise their weapons.

"Noon," I say. "Three days from today."

And that's that. Walking in a tight knot, the man and his guards scuttle quickly to the helicopter. Just as they reach the stairs, a GreyDevil moans and stumbles toward them. Two of the guards raise their weapons. There is a deadened *whup!* sound, the GreyDevil's chest caves in like it was kicked by an invisible boot, and down he goes. *That was no rubber bullet*, I think, and then I feel a chill as I think, *Coulda been Dad*. As more GreyDevils break into a mad shuffle toward them, the five men run up the steps, the hatch seals behind them, the blades spin, the dust boils, and they are in the air and sailing back over the ridge. A cluster of GreyDevils stands in the spot where the helicopter launched. Their heads are tipped back, and they are moaning toward the sky.

"What's up with the GreyDevils?" I ask Toad.

"The URCorn," says Toad. "They can smell it in the Bubblers. Comes out in their sweat. They'd eat 'em alive to get at it."

I look at Toad, my eyes wide. "But if that's true, how did Dad . . ." And then my eyes go even wider. All those times I

teased Dad about eating garlic and how it made him smell—
he was doing it on purpose, to hide the scent of the URCorn
and protect himself from GreyDevils!

"Garlic! Toad! Dad needs—"

Toad grins, and then he nods. "A dozen of Arlinda's best
cloves. In the bag with his corn."

Three days. It's gonna feel like forever. Dad is out there alone,
and the Bubble Authorities won't stop looking for him. But
at least I can relax about one thing: he smells like garlic, not
URCorn.

55

ON THE MORNING OF THE THIRD DAY, I CLIMB SKULLDUGGERY RIDGE
and raise the dinner flag. Upside down.

> When it is time, I will be ready. Just invite me to an upside down dinner for lunch.

I look out across the valley. Dad's out there somewhere. Watching this hill.

I hope.

What if he doesn't see the flag? What if right this moment some Bubble Authorities goon has him in his sights? What if he's just now waking up beside some bonfire, in a heap of GreyDevils?

I hike back down to Hoot Holler, and we wait.

When they arrive, it's quite a show. I climb up on the tilapia tank ladder so I can see over the fence. The military vehicles come first, big-wheeled trucks and vans and transports that arrange themselves around the giant BarbaZap gate that guards the entrance to the Sustainability Reserve, where the new planting of URCorn is several feet tall, and tiny ears of corn are already starting to form. Then comes a large helicopter escorted by four smaller helicopters. The small helicopters hover while the large helicopter lowers itself within the Sustainability Reserve, then the choppers retreat to four separate corners of the sky. The helicopter rotors stop, the hatch goes up, and the steps slide down.

And out steps Ma. My heart leaps, and I get a lump in my throat.

And right behind Ma, Lettuce Face, in a pair of baggy coveralls that make him look even skinnier.

And behind him, fat and sweaty as ever and wearing his regular old squeezy suit, the Fat Man.

Dad is still nowhere to be seen.

Toad and I step out of the gate together. Arlinda is right behind us, holding Dookie tightly by the hand. All morning Dookie has been walking in circles, saying *"Shibby-shibby-shibby"* over and over. I tried to calm him down but nothing worked. And he's right. It's shaping up to be a *shibby-shibby-shibby* kind of day.

When Dookie sees Ma, he says, plain as day, *"MA!"* and

jerks against Arlinda's hand. It's all she can do to hold him. I can't blame him. I want to run to her too.

Ma moves toward the BarbaZap gate, Lettuce Face and the Fat Man on either side of her, each gripping one of her arms. Ten feet from the entrance, they stop.

"WHERE'S YER OLD MAN?!?" hollers the Fat Man.

"Oh, he'll be . . . ," I start to say, but my voice cracks, because I have no idea where he is and suddenly I'm realizing how real this is, and how crushing it will be if he doesn't show. I clear my throat to try again when a voice behind me completes the sentence I could not.

". . . here."

I turn, and there he is. Dad, looking surprisingly healthy as he moves around me so we are standing side by side.

I expected to be nervous standing there with Dad, but I'm not. I have been preparing for this moment a long, long time, and I'm glad it has come. It's better to be *doing* than *waiting*. I peek back at Toad and Arlinda. They too stand shoulder to shoulder, and when Toad catches my eye he winks.

"AWRIGHT, let's GO here!" It's the Fat Man, hollering at me.

"Keep your cool there, ButterButt," I say. I figure if he's gonna talk big, I'm gonna talk big, too. If this whole thing goes terribly wrong I want to go out in a way people will remember. "We're gonna do this my way."

"Gettin' ordered around by a blankety-blank girl!" he grumbles.

"Get used to it, GreaseTrap," I say. "Ma—you all right?"

"Yes, Maggie," says Ma, but her voice is terribly soft.

Down the road I see a few GreyDevils appearing. Perhaps with all the commotion they think the cornvoys have returned. The soldiers encircling us are beginning to look over their shoulders.

"Okay, here's how it's gonna work," I say.

"You didn't really think we were gonna play by your silly, frilly little rules, did yuh?" says the Fat Man. "Thanks for findin' yer old man. We'll take him now."

For the first time, I feel uncertainty. It's one thing to talk tough about trading in your Dad, it's another thing to do it.

"I'm not going in," says Dad.

"Oh, yer goin' in," says the Fat Man.

"Dad . . . what about Ma?" I say. "The trade?"

"You don't want *me*," says Dad to the Fat Man, ignoring me. "You want your—my—*our*—*secret*."

The Fat Man just stands there glaring. Lettuce Face stomps his foot like a tiny dancer.

Dad continues. "You're terrified it'll get out."

"QUIET!" thunders the Fat Man. "If that were true, we'd have snuffed you the minute you stepped through that gate."

"I knew that was a possibility," says Dad. "But I was willing to gamble that you need me alive until you're dead sure the secret is safe . . . and it's not."

Now the Fat Man's fat face is turning purple.

"Nah, you'll keep me alive because my daughter, *Ford Falcon*, has set the dead man's switch."

"That's right, GreaseGuts," I say. When Dad said "my daughter," I felt a rush of pride. Then, quietly, under my breath and out of the corner of my mouth, I say, "What the heebie-jeebies is a dead man's switch?"

Dad answers in a clear, firm voice, so everyone can hear him, even over the sound of the approaching GreyDevils. "A dead man's switch is something automatically set in motion upon the death or incapacitation of someone . . . in this case, if anything happens to me, it triggers something that will make these two fellows very uncomfortable indeed."

I look at Dad again. He is standing up straight. I have never seen him look more in command. Now he speaks to the Fat Man and Lettuce Face again, and this time the slightest taunting tone has crept into his voice.

"You never did find the four vials, did you?"

The Fat Man's face turns an even darker purple, and Lettuce Face's face goes even paler, beyond wilted lettuce to anemic lizard belly.

The GreyDevils are beginning to swarm. "It's all those Corn-Eaters," says Toad. I've never heard him use the term before, but I can figure what he means: all those soldiers are from the Bubble, meaning they've had Activax, and with this many of them gathered and nervous and sweating, the GreyDevils can smell the URCorn coming from their pores. At this point the soldiers have stopped paying attention to us completely and have turned their eyes and their weapons toward the shuffling mob.

"You're out of cards, Lard-O," I say. Actually I'm not sure exactly what cards *we* have—but it seems like the thing to say. "Time to turn over my ma. Let's get this done before we're neck deep in GreyDevils."

I can see the Fat Man would like nothing better than to feed me to the GreyDevils, but he nods toward the security guard in charge of the BarbaZap gate, and when the man presses a button, the big gate slowly swings open.

"We're still takin' yer old man!" screeches Lettuce Face.

"We'll see," I say. "First, we get Ma."

And then, as Ma steps forward, everything comes undone.

56

AFTER ALL OF OUR EXPERIENCE ON THE *SCARY PRUNER*, TOAD AND I knew the GreyDevils were getting set to swarm, but when they see the BarbaZap gate begin to slide open, they go bonkers in a way we've never witnessed. It is like unlocking the door to a five-hundred-acre free buffet.

The soldiers start firing almost immediately and it's horrible, the *whup* of the bullets hitting the moaning GreyDevils, but there are so many of them they just keep coming, and I can actually feel the earth vibrating as they tromp forward in their slow-motion stampede. The security guards, seeing the GreyDevils inbound, have thrown the switch that reverses the gate. It's beginning to roll closed.

Dookie yanks his hand free from Arlinda. He is jumping up and down and trembling and spinning in circles, and saying "*shibby-shibby-shibby* . . ." over and over.

"Dookie!" I holler, trying to grab him by the shoulders. "It's okay!"

For just a moment, he freezes, as if I've gotten through to him. Then he ducks under my arms and takes off running.

Straight toward Ma.

Straight toward the closing gate.

The BarbaZap! I think.

"Henry!" hollers Dad, and we both run after him. He has a head start, though—we're not going to get to him in time.

Suddenly, Dookie stops in his tracks, looks straight up at the sky, and falls twitching and shaking to the ground.

A seizure! And he is lying directly in the path of the closing gate, a moving wall of BarbaZap snapping with deadly electricity. I am running as hard as I can and keeping right up with Dad, but even as we run I can see the killer gate slowly but surely closing in on Dookie's outstretched hand.

"DOOKIE!" I scream, knowing that the second the steel touches his fingers he'll be electrocuted.

I hear a sound behind me like an avalanche of stones, and even as I run I turn to look and I see Toad's silo, his Leaning Tower of Pisa, teetering and now tipping like a giant sequoia. After another season of nonstop cornvoy trucks, the rumble of the soldiers' gunfire and the vibrations of the hundreds of GreyDevils have been just enough to finally topple it. As it sweeps toward the earth it throws a dark shadow across the narrow Cornvoy Road, and the topmost section smashes earthward straight through the BarbaZap fence. Wires screech and howl as the steel rips and twists, then with an earthshaking *thud* the entire length of the concrete silo hits the dirt. An angry buzzing, snapping sound erupts, sparks fly high into the sky, and the gate stalls, millimeters from Dookie's hand. The falling silo has shorted out the electricity.

"Snooky holer-tables!" hollers Toad, pumping his fist when he sees the damage the silo has done, all those years after the government bulldozers bumped it. "That fight is *fit*!"

And then out of the smoke and pulverized concrete dust I see the GreyDevils come pouring toward us.

They have overrun the soldiers and are coming for the open gate, where Dookie is lying. I reach his side and drop to my knees. He is blinking at me in that quiet, goofy way he always does when he's coming out of a seizure.

"Henry! Henry!" It's Ma, trying to get to Dookie, but the Fat Man is holding her back, trying to drag her to the helicopter.

I look over my shoulder and see the GreyDevils stumbling toward us in a dirty gray wave, their desperate eyes fixed on the gap in the gate, looking right past us to the rows and rows of URCorn, their cracked and crusty fingers reaching out and grasping before them. Their voices swirl and moan in a tornado of sound. There is no way we can get back to Toad and Arlinda.

"The helicopter!" yells Dad, picking up Dookie.

Now the Fat Man is dragging Ma to the chopper. She is fighting him and reaching toward us, but he is jerking her backward mercilessly. Lettuce Face has already leaped into the chopper and is yelling, "Go! Go! Go!" at the pilot.

We catch Ma and the Fat Man right at the door of the chopper. The Fat Man whirls and snarls at us, one arm wrapped around Ma's neck.

"Get back!" he growls.

"Dead man's trigger!" my father hollers. "It's locked and loaded!"

The Fat Man turns as pale as Lettuce Face.

The GreyDevils are pouring through the gate.

"Nowhere to go but up!" hollers Dad.

"I . . . ," says the Fat Man, then he curses and lurches up the stairs, dragging Ma with him but making no effort to stop us. Dad lifts Dookie into the helicopter, I climb in behind them, the engine roars in tune with the GreyDevils, and then we are lifting up, up, and away. Toad and Arlinda stare up at us until we can see them no more and the fields of URCorn tighten into rectangles of brilliant green and then we are roaring through white sky, back to the Bubble and who knows what.

But hey, I think, as I look around: it's the whole family . . . back together again.

57

WE SPEND THE NIGHT IN EMPTY ROOMS WITH SIMPLE BEDS. I PULL my mattress off the rack and sleep on the floor. Dookie sleeps beside me. Ma and Dad are in another room. The last thing I hear is the low murmur of them talking.

The next day we are moved to the square room with three white walls and one mirror wall. Dad has his arm around Ma while she holds Dookie and hums his favorite old songs. Ma's still terribly upset about his seizure. I forgot that she didn't know about those. I explain how it's been since the night of the attack.

As happy as we are to be reunited, you'd think we'd all be chattering like mad, but mostly we seem to be lost in our own thoughts. How do you go from having pie together on Toad and Arlinda's porch to escaping a horde of GreyDevils in a helicopter and everything that happened in between and then just pick up where you left off? Being thrown back together in this way, we don't really know how to begin. Plus, it's not like we are sitting around our own kitchen table.

I look at us in the mirror. Ma, Dad, and Dookie, and me off to one side. It's like a family portrait, only instead of smiling we're just waiting to see what happens next.

We don't wait long. The mirror changes to a window, and the Fat Man and Lettuce Face appear.

"Well, well," says Lettuce Face. "Isn't this nice. A family *reeeeuuuu*nion."

I dream of the day I can stick a Whomper-Zooka up this dude's snoot.

"You'll be turning us loose any minute," I say.

"Oh, I don't think so," says Lettuce Face. "We have your mother, and—although I could really do without you—we have *you* . . . and your odd little brother."

He points at Dad. "But most important, we have him."

Dad steps forward.

"Not all of me, you don't," he says.

I step right up behind him. "Skip the mystery talk, Dad. I'm sick of surprises and secrets. Every time I turn around there's another one. I never thought I'd say it, but I actually miss Hatchet. He's forever attacking me, but at least I know what's coming. Let's wrap this up and catch the next helicopter outta here."

Dad looks me in the eye for what seems a long time, then speaks.

"Final secret, Ford Falcon."

The white room is silent except for the sound of Dookie softly and slowly repeating, "*Shibby . . . shibby . . . shibby . . .*" Ma draws him in close to her chest so he can feel her humming.

Dad squares his shoulders.

"Without me, there is no URCorn."

"*SHUT HIM UP!*" screeches Lettuce Face.

"Doesn't matter now," says the Fat Man.

Dad walks right up to face the Fat Man through the glass. "I loved working for your company. I was doing experiments. I was playing with all the latest toys. I was using my nerd brain the way it was meant to be used. I worked hard, and I was rewarded for working hard. I could provide my family with all the things they needed and most of the things they wanted.

"And above all, I was proud to help feed the world."

I snort. "Yah, feed 'em crazy corn, and make crazy money for CornVivia."

"Yes," says Dad, turning toward me. "Some of which was used to buy your diapers and keep a roof over your head. There is nothing wrong with being paid well for good work. And, Maggie, in the beginning URCorn truly was miraculous. It did everything the old advertisements promised. In a time when the weather was going topsy-turvy and other crops were failing and millions were going hungry, we came to the rescue."

The Fat Man smiles, and says, "And we never had a fatter bottom line."

"You oughta know about a fat bottom line . . ." I couldn't let that one go.

"Maggie!" says Ma, shaking her head.

"Yes," says Dad. "The bottom line. That's where things began to go wrong. First came the Secrecy Signings. I signed, because I agreed: if CornVivia paid me to do research for them, it wouldn't be right if I sold that information to some other country.

"Then came the Security Chip. That scared me. But there was so much restlessness in the country by then. Millions without jobs. Troublesome weather. Talk of strange invasions. CornVivia wanted security for their secrets and I wanted security for my family. So I submitted to the chip.

"Finally came the Top Secret project. They said they needed me to invent a lock. A lock made of chemicals that would add one more layer of protection for the secrets of URCorn."

"Activax?" I ask.

"Yes," says Dad. Then, very quietly, he says, "Had I known what I was part of, I would have walked out of the lab that day and never returned."

Now he walks over toward Lettuce Face, who has been

standing there all this time with his thin little lips stuck out in a pout.

"It was the Patriotic Partnering that first made me doubt what I was doing," says Dad. "When the biggest food corporation in the country joined forces with the government, I felt trouble ahead."

Only the glass is separating him from Lettuce Face now. "I loved this country. We were free to do as we pleased, and with a little luck and a lot of hard work, you had a shot."

"The nation lives on!" says Lettuce Face, drawing himself up all snooty and haughty. "Sealed it! Before they could steal it! Jobs for all!"

"Yes," says Dad, "as long as you work for CornVivia or the government."

"Patriotic Partnering!" cheers Lettuce Face. "It saved this country!"

"Yes," says my father. "But for whom?"

"Dad . . . ," I say. "Seriously. Wrap it up. I'm ready to go."

"The year after I designed the lock, CornVivia announced that three things happen when you take Activax," says Dad, turning back toward Ma and me. "Number one, it allows your body to use URCorn. If you don't have Activax—as you know, from that day outside the gate—URCorn makes you very ill.

"Number two, Activax turns you into an URCorn addict— you get all the benefits, but if you stop taking URCorn . . ."

I know. I was the one who dragged him into the pig shed.

"And number three, if you eat corn designed by anyone other than CornVivia, you'll get sick too."

"So: like it or not, take the Activax, and you're a customer for life."

"Yes," says Dad. "And CornVivia is well on its way to becoming corn dealer to the world. But there are a lot of people who worry about that and want to stop it."

The Fat Man chuckles.

"But once the Activax is turned on, there is only one way to turn it off," says Dad.

"The key!" I say.

"Yep," says Dad. "The key to unlocking Activax lies in a code built on a strand of DNA. As you might imagine, I developed it under the strictest secrecy, in a hidden lab all by myself. So when it came time to generate the code, I took the DNA from the only donor available."

"You! You are the key!"

I look at Ma. She's gone pale. "But why have these two corn-burpers been chasing you?" I ask, pointing at the two men behind the glass. "They've already got your DNA—and can't they just make more of it in the lab?"

"Oh, they don't want me for *themselves*," says Dad.

The look on my face is similar to that of a GreyDevil that's been hit upside the head with a shovel, and Dad can tell I don't understand.

"Other corn companies, other countries, and even groups of people who are opposed to genetically finagled food in general have figured out how Activax and URCorn are locked together, and they've even figured out how the key works. They're only missing one ingredient: my DNA.

"All someone would need to do is to get a piece of me . . . a flake of my skin . . . one of my toenail clippings . . ."

"Eeew, Dad."

". . . or a strand of my hair."

My eyes pop wide open then. The four vials! I hear a high-pitched screech and look up to see Lettuce Face stomping his foot.

The Fat Man is just standing there, calm as can be, if you don't notice his hands, which are balled into fists the size of hams. Now he stabs one fat finger at Dad. "If you've revealed the code . . ."

"Not yet," says Dad. "All four vials are safely stowed. But one little scratch to my head—or to any of my family—and the word goes out. The dead man's switch will be thrown."

"We've heard a lot about this 'dead man's switch,'" says the Fat Man, "but why should we—"

"*LIES!*" screeches Lettuce Face.

"—believe you?" finishes the Fat Man.

"We can test it now, if you like," says Dad. "And within twenty-four hours you will learn that the Euro-Cornsortium, the Anti-Gen Collective—(which as you know is leading the charge to outlaw the international distribution of Activax)— and representatives of the Juice Cruisers Syndicate will all be holding a test tube containing a strand of my hair and a set of very interesting chemical equations."

As he finishes, the Fat Man grabs Porky Pig, rises from behind his desk, and with surprising nimbleness, rushes to the glass, raising the pig like he's going to smash his way through. He stops at the last minute, freezes for a moment, then pulls Porky in tight like he's hugging it.

And for the first time since I've met them, the Fat Man and Lettuce Face turn the same color: bright, angry red.

And then the window becomes a mirror, and there we are. A family. Together.

"Let's get out of here," I say.

Ma looks at Dad. Dad looks at Ma.

Then they both look at me.

"Maggie," says Ma. "We're not leaving."

58

I WILL ALWAYS REMEMBER THEIR EYES. THE SADNESS IN THEM as Ma and Dad stood there after those words. I feel like I have been hit in the stomach and shot through the heart, all at once.

Then Ma speaks.

"I was never suited for life OutBubble," says Ma. "We managed to keep our family together, to have our own ragged little happiness, but there was the constant fear of being discovered, the constant fear of how to keep your father safe and sane, the constant fear of my children being lost or hurt . . ."

"Maggie," says Dad, "your mother is the backbone of this family. It was she who held us together. It was she who protected your childhood in the worst circumstance available. Ma has paid the price for every bit of life our family has won, rough or otherwise. If we stay here, Ma can have her books, her window. She can live without worrying one of us won't come back from a trip to town or some secret URCorn plot. For the first time in her life she can allow herself some time for happiness."

"Happiness, Ma?" I can feel anger rising in me, and it is making me reckless. "Happiness? Here? In this glorified prison?"

"Maggie!" For a minute I think Ma's going to yell at me, but then she leans forward, taking both my hands in hers. "This is not a prison! I am free to spend my days as I please! I have books . . . all the books and time I could wish for, and your father as he was . . . the smart, strong man I fell in love with all those years ago."

"The smart, strong man who needs mutated corn to stay that way!" I snap.

If I expected Ma to get angry at that, I am wrong. Instead, she lowers her voice and speaks slowly, as if to be sure I listen carefully to every single word.

"Your father and I were up all last night discussing this. If we stay here—if we live in this place rather than some shack on a hill under a tree—the damage that has been done to Henry can be undone. His terrible seizures can be stopped. He may even gain the ability to speak—to live a *normal* life."

I push Ma away. I feel rage again.

"You're going to give him the Activax!"

Ma looks away.

"We don't know that, Maggie," says Dad, looking at Ma, then back at me. "It's just a possibil—"

"NO!" I yell. "He *is* normal! Normal for Dookie! We've loved him that way forever! Why change him now? You'll just have him hooked on that awful stuff! The same way you are! And how do I know you're not just staying so you can get all the URCorn you need? And is Ma gonna take the Acti-vax too? And what about me? I'm your kid! So you're gonna make *me* take it?!?"

Dad reaches toward me, but I push his hand away.

"You and Ma—after all this time—you're no better than all those people who lined up to come UnderBubble in the first place. This isn't a Bubble, it's a *prison*!" I spit that last word out.

For the first time in a long time, I notice Dookie. He has backed into a far corner of the wall, and he is looking at me with wide eyes, and he is whispering, "*Shibby . . . shibby . . . shibby . . .*"

I fly into a rage, yelling at both of them, saying things I can't unsay. About how they were weak before and they're weak now, and how this is all Dad's fault and how Ma should have let him go eat corn and die, and then suddenly Ma's eyes flash the way they do when it's time for her to remind me she's still my ma, and sharp as steel she says, "Maggie!"

I stop, and tears flash in my eyes. They're not sad tears, or angry tears, but frustrated tears. Ma gathers me in a hug. And then I feel Dad's arms around me too.

And then Dookie hugs us all, and hums a tune only Dookie knows.

59

THE DAYS HERE ON SKULLDUGGERY RIDGE PASS ONE BY ONE, AS they always have. I wake in the morning to the sound of parrots and one hacked-off rooster, I dig around in the dirt, I tend my chickens and garden, I work on my solar bear vest, I travel down to visit Toad and Arlinda and ride shotgun on the *Scary Pruner*. It's important to keep busy, Daniel Beard said, in the preface to his long-winded book: "*The baneful and destroying pleasures that offer themselves with an almost irresistible fascination to idle and unoccupied minds find no place with healthy activity and hearty interest in boyhood sports.*"

I agree with him, but I've had it with his boy blather. I told Toad I didn't think *The American Boy's Handy Book* of *What to Do and How to Do It* was really all it was cracked up to be, and I was surprised when he said I might be right. The next time we went to Nobbern, Toad came out of Magical Mercantile carrying a box of books labeled "Foxfire" and handed them to me. I've just started getting into them, but it looks like they're gonna be great. Instead of Daniel Beard's DIVERS WHIRLIGIGS they've got instructions on things like how to keep bees and make blast furnaces and bury your grandma.

Right now, though, I'm on the hood of the Falcon, leaning against the windshield Toad fixed for me as a welcome-home present. We pulled the replacement from one of his junk cars.

The sun is out. I've got Emily on my lap, and we're visiting with the Earl.

An odd little piece of equipment is visible through the new windshield. It sits on the dashboard, and it's about the same size as *The American Boy's Handy Book*. On one side is a small panel that gathers energy from the sun. On the other side is a screen. Two or three times a week I punch a button and the screen lights up, and there are Ma and Dad and Dookie. Dad made Lettuce Face and the Fat Man give us the communicator. They pretty much have to do what he says. He told them it's so we can visit even though we're apart, but they also know that we are keeping them honest. If ever I turn on the screen and something isn't right, the dead man's switch will be thrown.

We also have a secret phrase to let each other know if we're being threatened behind the scenes. Dad gave me clues to the phrase in a note before I came back OutBubble:

> Secret phrase is the set of twins in the first line of the second stanza from E's poem that could be about Toad's dog-killer.

I grinned as I thought of Monocle peeking cautiously around the barn while Toad jumped around saying "Snooky holer-tables!" and rubbing the knot on his head. Of course "Toad's dog-killer" meant Toad's boomerang. I didn't remember Emily writing any poems about boomerangs, but I giggled out loud and knew I had my answer when I searched the table of contents and came to the poem titled "Unreturning."

I turned to the page and read it. *Greedy* appears twice in the first line of the second stanza. So if Ma or Dad don't show up for one of our video meetings or if we're ever visiting and they say "greedy, greedy," I know to trigger the dead man's switch.

No one in Nobbern knows this, but before she kept track of BarterBucks, Banker Berniece was an accountant for CornVivia. She prided herself on good math and honesty. When her boss—a large fat man—pressured her to hide the fact that he was making some deals on the side, she quit and moved to a small town named Nobbern, and after Declaration Day, opened a bank that took BarterBucks. One day when I was describing her to Dad, it dawned on him that she was the woman who used to sign his paychecks, and who quit rather than do the Fat Man's dirty work. That's when he realized she could be the trigger of the dead man's switch.

Berniece doesn't know what is in the two safety deposit boxes I set up during my unusual visit. She only knows that I left both keys with her, and if she gets the signal from me, or if Toad or Toby walks in without me and says they're looking for the Fat Man, or if a month passes without a personal visit from me (just so the Fat Man and Lettuce Face don't decide to squash me like a bug), she is to open the box with the smaller number on it. Inside she will find a set of instructions on how to contact the three different groups Dad mentioned when we were in the white room. She will deliver the message, and not long after that, someone will ask Freda for a corncob pipe, a new customer will ask Magic Mike for a cross-eyed corny gift, and a third person will enter the bank and ask how many BarterBucks a test tube costs. She'll open the second box and find the pencil case with the test tube inside.

After that, even Dad isn't sure what will happen, but whatever it is, it'll turn loose big trouble for Lettuce Face and the Fat Man. They'll do pretty much anything to be sure it never happens—including taking extra-special care that nothing bad happens to me and my family.

And of course the fourth tube is in the cellar beneath the slate, just in case.

It's been hard for me to understand everything that has happened, but I keep working on it. It must be even harder for

Ma and Dad to understand my decision—how I could want to come back to this life of GreyDevils and junk hauling and sleeping in an abandoned old car on a hill when I could have everything neat and clean and safe and be with my family. At least I get to see them and talk to them on the little screen, and during the last URCorn harvest I hitched a ride with a cornvoy driver and visited them in the white room. Dookie is on a medicine that has helped his seizures, but Ma and Dad haven't given him the Activax, and I don't know if they ever will. Dad looks healthy and happy, and he says he's been given his own science lab again, but now he only works on his own projects.

And Ma? I was so angry with her that day in the white room. And I meant that anger. I was mad all the way from my steel-toed boots to my ratty hair. But back on Skullduggery Ridge, the very first time I pulled out *The Complete Poems of Emily Dickinson* and saw Emily's lonely silhouette on the cover, it reminded me how hard Ma worked to keep our family together all those OutBubble years, and how many times I wished with all my heart I could give her something better. I suppose we could argue about what the word *better* really means, but Ma . . . well, the last time I saw Ma she looked *contented*, and that's good enough for me.

I know this story isn't over. I know that the Fat Man and Lettuce Face aren't going to let this thing be forever. There are battles ahead that will make the GreyDevils look like two kids tickling each other. And there are so many unanswered questions: How is CornVivia getting the whole world hooked on URCorn? Are they dropping Activax from helicopters or putting it in the water? Where did the GreyDevils come from? What *are* the GreyDevils? Do the Juice Cruisers do more than just make PartsWash? And what about the people UnderBubble? I've still never been under and seen anything other than the inside of a white room and the top of one puny little dome. What's really going on in there? I'm not sure, but I'm willing to bet it's not all volleyball and ice cream cones.

Believe it or not, it was the Fat Man who helped me decide to return to Skullduggery Ridge.

It happened when Dad was giving his speech there right at the end, and the Fat Man grabbed Porky Pig like he was going to smash the glass, then didn't. In that moment I realized it wasn't the glass the Fat Man was protecting, it was that pig. For some reason he couldn't explain, the Fat Man liked things from the past. Things that weren't all based on fancy science and mystery. Things that gave him feelings that money and power couldn't. And somewhere deep inside me I realized I felt the same way about Toad and Arlinda and Hoot Holler and Skullduggery Ridge. More than safety, more than health, more than long life, I wanted a *full* life. A *free* life. And if that meant tearing apart old cars and carrying a ToothClub and doing battle with solar bears and getting knocked around by GreyDevils now and then, well, I guess I think it's worth it. "*I'd rather suit my foot / Than save my boot,*" wrote Emily Dickinson, and I think that's what I'm trying to say.

I look at the book of poems on my lap, and the decrepit old station wagon beneath me and the countryside spread out before me.

This.

This is Ford Falcon's perfect world.

"Cock-a-doodle . . . *aaack-kack-kack-kack*!"

Did I say *perfect*?

ACKNOWLEDGMENTS

MOM, FOR TEACHING ME TO READ AND FILLING MY WORLD WITH books. Dad, for raising us in a quiet country nonetheless resonant with stories and storytellers. The Chetek Library, where I went for stories when I was young. Tom and Arlene, for the real-world example. Brad and Donna, for the topography. Christopher Moore, for that note. Alison Callahan, from way back. Alissa, for managing. Tara, for patience and encouragement beyond reason. Chris H, Lisa B, Dan K, Blakeley, Matt B, Dave E, and Karen R, for grown-up help. JDV and Kyle, for spinning the compass. Dan, Lisa, Katie, and all CB staff. Colorado family, you are always a part of our story.

That little banty rooster who never could quite crow.

Above all, for enduring the rough-draft me in every way, every day: My wife and daughters.